Also by John A. Miller

Jackson Street and Other Soldier Stories
Cutdown

CAUSES
OF
ACTION

A Claude McCutcheon novel

JOHN A. MILLER

POCKET **STAR** BOOKS
New York   London   Toronto   Sydney   Tokyo   Singapore

This book is a work of fiction. Names, characters, places and incidents are products of the author's imagination or are used fictitiously. Any resemblance to actual events or locales or persons, living or dead, is entirely coincidental.

 A Pocket Star Book published by
POCKET BOOKS, a division of Simon & Schuster Inc.
1230 Avenue of the Americas, New York, NY 10020

Copyright © 1999 by John A. Miller

Originally published in hardcover in 1999 by Pocket Books

ISBN: 0-671-02332-2

First Pocket Books paperback printing September 1999

10 9 8 7 6 5 4 3 2 1

POCKET STAR BOOKS and colophon are registered trademarks of Simon & Schuster Inc.

Cover design and illustration by Matt Galemmo

Printed in the U.S.A.

For KO

CAUSES
OF
ACTION

1

Dawn eased over the East Bay hills like year-old motor oil draining slowly out of a crankcase. A heavy fog, drawn in through the Golden Gate by the summer heat bottled up in the Sacramento Valley, grudgingly gave way before the rising sun as early-morning commuters fortified themselves with hot coffee and a glance at the headlines.

The darkness in Claude McCutcheon's house was resolving itself into shades of gray when Claude woke up. He lay absolutely still on the futon, aware that something was wrong but unable to pinpoint the source or even define exactly what "wrong" meant. He had gotten in late the night before, sometime after 1 A.M., and was a little groggy from too few hours of sleep. He could have stayed in the City but didn't much care, as a general rule, for waking up in someone else's bedroom. Spending the night with a woman was a clear statement of intent, one that Claude seldom felt comfortable making. And anyway, the drive across the Bay Bridge after midnight was always a pleasant one, the traffic light and the feeling of leaving the darkened City behind, even for the dubious charms of the East Bay, strangely liberating.

He had no idea what had woken him up, but again there was an overwhelming feeling, an undeniable sense, that something was wrong in the little California bungalow. Keeping his eyes closed, Claude stilled his breathing, his ears straining for the slightest sound. The big Colt automatic was tucked away in the small Korean chest next to the futon, a round in the chamber, but for all the good it did him there, it might as well have been on the dark side of the moon.

He put the weapon out of his mind and concentrated on identifying everything in the house with his eyes closed. Almost immediately he felt the presence and heard the calm breathing of the cat, reassuring by its very regularity. Then, behind and above the familiar purring of the cat, what sounded oddly enough like a child whimpering registered on his consciousness. He slowly raised his eyelids. Standing next to the futon, not three feet away from him, was a young boy.

Relief washed over him.

"How did you get in here?"

The boy, perhaps four years old, didn't answer. Claude could see the tracks of dried tears on his face and a small envelope pinned to his sweater.

"What's your name?"

Still no answer.

Claude sat up on the futon. "Who brought you here?"

The boy pointed to the cat, sprawled on the comforter next to Claude. "Kitty."

Claude nodded. "Well, it's a start." He reached out and dragged the reluctant cat over. Oscar was a large, muscular, female cat of indeterminate breed that Claude had adopted from the Alameda County SPCA. She had a short temper and a generally surly disposition and, in all the world, loved only Claude.

Oscar took one look at the boy and shrank back. Her experience with children was limited and informed by a healthy skepticism toward all humans, even small ones.

Claude scratched behind Oscar's ears and felt the cat relax. "The kitty's name is Oscar. Would you like to pet her?"

The boy, wide-eyed, nodded.

Claude patted the futon next to him. "Sit down here and I'll put her in your lap."

The boy sat as directed and a second later was cradling the cat, who was purring madly.

Claude carefully unpinned the envelope. "First time you've ever held a cat?"

The boy nodded, raptly devoted to the cat in his lap.

Claude got up and slipped on a pair of cotton trousers. "You just sit there quietly and tell her you love her while I go make the three of us a cup of coffee."

The boy bent down and clumsily kissed the cat on the head. Quite to Claude's surprise and amusement, Oscar was positively cross-eyed with pleasure.

"You now have a friend for life," Claude told the child.

In the kitchen he started a pot of water boiling and took a container of coffee beans from the freezer. After grinding the beans he leaned against the counter and tore open the envelope that had been pinned to the boy's sweater.

Dear Claude:

I'm sure you never expected to hear from me after all these years, although to be honest with you it often seems like just yesterday that we were at Ft. Bragg together, messing with the Hawk, or in the Nam. Remember Ft. Lewis? Man, we were something back then, weren't we? Artie Gibson put me onto JoJo Watson, over at the VA hospital in the City, and JoJo told me where to find you.

I'm afraid I'm going to have to leave my boy Earl with you for a few days. His mother died two years ago and it's been just me and Earl since then. Earl's got no other family besides me so I'm trusting you to do right by him if it comes to that.

To tell you the truth, I'm not sure how things got so bad so fast. I won't try to tell you what all's going on since I hope to have things straightened out in the next couple of days and I can come get Earl off your hands.

I can't tell you what it means to me knowing that Earl's in your hands. I know it isn't fair to just leave him with you, not after all this time, but I got nowhere else to turn.

Jesse Hamilton

Jesse Hamilton? Claude thought, glancing back at the futon where the boy sat, still entranced by the purring cat on his lap. An image came instantly to mind: three young men, two of them barely out of their teens, sitting on top of a sandbagged bunker drinking lukewarm coffee out of canteen cups. They had been in Vietnam only a couple of months: Claude, an OCS second lieutenant; Jesse Hamilton, the platoon sergeant, a brand-new E-6 no older nor more experienced than Claude; and Artie Gibson, a squad leader with the rank of corporal. They were the platoon's ruling triumvirate: Claude and Jesse by virtue of their rank; Artie because he was four years older than either of them, the oldest, most experienced man in the platoon.

Claude smiled, seeing in his mind's eye the three of them smoking cigarettes and strategizing. In base camp they sat together every morning after Claude met with the company commander, talking about what the platoon was expected to do, trying to translate theory into reality. The platoon was chronically understrength, whether from disease, casualties, R and R, or whatever creative excuse a soldier could come up with to avoid leaving base camp, and they were constantly shifting men between squads to fill gaps. General Westmoreland most certainly would not have approved of the exceedingly casual relationship—indeed, the friendship—that developed among the three of them, but then again neither he nor any member of his West Point–educated staff provided an alternative, workable model for use by junior officers in the field. Claude could hear their voices, now bantering, now serious, without even closing his eyes.

That afternoon, after three days in base camp, they had been alerted they were going back out on patrol.

"Cohen reported for sick call this morning," Jesse said, looking up from the small notebook in which he kept the platoon duty roster. "Mac"—the platoon medic—"said it looks like malaria. That puts us nine men"—almost a full squad—"under TO and E."

Jesse was tall and slender, almost elegant if a man could be said to look elegant in jungle fatigues and boots, with piercing black eyes and startlingly white teeth. He carried himself, whether in base camp or in the field with a full rucksack on his back and an M16 in one hand, with a formal demeanor that made him seem a good deal older than he was. He demanded, and received, respect from not only the men in the platoon but his fellow NCOs in the company's other platoons. Only twenty, he took his responsibilities as platoon sergeant quite seriously, determined to take full advantage of every opportunity the army was prepared to offer him.

"What about all those replacements from brigade we supposed to be getting?" Artie asked, a broad smile on his face. "The last issue of the *Stars and Stripes* I saw said that President Johnson was every day saying what a fine job we're doing fighting the hated Cong." He paused to snag a cigarette from Jesse, lighting it with a flourish with Claude's Zippo. "I expect we'll see thousands of volunteers filling up the ranks any day now."

While both Jesse and Claude tended to be serious, Jesse by nature and Claude by virtue of his position as platoon leader, Artie was the leavening in the mix. Shorter than both Claude and Jesse, Artie was deceptively slight, a powerful young man who stabbed at the earth with his feet when he walked. Not afraid to speak his mind, Artie was by far the smartest of the three of them, gifted with both a keen, if unschooled, intellect and a streetwise cynicism that let him see things Claude and Jesse might have missed. That intellect and cynicism ultimately saved

Artie, for while Claude and Jesse became hardened and, to some extent, damaged in Vietnam, Artie retained a perspective that recognized, amidst the horror, the comic futility of what they were doing.

"No replacements," Claude responded, shaking his head. "Zimmerman"—their company commander, a first lieutenant—"told me this morning to quit asking."

"Kitty."

The sound of Earl cooing to the cat brought Claude back to the present. *Don't suppose you know what your dad's gotten himself into, do you, Earl?* he wondered, stifling a yawn. Claude caught sight of himself in the mirror, seeing an unlined, comfortable face looking back at him. Although gray was beginning to show in his dark blond hair, his broad shoulders and trim, athletic body caused most people to underestimate his age by at least ten years.

A gurgling sound announced that the coffee had finished brewing. It was a dark Sulawesi-Kalosi, roasted by a small coffee importer in Berkeley's gourmet ghetto, and it smelled as exotic as it sounded.

Through the window he could see his next-door neighbor, Sally Pinter, in her kitchen. He waved and motioned for her to come over. She smiled and nodded. He was wondering what he had to feed a boy for breakfast when Sally let herself in the back door.

"Where's Bud?"

"He had to drive over to Modesto yesterday. His mother fell and broke her hip, of all things, and he's going to be over there for a few days getting her set up with a home health-care service."

"Sorry to hear it," Claude said.

"Better there than here." Sally laughed and then looked a little sheepish. "I guess that didn't sound very nice, did it?"

"Little Pete doing okay?" Claude asked, ignoring her last comment.

Pete was Bud and Sally's two-year-old.

"Doing great. He's sound asleep."

"Come here a minute."

Claude stepped back and motioned for her to follow him. At the edge of the large shoji screen that marked the slightly raised sleeping alcove, he stopped and pointed. The boy was still cradling the cat.

Sally's eyes widened. "Who is that?"

Claude nodded his head back toward the kitchen. There, his voice low enough so the boy couldn't hear him, he told her the gist of what the letter contained.

"You mean you just woke up this morning and he was here?" Sally asked incredulously.

Claude poured two cups of coffee. "You got it."

"What are you going to do?"

"I'm not sure yet." Claude took a sip of his coffee.

"You mean you're not going to call the

police?" Sally shook her head, incredulous. "Or the child-welfare people?"

Claude frowned. "Are you kidding? The county social workers? They're the last people I'd want to turn a young boy over to. Look." He jerked his thumb in the direction of the sleeping alcove. "This boy's father left him here, for what reason I'm not exactly sure. But until I find out, I'm sure as hell not just going to turn him over to a bunch of hard-hearted bureaucrats." Claude finished his coffee. "I need to ask you to do me a favor. Let me leave the boy with you for a couple of hours this morning while I check into a few things."

Sally took a sip of her coffee. "I suppose."

"I'd truly appreciate it. Lord knows I don't have the faintest idea what to feed a boy for breakfast."

"I don't guess you would."

Claude smiled. "Why don't you take him home now, give him something to eat, and I'll pick him up later."

Claude walked back to the futon and knelt down next to the child. "Okay, sport, time to get a move on. You're going to spend the morning with a neighbor lady of mine, Mrs. Pinter, while I try to find your daddy."

The boy looked up at Claude. "Kitty," he said, still clutching the cat in his lap.

Claude sighed. "Well, nobody said life was going to be easy." He winked up at Sally and looked back at the boy. "Tell you what, you be good for Mrs. Pinter, do everything she tells you to do, and you and the kitty can sleep together tonight."

The boy smiled. "Okay."

He got up, Oscar jumping safely off his lap just in time, and reached for Sally's hand.

"Oh, Claude, he's precious." A worried look crossed Sally's face. "Are you sure it's okay? I mean, isn't it illegal not to notify *someone?*"

Claude laid a hand on her shoulder and smiled. "Trust me. I'm a lawyer."

The old-fashioned gold-leaf lettering on the door read CLAUDE MCCUTCHEON, ATTORNEY AT LAW. Beneath the bold print, in smaller letters, were the words CONTRACTS, WILLS AND CODICILS, ALL CAUSES OF ACTION. As little law as Claude practiced, it still pleased him inordinately to see the words on the door.

His office was on the second floor of a small, two-story, stuccoed building on Solano Avenue in the city of Albany, a stone's throw from El Cerrito and Berkeley. Originally a single-family residence, the building had been converted to two office flats in the late 1970s when Solano Avenue was metamorphosing gradually from a residential to a commercial street. Within two or three blocks of his office Claude could buy a cup of coffee made from freshly roasted and ground beans, a baguette still warm from the oven, and food or clothing representative of a myriad of cultures. His immediate neighbors spoke English, Spanish, Lao, Persian, and several dialects of Chinese.

Walking up the stairs to his office, Claude guessed that Jesse had found out he was a lawyer now, but he somehow doubted that that was the reason he had left Earl with him. Claude paused for a second on the top step. *Christ,* he thought, *how in the hell am I going to find a man I haven't seen in thirty years if he doesn't want to be found?* Opening the office door, he smiled grimly, knowing that at least Artie Gibson, two years into an eight-year stretch at San Quentin, and JoJo Watson, obviously in detox once again at the VA hospital, wouldn't be too difficult to find.

"Mornin', Emma. How old is that coffee?"

"Good morning, Claude. I thought you were going straight over to Felix Mackie's this morning." Emma Fujikawa, Claude's part-time secretary, did not bother to respond to Claude's question about the coffee, which she knew he'd asked only to annoy her.

"A little something came up," Claude said. "Besides, I forgot to take the papers home with me yesterday. I must be getting feebleminded in my old age."

"I think the doe-eyed Ms. Ann Abbott has more to do with it than your age." Emma regarded her boss with a chastising look. "I thought you and she were no longer seeing each other."

"How do you know we're . . ." Claude

paused, knowing that mere denial was useless in the face of Emma's at times seemingly psychic knowledge of his personal life. He poured himself a cup of coffee. "She has proven to be rather, um, shall we say per*sist*ent, a trait she doubtless inherited from her father the oil baron."

"Humph." Emma had no intention of letting Claude off the hook. "I told you she was going to be trouble the first time she came to the office. If you had—"

"Yeah, yeah," Claude cut her off, thinking that it was just a little too early in the day to get into a discussion of his moral shortcomings with Emma. " 'If ifs and ands were pots and pans, beggars would ride.' "

Emma laughed. "Tell that to Ann Abbott. Maybe *she* can make sense out of it." She handed Claude a large manila envelope. "Here are the bank documents for Felix to sign." The telephone rang. "Law offices of Claude McCutcheon." Emma listened for a second, a broad smile playing across her face. She covered the receiver with her hand and looked up at Claude. " 'Is Mistuh McCutcheon theah?' " she mimicked in her not-too-close approximation of a heavy Texas accent. "The first call of the day from the Yellow Rose of Texas," she gratuitously informed Claude.

"Jesus," Claude replied sotto voce, drawing a finger across his throat to indicate that he did not wish to take the call.

"I'm sorry, Miss Abbott, Mr. McCutcheon just left the office. . . . Yes, I'll tell him you called." Emma hung up and smiled sweetly at Claude. "Mark my words, that young woman is going to have your head mounted over the fireplace back home in Dallas for all her University of Texas sorority sisters to see."

"It's Houston—"

"Whatever."

"—and don't count on it."

"Oh, wait," Emma said suddenly as Claude turned to leave the office. "You got a telephone call late yesterday afternoon while you were in the City, uh, 'counseling' the Yellow Rose. He wouldn't leave a number. Said he'd call back."

"Who was it? Anyone we know?"

Emma looked down at her message pad. "A gentleman by the name of Jesse Hamilton."

Bingo. "What'd he say?"

Emma shrugged. "Nothing. Just that he'd call you back. Who is he?"

"He's an old army buddy, a guy I haven't heard from or even thought of for . . . let's see now"—Claude calculated quickly—"it must be thirty years." He shook his head. "If he calls again and I'm out, be sure and give him my home number."

"What do you suppose he wants?"

"Don't know," Claude said over his shoulder as he walked out the door. As much as he hated doing nothing, he'd already decided that he had little choice but to give Jesse at least a day or two to get back in touch with him. He doubted that either Artie or JoJo would know exactly where Jesse had gone to earth, although Artie might have some idea as to why.

He shook his head.

What the hell am I going to do with a four-year-old kid?

Earl Hamilton was still very much on Claude's mind as he walked into Felix Mackie's gym, which was in the final stages of construction.

"I think we've finally got all the paperwork in order," he said.

"Just tell me where to sign," Felix rumbled.

"Don't you want to know what you're signing?"

Felix shook his head, his immense San Quentin arms folded impassively across his chest. "Don't mean shit to me." Anyone listening would have believed him without a doubt. "This place is either going to make it or it isn't, no matter what those papers say. If it makes it, I'll pay the money back. If it don't . . ." He shrugged. "Not even a bank can't get no blood out of a turnip."

Claude began laying documents on the counter, thinking that anyone so foolish as to try to get blood out of Felix would be in for a long day indeed. When the papers were signed, Claude stuffed them back into his small leather briefcase. "I'll drop the originals off at the bank and keep your copies with the file in my office."

Felix nodded. "I'll pay *your* money back as soon as I get the check from the bank."

"Whenever," Claude said casually. He had lent Felix enough money to keep operating while the application documents worked their tortuous way through the numerous bureaucratic levels of a minority-lending program. That Felix was a paroled murderer hadn't helped, although Claude had gone to some length to point out to a number of the bank's employees that the crime for which Felix had been convicted and incarcerated did not, in and of itself, necessarily reflect negatively on his fiscal responsibility.

"Nonetheless," Claude had, only half-jokingly, told the bank's minority lending officer, a young Stanford MBA with a new Porsche and little sympathy for people of color who needed to borrow money, "he's not a man I'd want to gratuitously piss off, if you get my point."

The young MBA had indeed gotten Claude's point.

"How come you never had me to sign a note or anything?" Felix asked, still referring to Claude's loan.

"Well, like you just said, I figured you'd either pay it back or you wouldn't. If I'd been worried about it, I would have never lent you the money in the first place."

Felix nodded. "Be a different place in here when I get my hands on that loan. How long will it take?"

"Probably another week or ten days, no more."

"You think it's safe for me to go ahead and order some stuff?"

"Yeah, it's a done deal. I don't doubt the bank's already scheduled a press conference to inform a disbelieving and incredulous world that it's actually going to lend money to a working man, and an African-American one at that."

A hint of a smile passed across Felix's hard face, come and gone so quickly few would have noticed it.

"What's so funny?" Claude asked.

"I was just thinking that they's lots of folks wouldn't believe it if they was to hear that a bank was lending money to Felix Mackie." Felix shook his head at the wonder of it.

"Have you thought of a name for your gym yet?"

Felix shook his head.

"You need a good, solid name. How about Felix's Place?"

"I'll let you know," Felix responded, clearly unimpressed. "You workin' out today?"

"No, I don't think so. I've got to get these papers"—he held up his briefcase—"to the bank and then . . ." Claude hesitated, not wanting to say too much. "Something's come up."

"Something always does," Felix rumbled from deep in his throat. "You better be careful."

"Sit right here," Claude said, putting Earl up on one of his kitchen chairs. "You can tell me all about your day while I prepare dinner."

"Kitty," Earl said, looking about the kitchen. He maintained a firm grip on a somewhat bedraggled teddy bear that Sally Pinter had given him that afternoon.

"What are you going to fix him for dinner?" she had asked when Claude picked him up.

"Something simple but nutritious," Claude assured her with a wink.

"Kitty's outside, no doubt looking for a rat to catch," Claude informed the child while filling a saucepan with a couple inches of water. "I thought that for dinner tonight we would try a little oatmeal."

"Oatmeal," the boy repeated, the beginnings of a smile appearing at the corners of his mouth.

"Do you like oatmeal?" Claude asked hopefully.

The boy shook his head vigorously.

"Too bad, 'cause that's what we're having. That and some raisin toast with strawberry jam. What sorts of things does your daddy fix for dinner?"

"Oatmeal."

"I thought as much. Do you know where your daddy is right now?"

"Kitty."

Claude took a quart of chocolate milk out of the refrigerator and poured a glass for Earl. "Can you use *oatmeal* and *kitty* in the same sentence?"

Earl drank half the glass immediately and looked up at Claude expectantly.

"Save the rest for dinner," Claude advised, busy with the bubbling oatmeal and the toaster. "Voilà." He placed a bowl in front of Earl with a flourish. "First, we put a pat of butter in it, to give you a head start on the road to cardiovascular disease, then we sprinkle brown sugar all over it, like so. Then, a little . . ." Claude paused, suddenly remembering he had forgotten to buy regular milk when he picked up the quart of chocolate and the raisin bread. "Oh, well, I always preferred my oatmeal with chocolate milk anyway. How about you?"

Earl, wide-eyed, looked from the bowl to Claude. He nodded yes.

Claude smiled, charmed by the absence of guile in Earl's face. *You better come get this boy quick, Jesse,* he thought, *before I start getting used to having him around.*

"We're going to do just fine," he assured Earl with a wink as the two of them began to eat. "Just fine."

2

Someone was knocking at the front door. Loudly. Insistently. And, what was worse, a heavy weight was on his stomach, pressing uncomfortably on his full bladder. Claude opened his eyes. Oscar was meat-loafed on his stomach, purring contentedly, while Earl, sound asleep, drooled on the pillow next to him. The knocking continued.

"Lord," Claude groaned. It had been a hard night, the first time in his life he had had to sleep with a child. Earl had tossed and turned all night. Claude sat up, dislodging the cat, and rose to his feet. "All right, goddamn it, don't knock the door down," he yelled as he walked around the shoji screen that separated his sleeping area from the water closet. He stood over the toilet and blinked his eyes several times to clear his vision as he relieved himself.

Ignoring the continued knocking on the door, he went into the kitchen, hopping from one leg to the other as he pulled on a pair of faded blue jeans. Through his kitchen window he could see Sally standing in her backyard. Claude waved and she pointed to the front of his house and made a knocking motion with her right hand. He nodded and shrugged. She smiled and made shooing motions with her hands.

"Mr. Claude McCutcheon?"

Two men in dark suits were at the front door when Claude opened it. That neither was smiling further annoyed him.

"What do you want?" Claude asked, none too courteously. "And where the hell do you think you get off hammering on my door like that?"

"I'm sorry if we disturbed you, Mr. McCutcheon," the taller of the two men responded, his tone of voice carrying no hint of regret, his words notwithstanding. His iron gray hair was crew-cut, and he had a high-mileage face with a nose that had been broken and badly reset many years ago. As if attempting to soften the image conveyed by his harsh, emotionless countenance, he wore an obviously expensive, Italian-cut suit of raw silk and gleaming black wing-tip shoes. He was a powerfully built man despite the presence of a growing paunch—the kind of man people instinctively moved aside for. "You *are* Mr. McCutcheon, aren't you?" he asked, not quite smiling.

"Who wants to know?"

"Mr. McCutcheon, we'd like to talk to you about a Mr. Jesse Hamilton."

Claude, startled by the completely unexpected mention of Jesse's name, thrust his chin forward aggressively. "Who are you guys, anyway? If you're cops, let me see some ID."

The taller one reached into the breast pocket of his suit jacket and pulled out a billfold. Opening it, he showed a green identification card to Claude.

"My name is Barton Jones. We're"—he nodded in the direction of his unnamed companion—"with Sentinel Microsystems. May we come in?"

Claude shook his head. "No. At least not until I know a little more about exactly what it is you're after."

"Well, Mr. McCutcheon, we badly want to talk to your friend Jesse Hamilton about—"

"What makes you think he's my friend?" Claude interrupted.

Jones smiled, a thin, mirthless pulling back of his lips that came and went like a nervous tic. "Perhaps he isn't your friend. In any event, we badly would like to talk to him and we wondered if you might know how we could get in touch with him."

"What do you want to talk to him about?"

Again the fleeting smile. Jones reached into his breast pocket and pulled out a business card that he gave to Claude.

"Good day, Mr. McCutcheon." Jones touched his right index finger to his forehead in a mock military salute. "I hope we didn't disturb your morning routine."

The two men turned and left without another word.

Claude watched until they reached the end of the sidewalk and got into a blue van. The anger he'd felt at being awakened had been replaced by a growing sense of unease.

He didn't know who those two men were, or what Sentinel Microsystems was, but his gut was telling him that Jesse Hamilton was indeed, as his letter had said, in a lot of trouble.

He walked into his kitchen and picked up the telephone, quickly dialing the number of the Albany Police Department.

"Yeah, let me speak with Lieutenant Beck, please." Claude idly rubbed his left hand over his bare stomach while he cradled the telephone receiver in the other. Bernie Beck and Claude were old friends, neither hesitating to call the other for a favor or lunch. Even though Bernie had risen to officer's rank within the Albany Police Department, he still made it a point to get out of the station regularly and walk the streets.

"Lieutenant Beck speaking," Bernie's "official" voice boomed over the telephone.

"Bernie, Claude here."

"Claude McCutcheon. What's going on?"

"Something screwy just happened, Bernie, and I need a favor."

"You always need a favor, Claude," Bernie teased. "When are you going to call up and ask if maybe *I* need any favors?"

"This is such a small thing I hate to even call it a favor, Bernie. You won't even have to put down that doughnut you're probably eating. An old army buddy of mine tried to call me the other day. He missed me at the office and told Emma that he'd call back. I haven't heard anything further, but this morning, just now, a couple of stiffs from some company called Sentinel Microsystems showed up on my doorstep rousting me about him."

"What'd they say the problem was?"

"They didn't. Look, I thought maybe you could check the wire, see if my friend's name turns up."

"When was the last time you talked to him?"

"Believe it or not, we haven't spoken for probably thirty years, but the guy was a straight shooter, a good guy."

"What's his name?"

"Jesse Hamilton. J-E-S-S-E. Hamilton like it sounds."

"All right, give me a couple of hours. I'll see if anything turns up on the computer."

"I appreciate it, Bernie."

Claude hung up and stood at the counter,

tapping his fingers on the wooden surface as the tension began to leave his body. He took a small quantity of coffee beans out of the freezer and placed them in his coffee grinder. When the beans were properly ground, he folded a filter and filled the coffeemaker with water. The first drops of coffee were dancing in the bottom of the pot when his neighbor, Sally, without bothering to knock, came in through the kitchen door.

"Come in," Claude said dryly. "Coffee'll be ready in a minute."

"I've already had two cups, but I guess another one won't hurt. Bud's still in Modesto at his mom's, and Pete finally got to sleep a few minutes ago. He had a fretful night."

"He ain't the only one."

Sally smiled. "Who was at the door?"

"Two vacuum cleaner salesmen." Claude blew on his coffee to cool it. "I expect they're over at your house knocking on the front door even as we speak."

"You're so *mysterious*," she said, rolling her eyes for emphasis. "What did you and Earl have for dinner last night?"

"Oatmeal."

"Oatmeal?" Sally shrieked, laughing out loud.

"There's nothing wrong with oatmeal," Claude assured her, feigning indignation. "It builds strong bodies twelve ways."

"That's white bread," Sally corrected, still giggling.

"Whatever." He nodded at her cup. "More coffee?"

"No, I'd better be getting back. Pete'll be waking up any minute."

Claude nodded. "How about taking little Earl for me again this morning? He's not too much trouble, is he?"

"Lord no. I just hope Pete grows up to be such a sweetheart." Sally paused for a second and chewed on her lip. "Any word from his daddy?"

"Not yet. I'm sure I'll hear from him real soon, though."

"Good. A boy this age needs to be with his family."

"Don't I know it."

Which was why, as soon as Claude got dressed, he was going to go find out a little more about Sentinel Microsystems.

Claude walked into Kate's Diner and winked at the young girl manning the elaborate copper-and-steel espresso machine. She was wearing a T-shirt that proclaimed in large letters SERVICE WITH A SMIRK. He looked around the small café and spotted the owner, Bette Beal, presiding over the large Wolfe range behind the counter.

"Hey, Bette," he called out, "how's tricks?"

"Claude McCutcheon, as I live and breathe," Bette Beal shot back sarcastically. She was a tall, heavyset woman with short, jet-black hair dressed with Brylcreem and combed back in a classic fifties ducktail. She had on a thin white

T-shirt with the short sleeves rolled up over her shoulders, revealing tattoos on both of her meaty upper arms. On her right arm was the Marine Corps emblem with the words SEMPER FI and on her left was a simple red, bleeding heart with MOM emblazoned beneath it.

Appearances were deceiving, though, because Bette was a 1978 Stanford graduate with advanced degrees in mathematics and computer science. After graduation she and a friend from Stanford's Business School started their own CAD software-development firm. Five years later they sold the company to a subsidiary of Lockheed, and Bette came out of the closet. She bought the café on Fifth Street in Berkeley and renamed it Kate's Diner in honor of her grandmother. Originally a blue-collar greasy spoon catering to the neighborhood's working men and women, the café became an instant success after Bette learned how to cook and raised prices.

"Is the coffee fresh?" Claude asked, knowing it would annoy her.

Bette sneered. "Does a hobbyhorse have a hickory dick?"

Claude gave her a thumbs-up and sat at the counter. "Gimme the whole nine yards."

By the time Claude finished eating, the breakfast crowd had thinned out considerably. "Hey, Bette," he said, nodding toward an empty booth at the rear of the café, "let me buy you a cup of coffee."

Bette handed the steel spatula she was holding to an anorexic young woman who had been assisting her at the range. "Sounds good to me, McCutcheon," Bette responded. "My dogs are starting to bark."

They walked back to the booth and sat down. One of the waitresses brought over two clean mugs and a pot of coffee. "Thanks, darling," Bette said to her. She took out the pack of Camels she had folded, seamanlike, into one of the short sleeves of her T-shirt and offered one to Claude. They each took one and Claude lit them with his battered Zippo. After both cigarettes had been lit, Bette reached over and took the lighter out of Claude's hand. She turned it over and read the inscription, running her index finger over the small paratrooper's wings.

"Nice," she said, handing it back to him. "I didn't know you'd been across the Pond."

Claude shrugged. "Long time ago." He put the lighter back in his pocket.

Bette took a drag on her Camel. "I like you, Claude. You treat people around here with respect. We're not exactly friends but I suspect we could be if it got right down to it." She leaned back in the booth and took a sip of coffee. "What's on your mind?"

"I need a little help, Bette. A guy I know seems to be having some trouble with a company down in the Silicon Valley."

"Yeah? What sort of trouble?"

Claude shrugged. "I don't know. The company's called Sentinel Microsystems. One of their security people, guy by the name of Jones, Barton Jones, was asking me some questions about my friend."

"What do you want from me?"

Claude stubbed out his cigarette and took a drink of coffee. "I was hoping you might have a friend or two from your days as a heavy hitter in the Valley. Somebody who might know something about Sentinel."

Bette smiled. "What'll you give me if I ask around?"

"What do you want?"

"Unfortunately," she said, laughing, "what I want you ain't got. But not to worry. I'll nose around a little bit, see what I hear. How's that?"

Claude winked. "You're a peach."

Bette hefted herself up from the booth. "Yeah, right. Don't forget to stop at the cash register on the way out."

Claude was whistling as he walked out the door.

"Anything going on?"

Emma looked up when Claude walked into the office. "The Yellow Rose of Texas called and wants you to call her back as soon as possible."

"Great. I take it Jesse Hamilton hasn't called again."

Emma shook her head. "No, he hasn't. Oh,

and Lieutenant Beck called a little while ago. He said it was important."

"Thanks. Get him on the line for me, would you?" Claude went into his office and closed the door. The telephone rang almost as soon as he sat down at his desk.

"Lieutenant Beck is on line two," Emma informed him.

"Thanks." Claude switched lines. "Bernie, thanks for getting back so soon. What have you got?"

"Jesus H. Christ," Bernie Beck almost shouted. "What in the hell's going on with you, Claude?"

Claude took the receiver from his ear and looked at it, as if its appearance might somehow explain his friend's surprising words. "Bernie, I don't know what you're talking about."

" 'Don't know' my ass. Look, Claude, something queer's going on here and I don't like being caught in the middle. You call me up first thing this morning saying some friend of yours is in trouble. Next thing I know the wire from the FBI lights up wanting any information the Albany PD might have on a certain Mr. Claude McCutcheon. What the fuck's going on?"

FBI? Claude shook his head. *What the hell . . . ?*

"Jesus, Bernie, you know I wouldn't back-door you. Like I told you this morning, the other day I missed a call at the office from an old army buddy I haven't seen or heard from in almost thirty years. Then this morning I get an unannounced visit at home from a couple of dickheads from a computer company down in the Silicon Valley who show up at my doorstep rousting me about the same guy, implying they think I'm involved with him."

"Involved in what?"

"Well, hell, if I knew that, I wouldn't have called you for information. Look, Bernie, obviously this old pal of mine is in trouble. That's probably why he tried to call me yesterday—I am a lawyer, remember? As to the FBI, who knows what they're after? Did you find out anything at all about him?"

"No. There's not a want or warrant out on him anywhere in California that I could find. I ran his name through all the computers and didn't come up with a thing. The guy doesn't even have any outstanding parking tickets."

Claude nodded. That sounded like Jesse. "Okay, Bernie, thanks."

"You're welcome." Bernie paused, and Claude could hear his friend weighing his next words. "Hey, Claude—have you thought about how these men from the computer company got to you so quickly after your friend tried to telephone you?"

"What are you getting at?"

"Electronic surveillance. Somebody must have a tap on your friend's phone. And if they have a tap on his phone . . ."

"I get the picture."

"My advice is to stay in touch. And be careful."

"Thanks." Claude hung up, wondering who else was listening.

"I thought you'd left." Claude looked up at Emma from the small pile of paperwork he was shuffling through. No wonder those big-firm lawyers worked eighty hours a week. They had to, just to keep up with the paperwork.

"I was just getting ready to go." She nodded her head back toward the outer office. "You won't believe who just walked in."

Claude turned back to his stack of papers. "Elvis."

"If that's the best you can do, I better go ahead and tell you: an FBI agent"—she rolled her eyes dramatically—"is waiting to see you."

"Do tell." Claude pushed back from his desk and smiled. *Now we're getting somewhere.* "Show him in."

Emma smiled like a woman whose two-dollar hunch bet on the last race of the day had come in first at fifty-to-one. She turned and left the office.

Uh-oh, Claude thought, knowing that when Emma smiled that way she had something on him. Or thought she did.

Emma returned with the agent. "Mr. McCutcheon," she said formally, "this is Special Agent Johnson."

Johnson was a tall woman with a hard, athletic body, hazel eyes, and chestnut hair. She wore a smartly tailored linen suit, low-heeled shoes, and carried herself with an authority that Claude guessed didn't just arise from the fact that she worked for the FBI. *I wonder where she carries her gun,* he thought.

Surprised, Claude rose from his desk and extended his right hand. "I'm pleased to meet you, Agent Johnson. Please"—he gestured toward the small leather sofa in one corner of the office—"have a seat. Would you like a cup of coffee?"

"No, thank you. Mr. McCutcheon, the reason I—"

"Please"—Claude smiled and sat on one of the two leather club chairs facing the small sofa—"let's use first names. It's Claude, not Mr. McCutcheon."

Agent Johnson considered the propriety of the request for a second and then nodded. "You may call me Rita."

"Rita," Claude repeated, liking the way the sound rolled off his tongue and lips. "I like it. What can I do for you?"

"First, I apologize for dropping in without an appointment. I was in the East Bay and thought I might catch you."

Yeah, right, Claude thought, *you were just in the neighborhood. Let's cut to the chase.* "I presume you're here to ask me if I know the whereabouts of Jesse Hamilton."

If Johnson was surprised by the question or the directness, she did not show it. Instead, she smiled at him and cast a cool gaze around his office. "This isn't quite what I expected."

Claude smiled back. "A small space, but not uncomfortable," he said teasingly, leaning back in his chair and crossing his legs.

"What does your law practice consist of?"

Claude shrugged. "A little of this, a little of that. To be honest, I don't practice a great deal of law at any given time. Or at least I try not to."

"If you don't mind my asking, how do you support yourself?"

"I live frugally," Claude answered, not offended by her directness but not inclined to provide any information about himself. "Are you sure you wouldn't like a cup of coffee?"

"No, thank you. Your presumption that I was here to ask you about Jesse Hamilton's whereabouts is correct. Do you know where I might find him?"

"What exactly is the nature of your interest in Jesse, if I may be so bold as to ask?"

Rita leaned forward. "The FBI is investigating an alleged theft of intellectual property from Mr. Hamilton's employer, Sentinel Microsystems. We would like to ask Mr. Hamilton some questions in connection with our investigation."

"Is Jesse a suspect?"

Rita shook her head noncommittally. "I cannot discuss the details of our investigation. Suffice it to say that for the time being we just want to talk to Mr. Hamilton."

"How did you connect me to Jesse Hamilton?"

Rita thought for a second before answering. "We obtained a court order to place an electronic monitoring device on his home telephone. One of the last calls he made before dropping out of sight was to your office."

Claude smiled. "I'd say that you want to more than merely talk to him if you've already gone to all the trouble to convince a federal magistrate to issue a court order authorizing a tap on his telephone."

"Do you know where we might get in touch with Mr. Hamilton?"

"I do not. But I will tell you this." Claude leaned forward in his chair. "I've known one or two thieves in my life, and I don't believe that Jesse Hamilton is one."

Rita stood up and took a business card from her purse. "If Mr. Hamilton should get in touch with you, I would appreciate it if you would give him my name and telephone number."

Claude stood and took the card. "Count on it."

3

This is Jesse Hamilton. I'd like to speak with Mr. Mellon, please."

Jesse stood at a pay phone in the San Francisco Public Library. He was an imposing man, tall and handsome, and his full beard was flecked with enough gray to make it more than a little distinguished. He wore a black beret, both because he liked the way it made him look and to cover the fact that he was starting to go bald. Both Alice, his late wife, and Louise, the woman who had gotten him into all this trouble, had advised him to shave his head, but he had refused, figuring he'd be too long a time bald to go hurrying it up with a razor.

"What's that?" The telephone receptionist at Sentinel Microsystems said something about needing to page Mellon. "Yes, thanks, I'll wait."

He felt an anticipatory thrill of fear at the thought of what he was doing, now that he had irrevocably made up his mind. J. Watson Mellon was Sentinel Micro's chief executive officer and a renowned scientist and businessman in Silicon Valley. There would be no going back, Jesse knew, once Mellon and his partners realized that he intended to play hardball. He knew enough about Sentinel Micro, from what little Louise had told him before she died and what he had been able to piece together on his own, to worry a little about what he was doing, but he also knew that a little worry wasn't necessarily a bad thing.

Artie Gibson, of course, thought he was crazy. Jesse smiled, thinking about his last visit with Artie, out at San Quentin.

Jesse had always tried to get up to see Artie at least once every six weeks or so, and even if the visits more typically occurred at intervals closer to bi- or even trimonthly, it was the thought that counted.

"How's the boy doin'?" Artie always made it a point to ask after Earl.

Jesse nodded. "Boy's doin' just fine. He never has much to say, but he's doin' just fine. How about you?"

"You know me, Jesse, same old shit." Artie had spent a fifth of his life behind bars, and was now in the second year of an eight-year, plea-bargained sentence. The judge, disturbed by the exceptionally high IQ scores in Artie's probation report, had gone to some length to tell him that the next time, under California's three-strike law, it would be life without parole. "What's up? You look like a man with something on his mind."

"I need someone to leave Earl with for a week or two, maybe longer."

Artie pursed his lips but otherwise showed no emotion. "Trouble?" he asked unnecessarily.

Jesse nodded but did not speak.

"Bad trouble?"

"Bad enough." Jesse leaned in close to Artie and began to speak, his voice low and his eyes busy, trying to make sure their conversation wasn't overheard. "You know that thing I told you about at Sentinel? It's come unglued a little bit."

"What'd I tell you?" Artie asked, irritation evident in his voice. "Didn't I tell you not to trust nobody on a deal like that?"

"I need to lay low for a while," Jesse continued, ignoring his friend's implied criticism, "give me a chance to play the hand out. Unfortunately, I can't afford to leave Earl in the deck."

Artie smiled. "You fixing to do some bluffing?"

Jesse nodded. "Sentinel has raised the limit, and I've got no choice but to stand pat and call.

Make 'em think I've got something besides a pair of deuces. If I can stay alive long enough, under cover, they'll have to play my game. Dealer's choice."

"Shit." Artie's tone of voice said it all.

"I don't like it either, but, like I said, I've got no choice."

"Who you got in mind for the boy?"

"Claude McCutcheon."

"You seen him lately?"

Jesse shook his head. "Not since the Nam. How's he doing?"

Artie laughed incredulously. "Man, you are some piece of work. You just gonna drop that boy off with a man you ain't said shit to for thirty years and expect him to cover for you?"

"I covered for him, lots of times."

"That was different, and you know it. We all covered for each other back then. That was the deal."

"You talk to him much?"

It was Artie's turn to shake his head. "No, not for a year or so. He offered to help out the public defender's office at my trial, but the DA was willing to plead me down so there wasn't any need. Last I knew he was still over in the East Bay. Tell you what to do. Find JoJo Watson. He'll know how to get you in touch with Claude."

"JoJo Watson," Jesse mused. *Another thirty-year-old name.* "How's he doing?"

"Not good. He's got a room over in the City—

dump called the Excelsior. If he's not there, check out the VA hospital."

"The VA?"

"Yeah, he goes in once a year or so for detox treatment. Never does much good, but it keeps him alive." Artie grunted sourly. "Barely. If he's out at the VA, take a little touch of something with you when you visit. He'll need it."

Artie had been right.

JoJo Watson was forty-nine years old and easily looked sixty-nine. Although white, a lifetime of cigarettes, hard drugs, and alcohol, combined with a liver that had all but thrown in the towel some years earlier, had turned him an odd, rather unpleasant shade of brown. He was undergoing alcohol and heroin detox for the umpteenth time, and it was pretty clear to Jesse that he didn't much give a good goddamn about anything. The two men had sat in a fog-darkened solarium on the fourth floor of the VA hospital, JoJo in a wheelchair, Jesse in a folding chair he had pulled away from a card table.

"So, JoJo, 's up, man?"

"Not much, Jesse, how about you?"

As if they had seen each other just last week.

Jesse shrugged. "You know me, JoJo, same old shit." He nodded, more to himself than to JoJo, and looked down at his hands. He started to make a joke about JoJo and him ending up the same color but thought better of it. "Been a while, hasn't it?"

"Christ, I reckon."

Both men fell silent, thirty years covered in fewer syllables than it takes to buy a pair of shoes. After several minutes in which each man drifted alone with his recollections of the other, Jesse spoke again.

"I was wondering if you knew what ever became of Claude McCutcheon?"

"Why do you ask?"

"I'll be honest with you, JoJo, I could use some help."

"What sort of help?"

Jesse smiled. "Do you know how I can get in touch with him?"

"Maybe, maybe not. How did you know to find me here at the VA?"

"Artie Gibson told me that you get sent here once a year or so to get dried out."

JoJo laughed, a short bark devoid of humor. "The VA takes care of its own, you know what I'm saying?" He nodded toward the space that should have been occupied by his right leg. "Of course, some might say the price is a little steep. You stay in touch with Artie?"

"Little bit." Jesse smiled. "We don't exactly exchange Christmas cards or nothing."

JoJo chuckled. "Christmas cards. I heard that." He started coughing, a wet, hacking sound that would have ruined appetites at a free soup kitchen. Regaining his breath, he looked at Jesse with watery eyes. "They took my smokes away and it's about to kill me." He hacked twice more to underscore his point. "I haven't seen Artie since before he went into the joint. Any chance of him getting out before much longer?"

"I doubt it, JoJo. The judge gave him eight years and I'm guessing this time he's in for all eight." Jesse shook his head. "It's been too long since the war for men like us, you, me, and Artie, to catch a break, you know what I'm saying?"

"He used to come down to the Tenderloin, make sure I was getting something to eat. Him and Claude both." JoJo shifted nervously in his wheelchair. "Where they got him?"

"San Quentin. Could be worse though."

"How's that?"

"Could be doing hard time up at Pelican Bay." Jesse gently nudged the conversation back on track. "How about Claude McCutcheon?"

"He's got an office over in Albany, across the Bay. You didn't have to come all the way out here—he's in the phone book." JoJo ran a trembling, spidery hand over his face. "You wouldn't happen to have anything on you, would you?"

Jesse looked around to make sure the solarium was free of orderlies or nurses and passed JoJo the half-pint bottle of no-name vodka he had bought at the Safeway down on Clement.

JoJo drank it all without taking the bottle from his lips or blinking his eyes. "I don't suppose you'd have another I could save for later?" he asked as he handed the empty bottle back to Jesse. Color flooded into JoJo's cheeks, giving him, for a few startling seconds, the incongruous look of a man in the full blush of good health.

"No, man, that's it. Hey, I appreciate you telling me about Claude."

"Would you have give me the vodka if I hadn't?"

Jesse nodded. "You know I would have, JoJo. We seen too much shit together, you and me and Claude." He looked around the solarium, empty except for the two of them and all the more depressing because of the fog blowing past the floor-to-ceiling windows. "Back when we was kids." He sensed more than saw the grove of redwood and blue-gum eucalyptus trees shielding the Palace of the Legion of Honor and the million-dollar homes with Golden Gate views at Sea Cliff from the squat ugliness of the VA hospital. "I guess not many of us from the old platoon have done too well for ourselves in the real world," he said quietly, more to himself than to JoJo.

Just then, a hard-edged voice came onto the telephone line, startling Jesse out of his reverie.

"Hamilton—this is Barton Jones."

Jesse shook his head as if Jones could see him. A vein began to throb in his forehead. "Get off the phone, asshole. I want to talk to Mellon."

"Forget Mellon. Here's the deal: return the disc and walk away. No ifs, ands, or buts. The people I work for don't negotiate. Ever."

"Fuck you," Jesse cursed, his voice taut with

sudden fury. His heart began to pound as the image of Barton Jones filled his consciousness. The *deal* was with Sentinel Micro, true enough, but the payback, the settling of a particular account, that was strictly between him and Jones. "If you and Mellon want to—"

Jones hung up on him. Jesse stared at the telephone receiver in his hand. A woman passing the bank of pay phones saw the look on his face and hurried on about her business. Finally he hung up the telephone and walked slowly from the library, not a little annoyed that he had let Jones hear his anger. He knew that for the plan to work, Jones and Mellon both had to believe that it was strictly business, strictly a matter of money. *Business first,* he thought. *Then . . .* Jesse smiled and nodded to a policeman on the corner as he waited for the light to change.

4

Claude nodded down toward little Earl Hamilton. "This here's my pal," he said to Bette Beal. He reached down and picked the boy up so Bette could see him over the counter.

"Well, goddamn," Bette said, leaning on her tooled-steel spatula. "I can't imagine who would trust you with such a good-looking baby."

Claude looked offended. "Earl ain't no baby," he said, winking at the boy. He leaned in across the counter and whispered conspiratorially, "He's a midget."

Bette laughed. "Did you gentlemen come in here to bullshit or to eat?"

Claude smiled at Earl. "We're here to eat, aren't we, partner?" He looked at Bette. "Give us a couple of chocolate shakes and two hamburgers. My pal here doesn't have a lot to say, but what boy did you ever know could turn down a shake and a hamburger?"

When their hamburgers arrived, Claude tied a napkin around Earl's neck. "The key to a good hamburger," he told the child, "is not to load it up with a lot of extraneous condiments. A little salt and pepper, one"—Claude held up a single finger for emphasis—"slice of tomato, maybe just a skosh mustard, and that's it." He then cut the hamburger in two so Earl could hold it better. "Lean in over the plate when you bite so the juice doesn't run all over your trousers. And don't be talking so much," he joked. "I can barely get a word in edgewise. Oh, I almost forgot: the way this milk shake deal works is, you get one drink of milk shake for every two bites of hamburger. That way, a little food gets eaten in the process." He winked at the boy, a smile on his face. "Mrs. McCutcheon didn't raise any fools."

Out of the corner of his eye Claude noted that Earl was beginning to imitate everything he saw Claude do, from the way he rested his forearms on the table to the way he arranged the french fries and hamburger on his plate. Claude smiled, remembering that most of his own mannerisms had been picked up watching his own father. He nodded at the boy's plate. "Good?"

Earl nodded back, a spot of mustard on the side of his face. "Good."

After they had eaten, Claude motioned Bette over to their table. She sat down with a sigh and smiled at Earl. "What'd you say your name was, sweetheart?"

"His name's Earl and as a general rule he won't talk to women he doesn't know well."

"I like him already," Bette grunted. "The trouble with most men, and I ought to know, is that they don't know when to shut up. Particularly around women. This good-looking boy"—she jerked a thumb at Earl—"is off to a promising start in my book."

"Have you had a chance yet to ask anyone about Sentinel?"

Bette raised her right arm and waved at one of the waitresses working behind the counter. "This is Delia, our house magician," she said, introducing the young woman to Claude when she came over. "Delia, this young man"—she nodded at Earl—"would love to see you pluck a dime out of thin air. Why don't you sit him up on the counter and show him a few tricks while Claude and I have a quick word or two."

"It's okay," Claude reassured the boy, "I'll be right here."

Bette scooted her chair closer to Claude's as soon as Delia and Earl left the table. "I talked to a friend of mine last night, a woman who used to work for Sentinel. Asked her to check around with anyone she might still know over there. It's going to take a little more time, but . . . Let me ask you a question: What do you know about this company?"

Claude held up his right hand, forefinger and thumb joined to form a zero. "Nada."

"Then I should give you a little background. Like damned near everything down in the Valley, it's a relatively new company. A couple of refugees from Bell Laboratories started it up in the early 1970s. They were specialists in microwave communications technology so naturally that was the direction the company initially took. They did okay, nothing special, until around the mid to late seventies, when they started doing more and more military work. They financed a major move into laser technology with venture capital money and, big surprise, the VCs made them take on a new CEO—guy by the name of, get this, J. Watson Mellon."

"Sounds Ivy League."

Betty snorted with derision. "He was. Is. A real first-class asshole. As the two geeks that started the company found out. Within a year and a half Mellon had forced the founders out and owned the company lock, stock, and barrel."

"Nice work if you can get it."

"Tell me. Under Mellon the company has gone exclusively for the military market. In addition to secure microwave communications gear, he's become a huge player in the laser-guided-weaponry industry." Betty paused and lit a Camel. "Anyway, that's a little background for you. As I was saying, my friend, the ex–Sentinel employee, called me back this morning and said the joint is jumping. Nobody seems to know anything, but her contact told her that security people are running around like cockroaches. Worse, the FBI has even been snooping around, talking to people."

"What do you think?"

"I think your friend's about to get his tit caught in a wringer." Betty leaned in and lowered her voice. "Sentinel has a reputation for meanness in the Valley, from the top down. Bigtime. People that know them don't fuck with them, you understand what I'm saying?"

Claude nodded. "I appreciate the information."

"Don't mention it." Bette stood up. "Come by again tomorrow. My friend was going to be talking later today to someone who still works there, someone who should be able to get a little more specific. It's tough getting anybody to talk, though. My experience was that the paranoia-induced pucker factor among most of the yuppies in the high-tech industry is so high you couldn't pull a pin out of their asses with a tractor."

"A felicitous image," Claude responded dryly. "Thanks again, Bette." He turned to Earl. "Let's go."

Claude took Earl home, intending to spend the afternoon playing with the boy. But almost as soon as he got home, the phone rang.

"Sorry to bother you at home," Emma Fujikawa said, "but just as I was leaving the office, you got a call from Sam Ratliff."

"What'd he want?" Claude asked. Sam, together with his two sons, operated a small construction and remodeling business in Berkeley.

"He wouldn't say, but he sounded quite agitated. I think you should call him back as soon as you can."

"I'll call him right away. Thanks, Emma." Claude hung up and immediately dialed Sam's number.

"Hello? Sam?"

"Jesus, Claude, I'm glad you got back so soon. Listen, you know that duplex we just started working on, over on Shasta?"

"Sure do."

"We started excavating for the foundation yesterday," Sam said, agitation clearly evident in his voice. "This afternoon, about an hour ago, the backhoe started turning up bits of what look like old skeletal remains, together with other junk like arrowheads, pieces of old pottery, and crap like that. What the fuck am I going to do?"

Claude shook his head. "Bad luck, Sam. Sounds to me like you've hit an old Indian burial ground. If I'm not mistaken, the state says that when builders run into something like that, they're supposed to shut everything down and notify an archaeological review board."

Sam groaned, a doleful sound. "Jesus Christ,

Claude, that'd kill me. You know I can't afford to go shutting down like that. How long do you think they'd tie me up?"

"You know what those pinheads over at the University of California are like. Hell, they'd probably want to be digging around over there with spoons and tea strainers for at least a year. And I'm not even sure the archaeologists are your worst problem."

"What do you mean?"

"You've heard the expression *multiculturalism?* Well, as soon as one self-appointed anthropological watchdog or another hears about your 'discovery,' they'll call the site a sacred burial ground and ask the city to revoke your building permit. And in Berkeley that's as close to a slam dunk as you're likely to get in this life. I'd say that if word of this gets out, you can pretty much count on kissing this project, as well as any money you've already got in it, good-bye."

Sam groaned again, a sound of real pain. "This is going to kill me, Claude. You know I'm not big enough to finance having this project shut down for any length of time, let alone have it killed altogether. This could bankrupt me. What can I do?"

Claude thought for a minute. "Who was running the backhoe?"

"My youngest boy, Raymond."

"Anybody else know about this besides you and your boys?"

"No. I left both Ray and Sam junior over at

the site. I told them to cover the hole with a tarp
and not let anybody see a goddamn thing until I
talked to you."

"Good. Here's what I would do if it was me.
Get back out there and start excavating. Load all
the dirt into your dumper and haul it the hell
away as soon as possible. Then you and Sam
junior and Ray sift through it and pull out anything that might be identifiable as bones or arti-
facts like pottery, arrowheads, or beads. Take
that stuff and throw it in the Bay. Then you can
get rid of the dirt like you normally would."
Claude paused for a second. "But you better
move quickly. And for Christ's sake, keep any
passersby moving along until you get everything out of there. Somebody's sure to call the
city if they even suspect something isn't
kosher."

"Man, I appreciate this. I told the boys you'd
know what to do."

"My pleasure. You can pay me back by having one of your boys come by the house and
help me put in a new bay window off my
kitchen."

"You got it. Just let me know when."

Claude hung up the phone and turned to
Earl, who was staring up at him, a questioning
look on his face.

"So maybe you want to be a lawyer when
you grow up too, is that it?" He picked up the
boy and sat him up on the counter next to the
stove. "Son, I'm going to teach you how to

cook something so good you're going to want to run around the house three times after you've tasted it."

The little boy looked around the kitchen from his new vantage point. "Kitty."

"Don't you worry about that kitty," Claude said, gathering his gear together, "she can take care of herself. What we're going to be making here today is Brunswick stew, a taste of the Old South. Now, the first thing we're going to need is a fat hen, one of which I just happened to have picked up on my way home." Claude looked at Earl. "Are you paying attention to all this?"

"Kitty."

"No, we're not going to cook the kitty. The first thing we have to do is boil this hen until the meat comes plumb off the bones. Then we'll let the broth sit overnight." Claude pointed a wooden stirring spoon at his audience. "Good Brunswick stew is a two-day proposition, one never to be undertaken lightly. Tomorrow's going to be a busy day in the kitchen, you can take my word for it. Tonight, however, we'll order in a pizza and watch the A's whip up on the Orioles on the television. What do you think of that?"

"Kitty" was the now-predictable response.

Claude shook his head. "Son, the girls are never going to love you if you can't cook." He lifted Earl off the counter and onto the floor. "I'll get this hen aboiling and you see if you can find the kitty. Good luck," he added, knowing that Oscar had recently abandoned the house for the relative tranquillity of the backyard.

The game went extra innings before the A's won it with a suicide squeeze in the bottom of the twelfth.

"Man, I love those fuckin' A's." Claude yawned.

Earl was asleep on the sofa, where he had nodded off after two slices of pizza and five innings of baseball. Claude got up and turned off the TV. "Come on, sport," he said, gathering up the sleeping child, "let's you and me go to bed. We'll clean up the pizza and beer bottles in the morning."

In the sleeping alcove Claude laid the boy on the far corner of the futon and pulled the down comforter carefully up around him. He walked into the kitchen and made sure the window was open for Oscar. The Pinters' house was dark, and Claude stood quietly at the sink for a moment, reflecting on the unexpected twists and turns that make up a life.

Lord, he wondered, *what in the world am I going to do with this boy?* The bold words with which he had reassured Sally Pinter the morning Earl had been left with him sounded foolishly hollow in the quiet of midnight. Now that a couple of days had passed and there had been no word from Jesse, he knew that he could no longer passively wait and hope for the best. He was going to have to find JoJo Watson. It might take the better part of an afternoon, but he was confident that JoJo was somewhere over in the City, down in the Tenderloin, scuffling for his next hit, his next bottle of fortified wine or, better yet, vodka. Jesse had talked to Artie Gibson, too, at San Quentin. *There was always a fine line between us,* Claude thought, *me and Artie.* Nothing really conscious, nothing you could ever put your finger on, just a reserve between the two men, going all the way back to Vietnam. Years later, when Claude started helping a few veterans in the Bay Area, they had run into each other again and had gotten close, much closer than they ever could have been in the army. *Maybe Artie can tell me something.*

He wondered what additional information Bette Beal's friend would be able to gather on Sentinel. He wasn't at all surprised at what she had told him that morning, based on his reaction to Barton Jones. *I need to know more about them.*

And Miss Rita of the FBI. Claude smiled, remembering how the subtle smell of her perfume had lingered in his office after she left. *What does the FBI really know about all this?* he wondered. *And, more importantly, what don't they know?*

Claude turned from the window and walked quietly back to the futon. In three minutes he was sound asleep.

* * *

The dream itself never changed, just the
characters. Claude had been having it for so
long that it was almost welcome, an old friend
visiting him most every night. Tonight it had
been the Mabry brothers, Kenny and Orville.
The dream was a little unusual because Claude
knew that Orville, or Buddy as everyone called
him, had never been in the Nam. Nonetheless,
there they were, the three of them, lounging
about a firebase in the rolling hills of I Corps,
up near Phu Bai. Buddy, a state prison—educated gunsmith of some local renown in North
Carolina, had made certain unauthorized modifications to Claude's standard-issue M16, modifications that, he said, would result in greater
firepower. He handed the automatic weapon
back to Claude and gave him a tobacco-stained
smile. *That sumbitch'll grind 'em out all day*, he
said, scratching contentedly at his crotch. The
scene switched instantly to night, and Claude
was on the perimeter, alone in a bunker with a
horde of North Vietnamese regulars clambering
over the concertina wire directly in front of
him. Mortars coughed, filling the sky with para-
chute flares, millions of candlepower bathing
the land in a cold, white light. As he confi-
dently brought his rifle to bear on the nearest at-
tackers, he discovered, to his horror, that
Buddy's modifications had rendered his
weapon useless. *Goddamn it*, he yelled as he
desperately worked the action in an effort to
unjam the M16. He could see men fighting all

around him, could hear the screams of the wounded and dying, but could not for the life of him get his rifle to fire.

Claude was not sure of when exactly he crossed the line between dream and reality. He was in the middle of the dream one instant, then awake, sweating on the futon, the next, alert but confused, his sense of time and place disabled. Disoriented, the darkness in his house suffocating, he lay quietly on the futon and listened to his pounding heart, gradually realizing that the jammed rifle was a dream and that he had watched Buddy Mabry and his brother, Kenny, die on a dirt road in South Carolina many years ago. Seldom did he sleep through the night—the hours between 1 and 4 A.M. were typically fitful at best, given over to tossing and turning, snatches of fretful sleep interspersed with wakefulness. He heard the boy, Earl, breathing softly, and it brought a smile to his face. *What do children dream of?* he wondered, somewhat amused and not a little surprised at the strong feeling of parental protectiveness he was already experiencing. *I'm beginning to understand how a man can love a child so much that he would leave him with someone he hadn't seen in thirty years.*

Fully awake, Claude decided to get up and go into the kitchen for a drink of water. Rolling over onto his side, he sat up on the edge of the futon, taking care not to wake Earl. Just as he started to rise, he heard a muffled voice in the darkness of the great room.

He quickly reached into the small Korean chest that sat next to the futon and grasped the heavy Colt .45 he kept there. He swung the weapon around, automatically thumbing the hammer back as he did so.

A dark shadow fell across the sleeping alcove, followed by the indistinct form of a man. Claude fired without thinking, the big Colt kicking back in his hand as the recoil mechanism ejected the spent shell casing and chambered a new round in less than a heartbeat.

5

He's deader than a doornail, Lieutenant." The EMT looked up from the body to Albany Police Lieutenant Bill Anderson. "Looks like one bullet through the sternum and into the heart. No exit wound, so I suspect the bullet disintegrated on impact. I'll bet the inside of that chest looks like a disaster area."

Anderson grunted and turned to the photographer. "You get enough pictures?"

The photographer nodded and began packing away his Nikon. "You mind if I smoke?" he asked Claude. "It helps calm my nerves."

"Help yourself," Claude replied with a yawn **and** a look at his watch. "Smoke 'em if you got 'em." It was 3 A.M. and he felt as if he had been up all night.

"All right, get it out of here," the police lieutenant said, indicating with a jerk of his thumb that he wanted the body placed in a body bag and removed.

The EMT nodded and motioned for the ambulance driver to lend a hand. Together they rolled the body into the heavy-gauge polypropylene bag and zipped it shut. They strapped it on a telescoping aluminum gurney and wheeled it back through the living room and out the front door.

"Tell me again how it happened," Anderson said, turning back to Claude.

"I've told you twice already."

"I know, but I'd like to hear it again." Anderson smiled. "Humor me."

Before Claude could answer, Lt. Bernie Beck, his pajama bottoms showing at the cuffs of his trousers, walked in. He neatly sidestepped the large pool of blood that had partially soaked into a small Oriental rug. He pointed at the stain. "You're going to have a tough time getting that blood out of there," he said to Claude.

"I know it," Claude said.

Anderson greeted Beck with a firm handshake and looked down at the carpet. He shook his head. "No fuckin' way. That bloodstain's never going to come out," he said to Claude. "You're going to have to replace the rug. I hope it wasn't too valuable."

"Valuable enough," Claude replied sourly, thinking it exceedingly unlikely the decedent's next of kin would offer to pay for a replacement.

Anderson grunted unsympathetically and looked at Beck. "What are you doing here?"

"He gave me a call at home," Bernie said, indicating Claude with a nod of his head, "right after he called the station. We've known each other for a long time so I thought I'd come on over and see if there was anything I could do to help out. You don't mind, do you?"

"Oh, hell no. The more the merrier. Not much to do, though. Your friend Mr. Mc-Cutcheon here couldn't identify the intruder. He was a Caucasian male, thirty-five to forty, nondescript clothing. One shot from a Colt .45." He pointed to the pistol that Claude had laid on the floor next to the body. "A heart shot, dead-on."

"Was the intruder armed?" Beck asked.

Anderson nodded. "Nine millimeter, still in his waistband. Got it bagged up for forensic. Nothing else. No ID, no nothing."

Beck turned to Claude. "Was he alone?"

Claude shook his head. "Hard to say. At first I thought a second man was in the living room, but I honestly can't say with any certainty that I actually saw or heard anything immediately after the confrontation." He shrugged. "My ears were ringing quite badly for a while after I shot. I doubt I could have heard very much for a minute or two."

"And you have no idea why the man you shot would have been prowling around your house at two in the morning?" Anderson asked.

"No. The only thing I can think of is that he was a burglar."

Anderson plainly disagreed. "I don't think so. This doesn't smell like a hot burglary to me. I don't know what the hell it was, but my gut tells me it wasn't a burglary. You got any unhappy clients that might have wanted to bump you off?"

"No. I've had a few *I* wouldn't have minded shooting, but none that I know of that were that unhappy with me. Besides, I don't really do that much lawyering anyway, and certainly no criminal work. Fact of the matter is, I haven't done anything that would cause someone to get *this* exercised about."

Beck took Anderson's arm and led him into the living room where the two men talked for several minutes. When they came back to the bedroom, Beck addressed Claude.

"I think we've probably got enough to go on for the time being. If you think of anything else, a disgruntled client, someone you were rude to in the checkout line at the supermarket . . ."

"Bernie, I told—"

"I know, I know, you don't have a clue who might be behind this, but humor me. Go through your closed client files, talk to Emma, do whatever it takes to jog your memory. If this wasn't just a burglary gone south—"

"And I don't think it was," Anderson reiterated.

"—then somebody came here on purpose. Lieutenant Anderson's going to be handling the investigation, but you can call either one of us if you think of something we should know, okay?"

Claude nodded. He bent down and started to pick up the Colt.

"Wait a minute," Anderson said. "We'll have to confiscate the pistol."

Claude looked up. "Why?"

"State law. That weapon was used in a fatal shooting and we have to run a complete forensic check on it. Don't worry, if everything checks out, you'll get it back."

"What about until then? I'll be the only one around here without a gun."

Bernie Beck laughed as Anderson bagged the pistol and the two of them prepared to leave. "Call 911."

Claude stood quietly in his darkened living room and watched the two police lieutenants drive away. When he was sure they were gone, he went to the armoire that sat along the back wall of the sleeping alcove and took out a short-barreled Smith & Wesson .38 revolver. It had been his father's pistol, one of the few tangible things he had gotten from the old man's estate. Although Claude seldom fired it, it was like an old and trusted friend.

After spinning the cylinder to double-check that it was loaded, he put it in the small Korean chest sitting next to the futon. When that was done, he walked through his kitchen, out the back, and over to the Pinters' back door. Sally opened the door on his first knock.

"Jesus, Claude," she said, white-faced, "is everything okay?"

Claude nodded and stepped into the kitchen with her. "No sweat, Sally, everything's hunky dory. As soon as they saw that it was a straightforward case of self-defense, they bagged up the body and left."

She sat down hard in a kitchen chair. "Jesus."

"I sure appreciate your taking care of Earl while the police were here. I'll get him off your hands now."

"All right." Sally led Claude back to her and Bud's small bedroom, where Earl lay fast asleep on their bed.

"He was no problem," she said to Claude. "I put him down as soon as you brought him over, and he went right back out."

Claude nodded, staring down at the boy. The kid was a sound sleeper, all right—Earl hadn't been bothered by the gunshot, hadn't even woken up until Claude had him out the back door. In the morning he probably wouldn't remember what had happened.

Not so Claude.

Whatever kind of trouble Jesse was in, Claude hadn't really considered it his up until this moment. But the kind of people who would go after a kid the way these killers had . . .

He bent down and took Earl in his arms.

Sally leaned against the doorjamb and shook her head. "Lord, Bud's not going to believe any of this when he gets home."

"Don't go spreading it around too much."

"You know I won't," Sally said, clearly a little irked. "I can keep a secret."

"I know you can." Claude smiled. "Thanks again, Sally."

"Sure. What're neighbors for?"

Claude was halfway across the yard to his door when she called out to him again.

"That boy's gonna be all right, isn't he, Claude?"

"Oh, yeah," he said, not even turning around. "You can count on it."

6

Claude managed to get himself and Earl bathed and fed by nine o'clock. Sure enough, the boy remembered nothing of the early morning's events. As soon as breakfast was over and the dishes were cleaned up, Claude called his office.

"Mornin', Emma," he said when his secretary answered the phone. "Look, I'm going to be a little busy this morning so I doubt that I'll get in until around lunch. Any calls or messages?"

"Just one. Special Agent Rita Johnson, of the FBI"—Emma paused dramatically—"just called and wants to see you today. I told her you'd call her back."

Good news travels fast, Claude thought cynically. "Call her back and tell her I can see her at four o'clock this afternoon. In *my* office, not hers. You got that?"

"Yessir, Mr. Benny," Emma responded in her best Rochester imitation. "Are you in trouble with the Bar Association again?"

Claude laughed. "Any other calls?"

"Nothing. Except, of course, the daily call from the doe-eyed Ms. Abbott wanting to know where you are. Where are you?"

"None of your business. Or hers, either. Listen, I want you to do one other thing for me. Call Nasrin Artoun and tell her I had a little accident over at the house. Ask her if she can come by today and take a look at a small antique Oriental rug she sold me a few years ago. It's stained and I want to know if she thinks she can do anything with it. The door'll be open so she can pop over anytime it's convenient for her."

"Accident? What kind of accident?"

"I'll tell you about it later. Anything else?"

"Don't forget your eleven o'clock court appearance before Judge Fuentes."

"Not to worry. I'll see you this afternoon." Claude hung up and turned to Earl. "Okay, sport, let's you and me take a little ride."

At his still-unnamed gym Felix Mackie acknowledged Claude with the barest nod of his head. If he thought it surprising that Claude had a little boy with him, he did not show it.

"Felix, I need to talk to you." Claude sat Earl on a weight bench near Felix's front counter. "I need a favor. A big one." Claude nodded toward Earl. "This boy's the son of a friend of mine, a friend from the Nam. He's gotten himself into some deep shit with a company over in Silicon Valley and he left the boy with me for safekeeping. Last night someone broke into my house and tried to snatch him."

Felix looked at Claude, his expression unchanged. "What'd you do?"

Claude lowered his voice so Earl couldn't overhear the conversation. "I killed him."

Felix raised one eyebrow a fraction of an inch.

"I want to leave the boy with you and Ruth," Claude continued, referring to Felix's wife. "I need a safe place for the boy while I straighten things out."

"Where'd you say the boy's father was?"

"I didn't. Nobody knows where he is, me included. But I can tell you a lot of people are looking for him, including the FBI." Claude paused. "I don't know what kind of trouble he's gotten himself into, but he was a good man when I knew him. We go back a ways."

Felix nodded. "Leave the boy with me. I'll call Ruth to come pick him up. You tell whoever sent that man over to your house last night to not even think about coming by me."

"I'll tell him personally." Claude walked over and picked Earl up from the weight bench and sat him on the counter in front of Felix. "Earl, this is Mr. Mackie. He's a personal friend of mine. I want you to stay with Mr. Mackie and his wife for a few days while I help your daddy, okay?"

Earl looked at Claude and shook his head. "Kitty," he said in a small voice as he began to cry.

Claude looked helplessly at Felix and then back at Earl. He took the boy into his arms and held him tightly for a moment. "I know this is tough on you, son, and I don't like it a bit better than you do, but you'll be just fine with Mr. Mackie and his wife for a few days. You can come visit the kitty real soon."

Felix nodded in agreement. "My wife loves children," he rather awkwardly assured Earl. "Look here. I'll call her right now and we'll go over there together."

Claude handed the boy to Felix and quickly left the gym.

Judge Rosa Fuentes, the presiding judge of the Contra Costa County Superior Court, was decidedly not amused by the matter before her. A Stanford Law School honors graduate and daughter of migrant farmworkers, she was generally regarded by most of the attorneys who appeared before her as utterly humorless. One of the youngest judges to be appointed to the bench in the state's history, at thirty-four she was now a seasoned jurisprudence veteran who took great pride in the efficiency—some said brutal efficiency—with which she ran the busy Contra Costa Law and Motion calendar. She pointedly glanced at her watch before looking down at the two attorneys standing before her bench.

"Do I understand, Mr. McCutcheon, that it is your intention to challenge the Redevelopment Agency's right to take your client's property?" Judge Fuentes's words quite adequately conveyed her incredulity.

"Indeed it is, Your Honor." Claude cast a contemptuous glance back toward the plaintiff's counsel's table at which sat the City of Richmond's Redevelopment Agency director, one Ernest Biden. "The Agency has failed utterly to demonstrate a need for the taking of my client's property beyond a publicly stated desire to 'protect' the citizens of Richmond from the presumed moral depredations of adult bookstores." Claude paused for effect. "I submit, Your Honor, that the citizens of Richmond far more need protection from their own Redevelopment Agency than from the legal and proper operation by my client of his lawful business, to wit, the sale of books, films, and miscellaneous articles of a, shall we say, adult nature. If I may quote from an opinion of the court of appeals of this great state: 'Since the nomad ceased from his wanderings, the progress of man has been reassured by his consciousness that his ownership of land'—and, I

might add, the conduct of his lawful business—
'was by the custom of his tribe or by the law of
his state rendered secure against the predatory
rapacity of the greedy and the malevolent.'"
Claude turned and pointed at a bespectacled,
rather puzzled-looking Ernest Biden. "There,
Your Honor, sits greed and malevolence."

Biden, his face suddenly flushed, jumped to
his feet. "Now see here—"

Claude's opponent, Ben Fong, Richmond's
city attorney, was having a difficult time hiding
his amusement. "Your Honor," he said, waving
Biden back to his seat and with his heart clearly
not in the game, "I must protest Mr. Mc-
Cutcheon's characterization of my client, the
Richmond Redevelopment Agency, as both
greedy and malevolent." He looked at Claude
and suppressed a smile. "Perhaps greedy *or*
malevolent, but surely not both."

"Do you have anything further to say?" Judge
Fuentes asked Claude, her tone of voice implying that she had heard quite enough.

"No, Your Honor. I intend to file a writ of
mandamus within the next few days."

Judge Fuentes looked at Ben Fong, who
merely raised his eyebrows and shrugged,
annoying the judge further. "You have ten days
in which to file your writ," she said to Claude.

"Thank you, Your Honor," Claude responded
courteously.

Although a number of other Law and Motion
matters were to be heard, the judge abruptly

rose from her seat. The bailiff, taken by surprise, looked up from the crossword puzzle she had been working on. "All rise," she commanded somewhat belatedly in a loud voice as the judge disappeared from the courtroom.

Claude smiled at Ben Fong. "I'd offer to buy you a cup of coffee but I need to get back to my office."

Ben wagged a finger at his old friend. "You really stepped off into the deep end this time. Fuentes's going to work you over like a cheap steak. You pissed her off big time with that mandamus bullshit."

Claude sneered for his friend's benefit. "To hell with her if she can't take a joke. If she gives me a hard time, I'll make a motion to disqualify her from ruling on my writ."

Fong laughed. "You haven't got the *cojónes* for it. Every judge in the county would have it in for you after that." He rubbed his hands briskly together in a gesture of gleeful anticipation. "I can see that this condemnation's going to be a slam dunk."

"Hell, my guy's going to lose anyway. I told him the best I could do would be to piss as many people off in the process as possible."

Ben nodded toward the judge's chambers. "I'd say you're off to a good start."

"How'd it go?" Emma looked up at Claude from behind her desk, where she was on her hands and knees.

Claude peered quizzically around the desk at her. "You don't have somebody down there with you, do you?"

"I dropped an earring," Emma said, rising to her feet with a grunt, the wayward piece of jewelry held triumphantly in her right hand. "And you'd better get that so-called janitor of yours to pay a little more attention to what he's supposed to be doing in here." She blew a large dust ball off the earring she had retrieved from under her desk. "Oh, and Ben Fong just called. He said you had gotten yourself in trouble with the judge again." She wagged a finger at her boss. "Haven't I told you a thousand times to behave yourself when you're in court?"

Claude laughed. "Yes, dear."

"What did the judge say?"

"She wanted to know where I bought my anteater-hide boots." He lifted his right leg to show off the expensive boot. "Said she'd never seen anything quite so nice. I expect she wants to buy herself a pair."

"Huh," Emma retorted. "I don't see why you can't wear ordinary shoes like everybody else. Did the sleazeball show up for your hearing this morning?" Emma was referring to the owner of the adult bookstore Claude was representing.

"He did," Claude said with a broad smile, "and as a matter of fact, knowing you to be a connoisseur of the unusual, he sent over a little something for your amusement."

Claude reached into his leather briefcase and, with a flourish, pulled out a purple satin bag from which he withdrew an anatomically correct, if somewhat oversize, twelve-inch sex toy.

"This is the African-American model," Claude said, holding it by the shaft between his thumb and forefinger. "Ahmad"—Ahmad Rasheed, Claude's client—"markets it as the Black Beauty."

Emma shrieked with delight and waved her hands in the air. "That's the most disgusting thing I've ever seen in my life," she crowed. "Let me hold it."

"I think the wart on the head is a nice touch," Claude said, handing the large, faux organ over to his secretary.

Just as Emma's fingers closed around the grotesquely compelling object, the office door opened and Emma's sister and brother-in-law walked in. The two visitors' eyes widened when they saw what Emma was holding.

A horrified Emma pointed the toy at Claude. "He did it," she said to her sister. When she realized what she was pointing with, she dropped the Black Beauty on her desk as if it had come alive in her hand.

"Betty knows me better than that," Claude sniffed. He shook his head sadly and turned to Roy Yamashita, Emma's brother-in-law. "I told her not to be bringing that thing to the office anymore"—Claude nodded toward the red-faced Emma—"but you know how it is with these liberated Japanese-American women."

Emma threw a paper clip at Claude. "You're a bad man. Just for that, you can take the three of us to lunch."

"Sorry, but I've got to be someplace else."

"What for?" Emma fixed a wary and suspicious eye on her putative boss.

"None of your business," Claude replied with a laugh.

"You haven't forgotten your four o'clock appointment, have you?"

"No, Mother, I haven't." Claude turned to Roy and Betty. "Listen, you guys have a nice lunch—I'll take a rain check."

"Humph," Emma grunted.

Claude walked into his private office and shut the door. Taking a seat behind his desk, he took out Jesse Hamilton's letter one more time, looked it over. Jesse mentioned talking to Artie and JoJo before he disappeared. *Not a good sign that JoJo's back at the VA.*

Claude flipped through his Rolodex, found the number he wanted, and dialed the VA.

"Ms. Thorne? Good morning, my name is Claude McCutcheon, and I'm trying to reach a patient there, a veteran named Joseph Watson."

"Watson, Watson," the woman murmured as she scrolled down the inpatient list on her computer screen. "That name rings a bell. Yes, here it is. I'm sorry, Mr. . . . ."

"McCutcheon."

"Yes, Mr. McCutcheon, I'm sorry, but Mr. Watson left the hospital yesterday afternoon."

"He was discharged?"

"Well, no, that's why I remembered his name. His doctor didn't discharge him; he left on his own, against his doctor's orders." She paused and clucked sorrowfully, not unlike a melancholy hen. "I'm afraid there's likely to be some difficulty should Mr. Watson seek treatment at this facility in the future. The VA has very strict rules regarding behavior like that."

"Thank you for your help," Claude said as he hung up, wanting more information but knowing he was unlikely to get any more over the telephone. He leaned back and put his feet up on the desk. *I don't get the feeling that JoJo is planning on checking back into the VA, at least not anytime soon.*

He checked his watch, thinking he would shoot over to San Quentin, see Artie. No, he decided. But maybe it was time to find out a little more about Sentinel, firsthand.

Driving south out of the City, Claude swung west and then south again onto I-280, following the lightly trafficked freeway through the brown hills of Burlingame and San Mateo. The main question on his mind as he drove was the nature and extent of the FBI's relationship with Sentinel. He was pleased that Rita Johnson, the FBI agent, had been honest about the fact that the electronic surveillance they had maintained

on Jesse was what had led them to him, Claude.
On the other hand, the visit from Barton Jones
had made it clear that Sentinel, unbeknownst to
the FBI, either had their own tap on Jesse's line
or, worse, had someone inside the investigation
feeding them information. Either way Claude
didn't like it and, believing the best approach
was a direct one, intended to tell Mellon just
that.

Sentinel's corporate offices occupied a small
but elegant redwood-and-glass, two-story building on the western side of I-280. The floors were
a combination of hardwood and unglazed tile,
and the walls were hung with obviously expensive art.

"J. Watson Mellon?"

Accompanied by Mellon's secretary, Claude
walked into the CEO's office and stood in front
of his desk. Behind Mellon a tinted, floor-to-
ceiling window revealed a stunning view of the
Los Altos hills. A mated pair of red-tailed
hawks called to each other as they soared at
opposite ends of a great circle in the strong ther-
mal updraft rising from the deep canyon just
beyond the window. Farther to the west, past
both La Honda and San Gregorio, lay the Pacific
Ocean.

Mellon rose from his chair and extended his
right hand. "That's correct, Mr. McCutcheon. It's
my pleasure to meet you."

Only Bette Beal's characterization of Mellon
as a real first-class asshole kept Claude from

smiling. Mellon was short and thin, almost elfin in appearance, with an exceptionally deep and resonant voice. It was an unsettling combination.

Mellon nodded toward Barton Jones, the only other person in the office. "I believe you have already met Barton Jones, my chief of security?"

Jones, sporting an expensively tailored three-piece summer-weight suit, leaned nonchalantly against a credenza to one side of Mellon's desk. He looked, Claude thought with grim humor, like a white Sonny Liston, pathetically dolled up to greet high rollers at a cheesy Las Vegas casino. The suit might be silk, but Jones himself was sow's ear all the way.

"I know who he is," Claude growled, ignoring Mellon's offer to shake hands. "He came by my house the other morning." Claude gave Jones no more than a rude, cursory glance, talking about him as if he weren't in the room. "I'm here to clear up a misunderstanding."

Mellon sat back down behind his desk. "Please." He motioned for Claude to sit down. "Would you care for a cup of coffee or tea? Perhaps a glass of chardonnay?" He smiled modestly. "I have an interest in a winery in the Napa Valley and last year's vintage was, I'm told by experts, quite extraordinary."

Claude shook his head. "No, thanks. I didn't come to visit. Somehow or other you people have gotten the idea that I'm involved with Jesse

Hamilton. Once and for all, I'm not. I don't like strangers asking questions about me, I don't like people eavesdropping on my telephone conversations, and I particularly don't like—"

"Please." Mellon smiled as he interrupted Claude and paused for a second as if in thought. "You're an attorney, are you not? Mr. McCutcheon, how would you like to be a Superior Court judge?"

"Knock off the bullshit," Claude snapped. "I don't want to hear it. I'm telling you people to back off."

"Mr. McCutcheon, it's not—"

"Just a minute." Barton Jones rudely interrupted Mellon with a wave of his hand. "The bottom line is this: your friend Jesse Hamilton is in possession of confidential, proprietary information that belongs to this company. You—"

"You're calling him a thief," Claude said.

Jones ignored the accusation. "You need to understand that Sentinel Microsystems is an extraordinarily powerful company, both economically and politically, and make no mistake about it, we're going to get back what belongs to us, one way or another."

"Mr. McCutcheon," Mellon interjected, "allow me to elaborate. If you were disposed to help us deal with Mr. Hamilton, to obtain the return of our property, we could show our appreciation in a very concrete fashion."

Claude snorted. "I told you, I don't want

what you've got. What I want is to be left alone."

Mellon smiled. "I was not making idle conversation a moment ago when I suggested that perhaps you might be interested in a seat on the Superior Court bench. I could pick up the telephone right now and call the governor on your behalf, and it would not be an overstatement to say that my doing so would be tantamount to your being so appointed."

"But the other thing you need to know and understand," Jones added before Claude could answer, "is that anybody who gets in the way of our effort to regain possession of our stolen property, whether directly or indirectly, will pay dearly."

Enraged by the threat contained in Jones's words and tone of voice, Claude turned and pointed at him. "I'm warning you: don't fuck with me."

He glared back at Mellon, who had risen from his seat.

"Mr. McCutcheon—"

"And don't you *dare*"—Claude tried and failed to keep the anger out of his voice—"fuck with the boy again. Do you hear me?"

Mellon stood impassively at his desk. "You're making a mistake, Mr. McCutcheon."

Claude turned and strode from the office.

JoJo Watson hadn't been too difficult to run down. As soon as Claude learned that JoJo had checked himself out of the VA, he called Anne Steinholtz, an old friend in the San Francisco city attorney's office.

"Anne, Claude here."

"Claude, it's good to hear from you. What have you been up to?"

"You know me, Anne, same old stuff. How about you?"

"Nothing new here. The usual slip-and-falls on city property, union disputes over how many city employees it takes to change a lightbulb, you name it. Oh, and you'll love this one—the city got served last week with a lawsuit claiming mental trauma caused by the sight of a cockroach on a Muni bus."

"Look at it this way—the crackpots ensure full employment for you and your uncounted colleagues who work in the city attorney's office. God alone knows what sort of foolishness the city would otherwise spend all that money on."

"Yeah, right," Anne chuckled. "Are you calling to ask me out? As in 'socially'?"

"Not quite. Listen, Anne, I need a small favor. An old army buddy of mine, Joseph Watson—everyone calls him JoJo—just dropped out of detox at the VA and disappeared into the City."

"Detox?"

"Yeah, alcohol, heroin, crack, you name it. Anyway, I'm a little worried about him and—"

"What's his name again?"

"Watson, Joseph Watson. I remembered that you were acting as a liaison between City Hall and several homeless advocacy organizations and thought you might make a call or two, ask if anyone has seen or heard of him."

"Is this good for a lunch?"

"At the North Beach Restaurant. With wine and dessert."

Anne had called back in ten minutes. "He's got a room at the Excelsior Residence Hotel, south of Market."

"I'm impressed."

Anne laughed. "The homeless folks are far more organized than most people give them credit for. As is, I might add, the city attorney's office. Anyway, someone who's been in the community as long as your friend Mr. Watson apparently has can usually be located with no trouble, just so long as it's not the police who are looking. When's lunch?"

"Thanks, Anne, I appreciate it. I'll call you soon."

"I've heard that before. Take care, Claude."

The Excelsior Residence Hotel was a six-story monument to societal meltdown three blocks south of Market Street in San Francisco. The not-so-grand lobby contained a mix of destitute elderly men and women getting by on Social Security and cat food, mentally disturbed young people on state and county general assistance who had no idea, on any given day, which planet they were inhabiting, and, by the looks of them, several young men in the final, heartrending stages of AIDS.

Inside the front door Claude greeted Jim Cavalini, a San Francisco plainclothes detective.

"Jim, thanks for meeting me. Sorry to be a few minutes late, there was an accident on the bridge."

"No problem, Claude. What's the deal?"

"An old friend, a man I served with across the Pond, has dropped out of sight."

"He lives here?" The detective's question covered a great deal more ground than a mere query as to domicile.

Claude nodded. "He lost a leg to a booby trap right at the end of his tour and never made the transition back to the real world. Booze, pills, heroin, whatever he could get his hands on—he's been in and out of detox the last several years at the VA, but it's never taken hold. A couple of us, old platoon mates, have tried to look after him from time to time over the years, but you know what that's like."

"When did you see him last?"

"He walked out of the VA yesterday against his doctor's orders. I know he's got a room here, but I couldn't get anyone on the telephone to tell me whether or not he was in. I thought we could get a key at the desk and check out his room."

The two men walked across the lobby to the chain-link fence—enclosed desk area.

"What room is . . ." Cavalini turned to Claude. "What's his name?"

"JoJo, uh, Joseph Watson."

Cavalini nodded and turned back to the clerk. "What room is Joseph Watson in?"

The clerk, a blade-thin young man with pierced ears, nose, lips, and eyebrows, curled his upper lip, revealing more gum than teeth. "That information is confidential," he sneered, having pegged Cavalini and Claude as dicks from across the lobby.

Cavalini looked at the clerk for several long seconds, letting tension build. Only when the clerk started blinking nervously did he speak.

"Get your ass out of there and take us up to his room," the detective rumbled, his voice low and threatening.

The three of them walked over to a rickety-looking, wire-cage elevator.

"What floor's it on?" Claude asked, looking at the elevator with the cynicism of a three-legged coyote contemplating a baited trap.

"Two."

"Christ." Claude motioned with his thumb toward the stairwell. "Let's walk up."

At the door to JoJo's room, Cavalini turned to the clerk. "Open it," he grunted.

"Jeez," the young man started whining while he fumbled with the large key ring chained to his pants, "I'm not supposed . . ." His voice petered out under Cavalini's unblinking stare as he found the correct key and unlocked the dead bolt.

Claude brushed by the clerk and into the room. A quick glance was all he needed to know that JoJo was past worrying about having burned his bridges at the VA.

7

"That your friend?" Cavalini nodded toward the body sprawled on the army cot, apparently the only piece of furniture in the room.

"Yeah," Claude murmured, "that's him."

Cavalini pointed to the hypodermic syringe lying next to JoJo's body. "I'd say he drove the spike one time too many."

The front-desk clerk came into the room, sniffing like a large, particularly unattractive rodent hot on the trail of a piece of cheese. "Christ," he said loudly when he spotted the body, "why do these miserable fucking winos always pick this hotel—"

Before he could finish his sentence, Claude

stepped up and slapped him across the face, snapping his head back with the force of the blow. His eyes widened in shock and his hand went up to his mouth, where Claude's blow, though open-handed, had forced one of his few remaining teeth partially through his lower lip and loosened it.

"What the fuck!" he screamed, blood flowing copiously from the corner of his mouth. "You can't hit me, you son of a bitch."

Claude, his eyes narrowed to slits and his lips pulled across his teeth in a terrible snarl, closed his right hand into a fist.

"Whoa, now," Cavalini said placatingly to Claude, stepping suddenly between him and the clerk, "easy, easy." He looked at the young man. "Get out of here," he ordered.

"Fuck you!" the young man shrilled, shocked at the pain of his cut lip. "You saw him hit me. What the fuck kind of cop are you anyway? You should be arresting the motherfucker, not hassling me." His voice had risen so high he was actually squeaking.

Cavalini laughed and then moved in close. His voice dropped and suddenly carried an undertone of serious threat.

"You want *real* heartache, keep running your big mouth, asshole."

Cavalini's left hand snaked out and he grabbed the young man's right arm at the wrist, turning it so that the inside of his elbow stood out.

The clerk yelped in pain and tried unsuccessfully to pull free.

"These are fresh tracks," Cavalini observed, nodding toward the inside of the elbow. "How'd you like to come downtown with me when I'm done here? Which reminds me, who's your parole officer? I'll bet anything he'd like to know that you're dirty."

The young man was suddenly frightened. "No way, man, no fucking way." He held up his free hand, palm out. "I don't know shit, you know what I'm saying? I opened the door and, like, went back downstairs, okay?"

Cavalini smiled. "You're smarter than you look." He released the arm he had held in a cruel grip and pointed at the door. "Take a hike."

"I'm sorry, Jim," Claude said quietly after the clerk left. "It's just that JoJo was a good man, even if he came to a hard end." He turned his head so his friend wouldn't see the tear in his eye. "It could have happened to any of us." *And almost had,* he thought as he walked over to the grimy window to feign looking out while he wiped his eye.

"Forget it." The detective reached into his pocket for a cell phone. "I'll call the coroner's office and get a team up here."

While Jim dialed and then spoke to his office, Claude looked around the room. All of JoJo's worldly possessions were in two grocery-store cardboard boxes. Claude quickly rifled through them and determined that nothing there appeared to have come from Jesse Hamilton. He looked back at the body and noticed a piece of paper tucked into the breast pocket of JoJo's shirt.

"What did you find?" Cavalini asked, folding up his phone.

"A telephone number." Claude held up the piece of paper so Cavalini could see it.

"Anybody you know?"

Claude nodded. "Another vet, lives over in the East Bay. Been in and out of the VA the past few years same as JoJo." He sighed and ran a hand over his face. "Listen, Jim, do you mind if I leave you with . . ." He nodded toward JoJo's body.

"Sure, Claude, no problem. The coroner's office should be here any minute. I may need a formal statement from you, but I can get that later."

"Thanks, Jim. Oh, and one last favor: Would you tell the coroner's people I'll take care of the body when they're done with it? For burial and everything."

Back on the street, Claude made a quick decision. *I should have enough time to drive up to San Quentin and talk to Artie,* he thought, looking at his watch, *and still make it back to the office by four o'clock.*

"Claude." Artie took Claude's right hand in his. "I was beginning to think you might have forgotten where I was hanging out these days."

Claude smiled and shook his head. "Not a chance." The smile faded. "I hate to show up with bad news, Artie—JoJo's dead."

Artie's face showed no emotion. "I'm sorry to hear it, but, you know, the shit he put in himself, I'm surprised it hadn't happened before now." He looked down at his hands. "I appreciate you getting word to me personally. How'd he die?"

"Looks like a straightforward overdose. God knows he's been trying for years. The coroner's office will do an autopsy sometime in the next week or so."

"Where they going to bury him?"

Claude laughed, a hollow sound devoid of humor. " 'They' aren't going to bury him anywhere. As far as I could ever tell, JoJo had no kin, at least none that cared enough about him to spend any money to get him buried properly. The coroner's office gets a healthy fee from the medical school for every so-called indigent they ship over for the students to dissect, so my guess is that's where he'd be headed if I hadn't been there when the body was discovered." Claude shook his head. "They probably use the proceeds from the body sales to fund their office parties. Anyway, I left word that I'd take responsibility for the body when the coroner is done with it."

"Where you going to bury him?"

"I should be able to get him a spot in the national cemetery down at Colma."

"I wish I had a little something I could throw in the pot, you know, help out with the arrangements and all."

"Not to worry. The VA always kicks in a little something, and I'll take care of the rest."

Artie continued to look down at his hands. "You think many people seen as much dying as we have?"

Claude shrugged. "Probably. Fortunately, we're just not as used to it anymore."

"I don't think JoJo ever got used to it. He told me one time that he took all that shit to get away from the sight of all those dead bodies we saw in Vietnam."

"He's away from it now."

"You think he found some peace?"

"I'll be honest with you, Artie, I don't know what he's found. Can't be any worse than what he had here, though. Oh, by the way"—Claude handed Artie a double-CD jewel case—"before I forget. A new recording of the Bach cello suites."

"Pablo Casals," Artie murmured, examining the case, "digitally remastered. Thanks."

"I saw a review in the paper last week and thought you might enjoy it." Claude smiled. "Everyone else was always listening to rock and roll and Motown, and all you ever wanted to hear was Bach."

"The voice of God." Artie paused and looked

closely at Claude. "Jesse leave his boy with you?"

Claude nodded. "Lots of people seem to be looking for Jesse. And the boy."

"Jesse didn't think too many folks even knew he had a son."

"Someone knows. A man broke into my house last night looking for him."

"Did the police get him?"

"In a manner of speaking. I killed him."

If Artie was surprised, he did not show it. "It wasn't Barton Jones, was it?"

Claude did show surprise. "You know Barton Jones?"

Artie shook his head. "I know of him. It wasn't him, was it?"

"No. My guess is that it was someone he hired, though. What do you know about Jones?"

Artie took a moment before answering. "I told Jesse it wasn't fair to just leave Earl with you. But he was afraid of this man, Jones, afraid of what he might do. Well," Artie sighed, "I might as well tell you what I know. First, though, what happened to Earl after you killed whoever it was come looking for him? Do the police have him?"

"No. I stashed him with a neighbor lady while the police were around, and yesterday I gave him to someone who can look after him while I try to find Jesse."

"Who'd you leave him with?"

"Felix Mackie."

Artie's eyebrows rose a fraction of an inch. "I think Jesse would approve."

"He's got no choice in the matter. Now, why don't you tell me what you know about all this."

"Everything started maybe six months ago. Jesse was dating a sister that worked at the same place he did down on the peninsula."

"Sentinel Microsystems."

Artie nodded. "She was a computer scientist of some sort and he worked out in the warehouse." Artie paused and smiled sardonically. "They didn't have too much trouble finding each other 'cause there aren't exactly too many colored folks working down in Silicon Valley, you know what I'm saying? Anyway, like I said, they started seeing each other pretty regularly. Then, about a month ago, she came to see him at home late one night, agitated, saying she wanted to leave something with him, some sort of computer disc. She wouldn't tell why, just said to keep it for her for a day or two, and she would get it back. Then, the next night, she committed suicide."

"Suicide?"

Artie nodded. "Police found a note and everything. Case closed. Except Jesse didn't think so."

"He think she was killed?"

"Yeah. See, about a month before she died, this Barton Jones showed up. Seems like Sentinel wanted to beef up security."

"Hired muscle."

"You got it."

"Why? What was Sentinel afraid of?"

"Word around the company was that someone was selling the technology—you know, corporate espionage. Jones was brought in to find out who it was. Anyway, he scared a lot of people, and after the woman died, Jesse asked me to ask around, see if anyone I knew had ever heard of the guy." Artie smiled. "Jesse'd been around enough to know that if a man's dirty, someone in jail, somewhere, will know him, or at least know about him. Anyway, it wasn't too long before a guy I know over in the City, guy who did time a while back at the federal pen in Leavenworth, came up with another guy who knew a little about Mr. Jones. Turns out this second guy is a vet who got a dishonorable discharge and felt that certain people didn't help him out like he thought they should. So, my friend asks him about Jones, and he's willing to talk a little."

"Jones is army?"

Artie shook his head. "Was. Retired now, with full retirement pay and benefits. Served in Vietnam about the time we did, full tour plus two voluntary extensions. Quartermaster Corps in Saigon." He chuckled. "Man got over. I guess guys like you and me and Jesse and JoJo weren't too smart to be out humping the hills while guys like Jones were living in Fat City."

"What'd he do in Saigon?"

"Made money. Lots of it. You ever hear of something called the Network?"

Claude shook his head.

"Me neither. Turns out it was a group of senior NCOs who controlled the rackets in Saigon and all over the country. Sold everything from pharmaceuticals to guns to the VC and North Vietnamese. Quick as shit was unloaded at the Saigon docks, they stole it and ran it into Cholon, where they dealt it through Chinese brokers. They ran all the NCO and enlisted men's clubs and whorehouses and massage parlors on all the big base camps throughout the country. Plus, they sold protection services to most of the big civilian engineering projects going on in Saigon, Cam Ranh Bay, Da Nang, wherever. Anyone pouring concrete in Vietnam paid off sooner or later. We're talking tens of millions of dollars here, maybe more."

"I heard all those rumors, but how in the hell could a bunch of NCOs, even E-8s and E-9s, operate on such a scale without attracting attention?"

Artie laughed. "You're not that stupid, Claude." He rubbed his thumb and forefinger together. "We're talking big money here, right? Big goddamn money. And a whole lot of it wound up in the hands of the generals, Vietnamese and American, who were running the war. Shit. Why do you think every goddamned general in the Pentagon wanted to get to

Vietnam? Their only concern was that the war might end before they got theirs."

"Where did Jones fit into all this?"

"At that time he was a relatively minor player. The guy doing the talking to my friend said that Jones's specialty was muscle, making sure no one got too nosy about what was going on."

"When did Jones retire?"

"Guy didn't know. Said the last he heard of him, several years ago, he was still in, assigned to some unit in Germany. Still working for the Network."

"What'd Jesse think of all this?"

Artie shrugged. "Enough to want to leave Earl with you until he figured out what he was going to do."

"Have you got any idea at all where I might reach Jesse?"

" 'Fraid not. See, when the sister got killed—"

"*If* she got killed."

"When the sister got killed," Artie continued, ignoring Claude's comment, "Jesse didn't have no idea what he was going to do with that disc she gave him. He stayed away from work, and pretty soon Jones put two and two together and figured that Jesse was in on it."

"In on what?"

Artie shrugged again. "Jesse didn't know, or if he did, he never told me."

"Why the hell didn't he just take the disc to the police?"

"I think he thought about that, at first, but

then when the police were so quick to call the woman's death a suicide, maybe he got scared. From what I told him about Jones, plus the death of his friend, hell, a man would be a fool not to think twice before standing up and waving his arms to attract attention to himself."

"There's something missing here, Artie. I mean, even if his friend were selling the company's high-tech secrets, I never heard of anyone getting murdered for industrial espionage. And in any event, from what you've told me about Jones, bringing him in on a matter like this seems like overkill, if you'll pardon the expression. Sort of like chasing flies with a sledgehammer." Claude paused for a second, choosing his next words with some care. "Listen, I know you and Jesse were close, but could Jesse have decided to freelance the disc after his friend died? Perhaps suggest a little cash reward from Sentinel for its safe return?"

"Could be," Artie replied carefully. "He didn't exactly share his thinking with me, other than the question of leaving little Earl with you for safekeeping. 'Course"—Artie looked down at his hands and then back at Claude—"you got to keep in mind that he was getting close to that woman, real close, before she died."

"You think he's after Jones more than the money?"

"Wouldn't you be?"

Claude stood up.

"What are you going to do?" Artie asked.

"Try to find Jesse before this Barton Jones or the police or anyone else does. If he gets in touch with you, I'd appreciate it if you'd advise him to call me. You and I don't need to be burying any more old friends."

8

There was a lot more to Claude McCutcheon than met the eye, Rita decided, pushing open the door to McCutcheon's small law office.

Maybe it was just prejudice talking, but she hadn't expected a lawyer in a small, solo practice on the periphery of a large city to be as competent as he clearly was. Most of the lawyers in McCutcheon's situation just couldn't do any better, couldn't get a job with a large law firm or corporation, and were forced to survive on a practice of cheesy divorces or drunk-driving cases.

McCutcheon was different, though. She'd been honest with him earlier—his office *had* confounded her expectations. Not just because of the bright red gladiolas on the table next to the sofa, nor the antique oak rolltop desk, nor the exotic, multihued hardwood floor, but the *feel* of the place—comfortable, masculine without being macho, substantial yet not overbearing. Far from the seedy, low-rent, out-at-elbow sole practitioner's office she had anticipated.

And then there was McCutcheon himself. Somehow she had pictured him as a suede-shoe artist in a shiny suit, a hustler operating on the fringe of the legal profession, arranging petty payoffs to the authorities, engaging sleazy investigators to photograph wayward spouses in tawdry divorce cases, filing dubious slip-and-fall lawsuits at the behest of professional plaintiffs. Instead, like the office itself, she'd sensed in Claude a straightforwardness, a substantiality without artifice. It troubled her. Her initial impressions had been confirmed by a brief talk with Lt. Bernie Beck of the Albany PD.

"Let me tell you something about Claude," Beck had said. "Folks around here, Albany, Berkeley, El Cerrito, all like him. A lot. He's helped a few young people get their businesses started and helped a few old ones settle their estates. Them as can pay, Claude charges. Them as can't, he doesn't. He's even helped a couple of paroled felons get jobs and just recently, in the past week or so, got a San Quentin grad set up in a new business, a gym, with a loan from a large bank. Simply put, he's a good neighbor."

Clearly a man worth finding out more about. So she'd convinced her boss, Joe Bradley, to put a tap on his phone for the last couple days. Not that that had yielded anything—McCutcheon was ridiculously circumspect on his phone, to the point where Rita began to think he actually knew it was tapped.

And then last night, when he'd shot a man breaking into his house. Connected with what was happening at Sentinel Microsystems?

She guessed so, as Claude's secretary showed her into the man's private office.

"Miss Rita," Claude said warmly, rising from behind his desk. He again motioned for her to sit on the leather sofa, and he settled himself into one of the facing chairs. "It's good to see you again."

"Claude." Rita kept her response polite, though he did seem to be genuinely pleased to see her. "I thought we should meet again, particularly after—"

"The unpleasantness at my house."

"Yes. Have you heard from Jesse Hamilton?"

Claude shook his head. "I haven't. But apparently the folks at Sentinel Microsystems believe otherwise."

"Why do you say that?"

"Let me rephrase that. Either Sentinel believes otherwise or there's another player in the game that I haven't been told about."

"What do you mean?"

Claude looked at Rita. "Do you think it mere

coincidence that someone broke into my house last night?"

"No, I don't think it was mere coincidence, but that's not the same thing as saying Sentinel was somehow behind it. Since they were the ones who contacted the FBI in the first place, I find it difficult to imagine that they would thereafter engage in breaking and entering for the sole purpose of obtaining information which, from their perspective, you may or may not have."

"I'd say it has gone beyond simple breaking and entering. It's now felony murder."

"Indeed it is. Tell me, do you honestly think Sentinel was behind it?"

"Let me answer your question with one of my own: What do you know about Sentinel's security guy, Barton Jones?"

Rita shook her head. "Nothing in particular. He briefed me on the alleged theft and shared what little personnel-type information the company has on Mr. Hamilton. Why do you ask?"

"If Sentinel was somehow involved in the break-in last night, he would have likely been the one who set it up."

"Really? Where did you get your information?"

Claude smiled. "Here and there. Seriously, though, there may be profit to be had in exploring Mr. Jones's background. I've been led to believe that it's an interesting and varied one."

Rita made a mental note to do just that.

"Speaking of the break-in last night, may I ask why you felt it necessary to kill the intruder?"

"Are you kidding?" Claude shook his head, clearly astounded at the question. "Let me set the stage for you. It's two o'clock in the morning, I'm sound asleep, and I wake up to find an intruder in my house. Case closed."

Rita looked troubled. "You could have frightened him away—maybe wounded him. Even criminals have rights."

Claude shook his head. "Not in my house they don't. Not at two o'clock in the morning."

"Do you always sleep with a gun beside your bed?"

"So many questions." Claude rose from behind his desk. "Let me propose something a little out of the ordinary. There's a wonderful Chinese restaurant just a block from here. Why don't we continue your investigation of Jesse Hamilton over an early stir-fried dinner?"

"I thought you hadn't seen him in thirty years. What could you know that might be helpful after all that time?"

Claude shrugged. "Some things don't change in a man. Things that might speak to his propensity for getting into or causing trouble."

Rita shook her head. "Thanks for the offer, but I don't think so."

"Are you sure? Look at it this way: you have to eat dinner anyway, and this is the best Chinese food you're likely to find on this side of the Bay." Claude smiled. "I would think that that in itself would be crucial information for anyone in the law enforcement business." He held his hands up. "Besides, as you can plainly see, I'm unarmed."

Like hell you are, Rita thought, looking up at him. *This is a bad idea. Why am I even thinking about it?*

"I'll pay for my own dinner," she said.

"I wouldn't have it any other way,"

The Hunan Palace restaurant presented little more than a small storefront on Solano Avenue. A childishly lettered piece of paper in the window listed the daily specials, and a bright red sign taped to the inside of the front door proclaimed that the Palace was OPEN. The dining room contained only eight tables, six of which, despite the early hour, were occupied. The air was redolent of garlic, ginger, and hot peanut oil. Two waitresses in incongruous western cowgirl outfits darted back and forth between the dining room and the kitchen. Overseeing everything was an elderly Chinese gentleman seated on a high stool next to the cash register.

"Why don't you grab that table," Claude said to Rita, indicating one of the two empty tables with a nod of his head, "while I go pay my respects to the old man."

"Is he the owner?" Rita asked, somewhat taken aback by the Palace's decidedly low-rent atmosphere.

"Yes and no. He started the place years ago. Came over from Hong Kong as a young man and worked himself damn near to death for over thirty years, living like a dog to save money. When he had enough, he began bringing his family over and putting them to work. Finally, when everyone was here and they had another small nest egg accumulated, he started this restaurant. It's strictly a family business. His son does the cooking, his daughter-in-law does the books, and the two girls waiting tables are his granddaughters. He's too old and tired to do much himself anymore, so they sit him up on that stool by the cash register to keep him out of the way."

Claude walked over to the old man and said something in his ear. The old man cackled and said something back in Cantonese, causing the nearer table of Chinese diners, who could hear the interchange, to break into laughter. Claude, smiling broadly, walked back to the table.

"What did you say to him?"

Claude winked at Rita, but before he could say anything, one of the waitresses came to the table. She addressed Claude in Cantonese, the same dialect the old man had used.

To Rita's astonishment Claude answered back in the same language. They spoke for a moment, Claude pointing once to the evening's specials board hanging by the galley doors to the kitchen. When the young girl walked back to the kitchen to give their order to her father, Rita smiled at Claude.

"I suppose I should ask what you've ordered, but somehow I get the feeling you know what you're doing. Did you learn Chinese in the army?" she asked, remembering that his military records made no mention of any particular language skills.

Claude shook his head. "I've helped the old man's family over the last few years with odds and ends—immigration and naturalization, landlord-tenant problems, that sort of thing. They pay me with language lessons now and again. I'm actually pretty bad at it, but since they seem determined to make a civilized person out of me, I do the best I can so as not to disappoint them. As to what I've ordered for dinner, you won't be disappointed. We're going to start out with hot and sour soup, mu shu pork, Szechwan crispy chicken, and then sizzling bean curds and prawns. How does that sound?"

Before Rita could answer, their waitress returned with a steaming tureen of soup, its spiciness all too apparent in the wonderfully complex aroma rising from its surface. Rita closed her eyes and inhaled. Claude spoke again with their waitress.

"Now what?" Rita asked.

"I asked her to give a glass of plum wine to the old man. And I ordered two bottles of Chinese beer for us." Claude took a spoonful of soup. "It's the only thing to drink when you're eating Chinese food." He smiled. "Dig in."

"This soup is wonderful," Rita said between spoonfuls. "And hot." She took a long sip of beer and felt herself beginning to relax. "Tell me about Jesse Hamilton."

Claude nodded, setting down his spoon. Rita noted with some surprise he'd already finished his soup.

"Most kids that go into the military try to blend into the woodwork, thinking that if nobody notices you, there's less chance you're going to get yelled at, assigned to work details, things like that. Jesse, though, was just the opposite. He was ambitious. He wanted to be noticed. He looked at the army as an opportunity, perhaps the best opportunity he was going to get as a young man. When he learned that the army had developed a new training program for noncommissioned officers, he immediately applied, and when he got the assignment, he graduated first in his class."

"Where was he from?"

"To tell you the truth, I've completely forgotten." Claude shrugged, helped himself to a little more soup. "I have no recollection whatever."

"So the first thing you remember about Mr. Hamilton is that he was ambitious."

"That's correct. And the second thing you should know is that he always made an effort to see that others around him succeeded. I'm probably not articulating this very well, but he felt that an integral part of his job as an NCO was to allow the men under him to develop and advance their own careers fully as much as he did his own. He never took credit for a job the platoon did well—he always singled out for praise the individuals who had performed at a higher-than-average level, those who did more than their share, or whatever."

"Mu shu?"

Rita looked up to see their waitress standing over them with two steaming plates.

"Right here," Claude said, clearing aside the large soup tureen and handing it to the waitress.

"Smells good, doesn't it?" he said to Rita.

She nodded.

"Which is not to say Jesse wasn't a hard-ass when necessary. He'd bend over backwards to help someone out, but you could not, pardon the expression, fuck with him. In Vietnam, when we were in base camp, he allowed a certain amount of goofing off, but when it came time to go on patrol, to take a walk in the woods, he had zero tolerance." Claude smiled. "In Jesse's platoon you did things his way—no ifs, ands, or buts. Everybody respected him, though, and no one, as far as I can remember, tried to transfer out."

"But you were the platoon leader?"

Claude set down his chopsticks. "Yes, although my recollection is that we were closer to being partners than anything else. Usually the relationship between platoon leader and platoon sergeant is a much more formal one, if for no other reason than the fact that the lieutenant is often fifteen or twenty years younger and therefore much less experienced than his platoon sergeant. Since Jesse and I were both the same age, and equally inexperienced, we developed a different, a much closer, relationship than otherwise might have existed. You might say that we made up the rules as we went along."

The Szechwan crispy chicken arrived, followed almost immediately by the sizzling bean curds and prawns. Claude ordered two more beers, and he and Rita slowly but surely began to make a dent in the serving platters. While they ate, each surreptitiously watched the other, quickly looking away whenever their eyes chanced to meet.

Rita finished the last of her beer with an audible sigh and, putting down her chopsticks with an unmistakable gesture of finality, looked over at Claude. "I couldn't eat another mouthful. I don't think I've ever had better Chinese cooking."

Claude, pleased, smiled broadly. "My sentiments exactly. How about a nice double espresso to cap your evening with that renowned desperado Claude McCutcheon?"

"Espresso? In a Chinese restaurant?"

"Lord, no. I was going to make it for you personally." Claude rose from the table and held a hand out to Rita. "I live only seven blocks from here and the walk will do us both good."

"Whoa, my agreeing to have dinner meant just that: dinner." Rita reached for her handbag. "And I intend to pay half the bill."

"No problem. Only, please don't pull out any cash in here. My honorable friend"—Claude indicated the old man at the cash register with a nod of his head—"would be shocked senseless. I'll take care of the tab and you can pay me outside."

Claude settled up at the cash register and met Rita outside.

"How much do I owe you for dinner?"

"Pay me at the house. I've never thought it a wise policy to exchange cash in public. It involves too many people in your business." Claude took Rita's arm and began walking.

"I never said I would have coffee with you—particularly not at your house."

Claude smiled. "It's the perfect opportunity for you to continue your investigation. Seeing my home and how I live will give you invaluable insight into my character. Plus"—he paused and looked at Rita—"if you'll allow me to make you an espresso, I'll tell you things about Jesse Hamilton that don't appear in any FBI files."

It was a pleasant evening, and a wonderfully indolent feeling came over Rita as she and Claude walked along. *Business,* she reminded herself. *This is not a social evening. This man is a key figure in an ongoing investigation, and the only reason you're going to his house is to further that investigation.*

Claude's house, a stuccoed and painted California bungalow, fit comfortably into a neighborhood of similarly well-maintained, small homes.

"Have you lived here long?" she asked as Claude unlocked the front door, wondering if his answer would jibe with the information she had received from Lieutenant Beck.

"I bought it in '78," Claude replied, stepping over the threshold and turning on the lights.

"Oh, my," Rita exclaimed, startled by what she saw.

The interior of the house had been completely gutted, its original standard two-bedroom, one-bath floor plan scuttled in favor of a single great room. All of the interior walls and ceilings had been removed, their structural function replaced by three massive, glue-lam beams running the length of the house. The beams were finished in a gleaming, Oriental red lacquer, and the roof joists were trimmed with all-heart redwood. The peak of the roof had been removed and a clerestory added along its entire length.

"Did you do all this yourself?"

"Mostly, although I did have a little help here and there." Claude laughed. "As you can probably tell, I've been tinkering around with it pretty much ever since I bought it."

The kitchen occupied one far corner of the great room and a slightly raised sleeping alcove the other. A toilet, pedestal sink, and antique claw-foot cast-iron tub were set apart by three shoji screens. A lustrously red-hued Brazilian-hardwood floor was laid throughout the great room except for the kitchen area, which was paved with unglazed Mexican paver tiles. Claude had removed the original plaster and lathing from two of the walls of the great room and built cedar-trimmed bookshelving into the studs. The sleeping alcove featured a futon on the floor and an old oak armoire. The only other furniture consisted of a matching leather sofa and club chair, and a hand-hewn-plank trestle table in the kitchen with four Shaker-style chairs.

"My God," Rita said, walking into the large room and noting the books on two walls, "it's like a library in here."

She went to one of the shelves and selected a calfskin-bound book, turning it over in her hands. She opened it and whistled a single, low note of appreciation. "A first edition of Lawrence's *Seven Pillars of Wisdom*," she said, more to herself than to Claude.

"Actually, it's one of the privately printed subscribers' texts," Claude said. "The texts were issued to subscribers in December 1926 and January 1927. T. E. Lawrence, an eccentric man to say the least, refused to divulge exactly how many such texts were printed and distributed." He took the book from Rita's hands and read from it:

> I loved you, so I drew these tides of men into
> my hands and wrote my will across the sky
> in stars

To earn you Freedom, the seven-pillared wor-
  thy house, that your eyes might be shining
  for me
When we came.

"He was also a poet," Claude added as he
replaced the book on the shelf.

"A book like that must be quite valuable,"
Rita said as she followed Claude into the
kitchen.

Claude shrugged. "I expect it's worth something," he said over his shoulder, "although it
doesn't much matter because I doubt I'd ever
sell it."

In the kitchen the large, uneven Mexican
paver tiles with their dark brown, rough-
textured finish gave a homey warmth to the
space. Through their respective kitchen windows Sally Pinter saw Claude and waved at
him. Her hand froze in midwave when she saw
Rita standing behind him.

"Friend?" Rita asked.

Claude smiled. "Neighbor. She likes to
come over for coffee during the day when her
husband's at work. Makes her feel, oh, I don't
know, maybe a little like a single woman
again."

"What does her husband think of it?" Rita
asked, not certain why she should care.

"I don't know." Claude busied himself with
the espresso maker. "I'll ask him the next time I
see him."

As Claude made two espressos, Rita walked around the kitchen, admiring the rustic, handmade crockery in Claude's open, doorless cupboards.

"Would you like to sit here in the kitchen or out in the living room?" Claude asked.

"Where would *you* like to sit?"

"Well, I've always liked visiting in the kitchen. Friends visit in the kitchen, company generally gathers in the living room."

"The kitchen it is." Rita sat at the dark, hardwood table. Looking at it closely for the first time, she knew it must be an antique. "Is this old?"

"Quite." Claude joined her with the two espressos. "It's from North Carolina and I was told that it came originally from Scotland in the late eighteenth century." He paused to sip his espresso. "The Shaker chairs are reproductions."

"It's exquisite," Rita murmured. She looked at Claude. "Besides T. E. Lawrence, who else do you particularly admire?"

Claude shrugged. "Richard Francis Burton comes to mind. A man truly to be admired if we can believe his biographers. He was an enigma of the highest order, a paradigm of nineteenth-century Western civilization."

"I don't believe I've ever heard of him."

"I'm not surprised," Claude replied, not unkindly. "I'm sure that Burton has for some time been considered politically incorrect by the politicians to whom public education is entrusted. Nonetheless, he was a colossal intellect whose achievements are almost unbelievable when considered against the backdrop of mediocrity that has become our standard today." He paused and smiled at Rita. "If you're interested, I'd be happy to provide you with a short bibliography."

"Tell me more about Jesse Hamilton."

Claude savored the strong taste of his espresso before answering. "There is a wonderful Zen Buddhist saying I try to remember whenever something is puzzling me: 'The finger pointing at the moon is not the moon.' "

Rita smiled politely but said nothing.

"By that I mean I think it would be a mistake," Claude continued carefully, "to focus your attention entirely on any alleged crime that Jesse may or may not have committed."

"How so?"

"Have you considered the possibility that in fact Jesse's the one who needs help here and not Sentinel?"

"What do you know that leads you to believe that your friend is in trouble?"

"Well, my nose tells me that something's not right here."

"Why do you think Mr. Hamilton tried to contact you?"

Claude shook his head. "I have no idea, I surely don't. As I explained at the restaurant, at one point in our lives we were as close as kids in the army can be, undying loyalty, that sort of thing, but we've remained entirely out of touch with each other ever since we got out."

"Until a few days ago."

"Yes, but remember, we never actually spoke—Jesse only left me a message."

"You served together in Vietnam. Perhaps something happened there that would cause him to feel a special bond, even if the two of you subsequently drifted apart."

"Who knows?" Claude smiled and looked down at his cup. "He may just have wanted to talk to someone with some sense."

"What will you say to him if he manages to get in touch with you?"

"Hard to know. Maybe I'll just listen to what *he's* got to say. Could be he's not looking for advice."

"Have you ever been married?"

"Never," Claude answered, looking up and meeting her eyes. "You?"

"No."

"How long have you been in San Francisco?"

"Just eight months."

They fell silent for several seconds, both keenly aware of the sexual tension that suddenly pervaded the room.

"Another espresso?" Claude finally asked, pointing at Rita's empty cup.

"No, thank you," Rita said huskily, her face coloring slightly but noticeably. She looked at her watch. "I'd better be going."

Claude immediately stood up. "It's been a delightful evening."

Rita shook her head emphatically. "It's been all business," she said firmly, "but not unpleasant."

"One question before you leave."

"Shoot," Rita responded, and then laughed. "Perhaps an infelicitous choice of words."

Claude smiled. "I'm unarmed," he reminded her. "The question: What are you doing for lunch on Friday?"

"Why?"

"There's somebody I'd like you to meet—somebody who might be able to give you some additional insight into this case. You could meet me for lunch at a place on Fifth Street in Berkeley called Kate's." He walked Rita from the kitchen back to the front door. "Would you like me to walk you back to your car?"

"No, thank you. What time Friday?"

"Noon would be just about perfect."

Rita stepped out onto the porch and down the two steps to the sidewalk. "I'll meet you there at noon. Good night."

Claude stood at the door for a moment before turning out the porch light and walking back into the house. He turned off the espresso machine and washed the two cups he and Rita had used, pleased that the evening had gone so well. The power of the sudden desire that had come up between them, the coalescing of vague feelings he had first noticed back at his office, before dinner, had taken him completely by surprise.

He had, of course, been physically attracted to her almost from their first meeting and had shamelessly used his old friendship with Jesse Hamilton to influence her to have dinner with him, but mere physical attraction aside, he was more than a little troubled at the obviously mutual desire, the charged, erotic atmosphere that had come upon them so quickly.

"Talk about pheromones," he said to Oscar, who came padding silently into the kitchen. Unimpressed, she sat on her haunches and began assiduously grooming one paw.

Leaning against the counter as he dried the cups and put them away, Claude smiled at what he thought must have been a rather transparent ploy to get her to have lunch with him on Friday, pleased nonetheless that she had agreed to meet him at Kate's. *Additional insight indeed*, he thought sardonically. *I could use a little of that rare commodity myself.*

9

"Mornin', Emma."

Dressed in blue jeans and a linen shirt, Claude stood at his secretary's desk. It was a little after ten o'clock on Friday morning.

"My God," Emma replied, concern on her face, "why didn't you tell me?"

"Tell you what?"

Emma pointed to the front page of the *Oakland Tribune,* unfolded on her desk. The headline proclaimed LOCAL ATTORNEY INVOLVED IN SHOOTING, accompanied by a photograph of Claude that looked as if it had been purloined from the files of the Department of Motor Vehicles.

"Jesus," he said, "where in the world do you suppose they got that picture? It looks like a police mug shot." He gave the paper back to Emma. "You'd think they could have done better than that."

"Why are you worrying about the picture?" Emma cried. "You could have been killed."

Claude laughed. "Then you'd have been in big trouble, wouldn't you, with no one to boss around."

Before Emma could answer, the phone rang. She picked it up and, after several seconds, rolled her eyes at Claude. "Could you hold the line for just a second?" She placed the caller on hold and looked up at Claude. "The Yellow Rose of Texas."

"Damn," Claude murmured, his mind racing. "I don't have time to deal with her this morning." He pointed his finger at Emma. "Tell her I'm over in the City visiting a sick friend today and that I'll call her first thing tomorrow."

"I'm sorry to have put you on hold, Ms. Abbott, how may I help you?" For Claude's benefit Emma pantomimed putting her finger down her throat and gagging. "I'm sorry," she continued after a short pause, "Mr. McCutcheon is not in the office today. . . . That's right. . . . No, he's going to be in the City all day today. I understand that a dear friend of his is under the weather. . . . Yes, I'll have him call you as soon as he comes in. Thank you." She hung up and stuck her tongue out at Claude.

"Thanks," Claude drawled. "Why don't you pour us a cup of coffee while I check my messages and make a call or two."

In his office Claude looked through his several telephone messages and decided that none of them needed calling back right away. Emma walked in with a cup of coffee.

"One of those messages is from Jack Anderson," she said, putting the cup on Claude's desk. "He said he's got a case he wants to refer to you. I think he's trying to return the favor for that probate work you sent him last year."

"Not interested," Claude said as he cautiously sipped the hot coffee. "I'll call him back later."

"You don't even know what he wants to send over." Emma heartily disapproved of Claude's disinclination to take on new clients. "It might be a good referral."

"Doesn't matter. Tell your nephew to hurry up and pass the bar exam and I'll bring him in here with me. He can handle all these new clients you seem so determined to saddle me with."

Emma's nephew had graduated from Cal that spring and was studying for the July bar exam. An honors graduate, he had been selected as a law clerk by one of the justices of the Ninth Circuit Court of Appeals.

"He'll have a hell of a lot more fun working for me than he will that octogenarian liberal he's signed on with, and more to the point, he'll learn how to make an honest living." Claude picked up the telephone on his desk and dialed a number. "Thanks for the coffee," he called out as Emma returned to her own desk, muttering that it would be a cold day in Hades when she allowed her nephew anywhere near Claude's office. "Jesus? . . . Yeah, Claude here. Listen, Jesus, I'm going to be down at Felix Mackie's new place on San Pablo Avenue in about twenty minutes. How about meeting me out front, and look, bring me a loaner, will you? I'll swap with you there. Thanks." He got up and walked out to Emma's desk. "I'm out of here. I'll be down at Felix Mackie's place for a workout and then lunch. In fact, take a long lunch yourself. I won't be back before three-thirty or so."

Jesus Ortega was waiting for Claude outside Felix's gym. A distant cousin of Rocky Martinez, a client and friend of Claude's, Jesus was what most people would have referred to as a shade tree mechanic. Jesus, paroled from the state correctional facility at Atascadero after serving eighteen months of a four-year sentence for grand theft, auto, had been referred to Claude by Rocky. Claude had helped him establish a garage out on the San Pablo Dam Road and had lent him the cash necessary to bring his wife and young daughter north from Hermosillo. Knowing that the young Mexican couldn't afford to pay him anyway, Claude declined to bill him for his services. When pressed, Claude admitted that he was looking for an older, pre-1960s Chevrolet half-ton pickup truck. Two months later Claude had his truck, a dusty gray 1955 that a cousin of Jesus's wife's sister-in-law drove all the way up from Mexico City. Claude paid $400 for the truck and immediately set Jesus to work installing a rebuilt short-block V-8 engine and transmission. He did nothing to the exterior, preferring the low-rent appearance of a working pickup. For the better part of a year Jesus had worked on the truck, slowly but surely replacing everything under the hood.

"How can I help you, amigo?"

"Two things." Claude held up two fingers. "First, the truck needs brake pads, and I want you to check the master cylinder as well—I think it might be leaking."

"Easy enough, my friend. What else?"

"I need a piece."

Jesus smiled, his mouth a blaze of gold. "What kind are you looking for?"

"You know me, Jesus, I'm an old-fashioned kind of guy. An army Colt .45 automatic. No knockoffs, no blems, and no trace."

"That's easy. My little Hector could handle it."

"How much?"

Jesus rubbed his chin for a few seconds and then held up four fingers.

Claude nodded. "When? Sooner is better."

"This afternoon?"

Claude smiled, pleased as always to be doing

business with a competent entrepreneur. He handed Jesus the keys to the truck. "I'll come out to your place. Three o'clock?"

"Sí." Jesus pointed to a battered 1976 Volkswagen Golf with Mexico City license plates and handed Claude the keys.

"It's not on any hot sheets up here, is it?" Claude asked sarcastically.

Jesus laughed but said nothing as he and Claude shook hands and exchanged keys.

A sign painter was hard at work when Claude entered the gym. Inside, Felix sat impassively behind his counter, surveying his domain with the nonchalant authority of absolute sovereignty.

"How do you like the name?" he asked Claude, nodding toward the almost completed sign: HOUSE OF IRON.

"I like it. It's a good name for a gym, downright Pennsylvanian. How's the boy doing?"

"He's not what you'd call a big talker," Felix replied, his arms folded across his chest. "Ruth's taken to him. Says she wants to talk to you."

Claude smiled, knowing that that was Felix's way of saying everything was okay. "Tell her I'll stop by and visit in the next day or so."

An hour later Claude walked into Kate's. He had finished his workout with a long, hot shower and was hungry.

"Claude." Bette pointed at him and nodded toward an empty table at the rear of the diner.

"Whoa, that feels good," Bette sighed as she sank into a chair next to Claude. "I haven't been off my feet since six-thirty this morning."

"The joys of sole proprietorship," Claude said as he handed her a Camel. "The boss always works harder than anyone else."

"You got that right." She flagged down one of her waitresses. "Bring us a couple of cups of coffee, darling." She accepted a light from Claude and sat back in her chair. "I got a little more information for you, but first, I want to know what the hell's going on."

"What do you mean?"

"Don't give me that wide-eyed look of innocence," Bette snorted. "First you come in here with some cock-and-bull story about a friend having personnel problems at Sentinel, next you show up with a young boy clearly in your custody, then, whammo"—she slammed a fist into an open palm—"I read in the paper that you've killed someone, an intruder, at your house. Believe me, I don't need Dick Tracy to tell me that you're already up to your *cojónes* in whatever's going on at Sentinel."

"Not quite up to my *cojónes* yet, but I'm getting that way. You're right about the boy. His daddy's on the run from the folks at Sentinel, and he left him with me for safekeeping. My guess is that the intruder I shot the other night was looking to snatch him for the company and force his daddy out into the open."

"Who's his daddy?"

"His name is Jesse Hamilton. Friend of mine." Claude paused for a second. "Well, not exactly a friend—an old army buddy. Guy I haven't seen for thirty years. He left the boy with me in the middle of the night with a note that didn't tell me a damned thing."

"Do the police know about the boy?"

Claude shook his head.

Bette raised an eyebrow. "I'd say you're taking a hell of a chance for just 'an old army buddy.' "

"I know it sounds crazy, but . . ." Claude's voice trailed off. "I think of the guys I served with in Vietnam—we're like family. And we can pretty much count on ourselves, and that's about it. Vietnam vets have been marginalized, cynically manipulated, used and discarded by politicians, conservative and liberal, from Kennedy forward. So, when someone like Jesse Hamilton turns to me for help"—Claude shrugged—"I help. Maybe not exactly like he expects, or would have wanted, but I do what I can."

"What'd your friend do to piss Sentinel off so badly?"

"I'm not exactly sure. The police seem to think it's a simple case of stolen technology—industrial espionage."

"Shit," Bette grunted. "The high-tech business supports the greatest number of paranoid personalities in the Western world. All those assholes seem to be able to do is sit around worrying about someone stealing their supposedly great ideas."

"Sentinel is doing more than just worrying— they've brought in the FBI, and, if the visit to my home the other night is any indication, they're more than willing to play hardball."

"Your friend has good cause to be worried. The latest information I've got isn't going to please you. Sentinel has brought in some serious muscle in the past month, a man by the name of Barton Jones."

"I've met him. I've also heard about him from another source."

"If what you heard is bad, it's probably true. My contact says that he's got everyone there scared shitless."

Claude suddenly stood up and waved toward the front of the diner.

"Who's that?" Bette asked.

"My lunch date. Come on up and I'll introduce you. And listen, Bette, thanks for the information."

Bette nodded and got to her feet. "My last piece of advice is to be careful how you use it." She put a hand on Claude's arm. "Unlike mine, your 'family' isn't getting any bigger."

Rita stood waiting for Claude next to the cash register.

"You smell good," he told her.

"That's the special of the day you're smelling," she replied with a smile, coloring slightly.

Before he could answer, Bette Beal walked up.

"Bette, I'd like you to meet Rita Johnson. Rita, this here's Bette Beal. She owns the place."

Bette extended her hand toward Rita and asked, inclining her head toward Claude, "How well do you know this clown?"

"I and Miss Rita are not yet what you might call a 'number,' " Claude interjected with a smile before Rita could answer.

"A 'number'?" Bette sneered. "I'll give you a number. Table number six, way in the back. I put your Miss Rita up front where all the ladies can see her and nobody'll get any work done today. 'Number' my ass," she cackled belligerently as she turned and walked back to the big range behind the counter.

Claude led Rita back to their table, greeting several of the waitresses as they passed.

"You patronize the *oddest* places," Rita whispered as they sat down.

"Wait'll you taste the food. There's nothing bad on the menu."

"Did you know that someone was watching your house last night?" Rita asked as they sat down.

Claude, about to ask the waitress what the luncheon special was, shook his head. He smiled. "I like a woman who gets right to the point. Would you like me to order for the two of us?"

"No." Rita looked up at the waitress. "I'll have the Salade Niçoise with the house raspberry vinaigrette dressing on the side."

"All of our tuna is certified caught in a dolphin-safe manner," the waitress volunteered.

"I expected no less," Rita answered, smiling at Claude.

"What would you like to drink?" the waitress asked. "The milk shakes here are, like, radical."

"Well, I'm nothing if not, like, radical," Rita said. "I'll try a coffee shake."

Claude, only slightly nonplussed by Rita's obvious *presence*, bought a moment's composure by appearing to study the menu. He handed it back to the waitress with a flourish. "Tell Bette to make me up whatever she thinks I might like. And bring me a decaf cappuccino." After the waitress left them, he said to Rita, "Now, what's this about somebody washing my house?"

In spite of herself Rita laughed. "Not washing, *watching*. When I left your house last night, I spotted a male Caucasian sitting in a Dodge about a half block from your house. The car had no license plates. Unfortunately, the man must have guessed that I had spotted him because by the time I came by again in my car, he was gone."

" 'A male Caucasian.' " Claude chuckled. "I love it when you talk that police talk." He shrugged. "Could have been someone taking the baby-sitter home."

Rita smiled. "Could have," she said, her tone of voice leaving no doubt as to what she believed.

"What did Bernie Beck think?"

"Why do you think I would have called Lieutenant Beck?"

"To see if it was one of his men."

"If it had been a policeman, he wouldn't have taken off just because I spotted him," Rita pointed out, impressed that Claude had so quickly surmised that she would have called the Albany police lieutenant. "But you're right, I did call Lieutenant Beck just to be sure, and no, it wasn't one of his people."

Rita paused as the waitress delivered the milk shake and cappuccino. The young woman placed the cappuccino in front of Claude without so much as a glance at him and then turned and smiled sweetly at Rita. "I put extra whipped cream in it for you."

"How can my hips ever thank you?" Rita asked, a question the young waitress found too amusing for words. She giggled and left the table, obviously smitten.

"If *Mr.* Right doesn't show up on schedule," Claude said dryly, "I believe *Miss* Right may be just around the corner."

"Don't be catty," Rita chided, then sipped her milk shake with relish. "Getting back to last night, it would appear as if someone doesn't believe you're as uninvolved with Mr. Hamilton as you say you are."

"So it would appear. Nonetheless, that doesn't change the truth." Claude took a sip of his cappuccino. "What do you believe?"

"I believe that the truth is frequently an extremely delicate if not downright endangered commodity in the law enforcement business. I also believe that the truth is, for many people, a fungible commodity. Lastly, I believe that you haven't told me everything you know."

Before the conversation could continue, the waitress arrived with their lunches. For Claude, Bette had prepared two chicken enchiladas covered with a stinging tomatillo verde sauce sprinkled liberally with feta cheese. Before grilling, the chicken had been marinated in lime juice and cilantro. The enchiladas were accompanied by a steaming black-bean-and-onion side dish.

As she was dressing her salad with Bette's special raspberry vinaigrette, Rita looked at Claude. "Why are you carrying a concealed weapon?"

"You don't miss much, do you?"

"Such things aren't terribly hard to spot when you know what to look for."

"Well, you're right. I am carrying a pistol, and until I get to the bottom of this business with Sentinel Micro and Jesse Hamilton, I intend to continue doing so. Someone tried to kill me the other night, remember?"

"You don't know that. In fact, if the intruder really was sent by Sentinel, it's far more likely they were looking for information. They would have nothing to gain by killing you. Besides, it's a felony to carry a concealed weapon without a permit."

"Who said I didn't have a permit?" Claude smiled. "Buy enough tickets to the Albany Policemen's Ball and anything's possible."

"Seriously, do you have a permit?"

"Of course."

"I don't like it. It scares me when private citizens carry concealed weapons."

Claude shrugged. "Each of us is ultimately responsible for our own safety and survival. Almost all law enforcement is *after* the fact: after the robbery, after the shooting, after the rape. You, as a federal agent, must know that better than most. If you don't believe me, call the police." Claude pointed to the telephone by the cash register. "Tell them you're a single woman living alone and someone, a man, is threatening you. They'll ask, 'Has he actually done anything to you?' and when you say, 'No, not yet,' the response will be, 'Call us when he has.' Or, even if you were able to harass an overworked assistant DA into cajoling a brain-dead judge into issuing a restraining order, how many murderers or rapists do you suppose would be put off by a piece of paper?"

"That's overly simplistic and you know it."

Claude smiled. "Perhaps, but would you honestly be willing to count on the police or the courts, to bet your life, if you felt truly threatened?"

Rita looked unhappy but didn't reply.

"Neither would I," Claude said.

They both ate silently for several minutes.

Finally, Claude put his fork down and looked at Rita. "We're getting off to a bad start here. I'll be honest with you. I was hoping we could forget all this Sentinel business for a while and just have a nice lunch together. What do you say?"

Rita smiled. "This wasn't exactly supposed to be a social lunch—as I recall, you were going to introduce me to someone who would be able to, I believe you said, give me some 'additional insight' into the Jesse Hamilton case."

"That's true—"

"But"—Rita held up a hand to interrupt Claude—"I don't think it would be a federal crime if we enjoyed lunch first."

Bette was busy at the Wolfe range when they were ready to leave, so Claude paid the waitress and told her to tell Bette that everything had been just fine. Outside, Rita laughed.

"What's so funny?"

"This is a first for me," Rita said, flourishing a small slip of paper. "Our waitress slipped this to me as we were leaving." She showed it to Claude. "Her name and phone number."

Claude, amused, shook his head. "If nothing else, she's got good taste."

"Where are we going?" Rita asked as Claude eased Jesus's Volkswagen into traffic. "And how long ago was this car stolen in Mexico City?"

It was Claude's turn to laugh. "As I said earlier, you don't miss much, do you? Where we're going is out to Point Molate. There's an old, privately run anchorage out there, on San Pablo

Bay. It houses a few houseboats, several commercial fishing boats, and a handful of sailboats whose owners are on waiting lists at the tonier yacht harbors. I know the harbormaster pretty well and I want you to meet his son."

Claude drove toward the Richmond–San Rafael bridge and turned onto a neglected, two-lane county road.

"The navy used to store strategic oil reserves out here," Claude said, pointing to numerous bunkerlike openings that dotted the rolling hills rising above the bay. "May still, for all I know."

They bounced farther down the potholed road, and Claude pointed out the remains of a large building that had been built on pilings extending out over the water. "That was the last active commercial whaling station in America."

Rita, fascinated, craned her head as they passed the burned-out hulk of a structure. "My God, I had no idea all this was over here."

"Most folks don't. All this land on both sides of the road is owned by either the navy or Chevron, and neither entity welcomes or encourages tourists or casual visitors to this end of the bay."

The road wound through the hills, past a small enclave of battleship-gray naval family-housing units, and up a steep rise. At the top of the rise Claude stopped so Rita could enjoy the view back toward Oakland and San Francisco. He pointed down below them, to the anchorage that was their destination. The road ended at the harbor, terminating in what was, for all intents and purposes, a junkyard. Claude parked the Volkswagen and escorted Rita to the faded wood planking that led to the harbormaster's office. At the office Claude peered through a window and rapped on the door. An old man opened it.

"Ben," Claude said loudly, "it's me, Claude McCutcheon. Where's Harry?"

The old man just stood there, cataracts visible in both eyes. Finally he turned back into the office and sat down in a cane-back chair with a bowed seat. "He went to shit and the hogs ate him," he suddenly shouted, cackling with an obviously demented glee.

Claude smiled at Rita. "Poor old Ben's lived out here since long before I can remember. I doubt he even knows what planet he's on anymore."

"I know something you don't know," the old man shouted with obvious relish, startling Claude.

"What's that, Ben?"

Before the old man could answer, a voice came from down at the end of the dock: "Claude McCutcheon!"

A trim, middle-aged man hailed Claude from the boat slips. He waved and came walking up the dock toward the office. "This is a pleasant surprise," he said, wiping both hands on a clean rag before extending his right hand toward Claude.

"Harry Morgan," Claude said, taking the harbormaster's hand in a firm grasp, "I'd like you to meet Rita Johnson."

Rita extended her hand. "How do you do?" she said, instinctively liking the sunburned, gray-headed man standing solidly in front of her.

"It's my pleasure, I'm sure," Harry said in a courtly manner, looking directly into Rita's eyes. "Any friend of Claude's is welcome here." He swung his gaze to include Claude. "Come on down to the houseboat. Hazel just put on a fresh pot."

"How's Rainer doing?" Claude asked as the three of them walked toward the dock. "I brought Rita out here to meet him."

Harry stopped abruptly. "Not so good. Hazel and I had to take him back over to the VA hospital in the City last week." He looked at Rita. "Rainer's my boy and Hazel's his wife." He paused and chewed on his lower lip for a second. "It'd probably be best if we didn't discuss or say anything about Rainer around Hazel. She's still pretty upset about it."

Claude nodded. "No problem. Would it be better if we just took off, maybe came back for a visit some other time?"

"Lord, no. Hazel'll be tickled to death to see you. I just wouldn't bring Rainer up if we can avoid it."

The houseboat in which Harry and his small family lived was one of the most fascinating homes Rita had ever seen. Built on a large concrete hull, the house portion was a two-story, redwood-faced, wood-frame structure topped by a cedar-shingled, octagonal cupola that sported handmade stained-glass windows. It was permanently moored to the dock and rocked gently on the changing tide.

"Hazel," Harry called out as they approached the houseboat, "look who's come to visit."

A dark, slender woman came to the Dutch door entrance of the houseboat. Quite pretty, she appeared to Rita to be in her late thirties.

"Claude McCutcheon," Hazel said, a smile lighting her face. "It's good to see you."

"We can't stay but just a minute," Claude said as they boarded the houseboat. "Rita here's got to get back to work. Hazel, I'd like you to meet Rita Johnson. Rita, this is Hazel Morgan, Harry's daughter-in-law."

"You must be awfully special," Hazel said, taking Rita's hand. "I do believe you're the first girlfriend Claude's ever brought out here to meet us."

Rita smiled but didn't say anything.

"You can stay long enough to drink a cup of coffee, can't you?" Harry asked.

"One cup," Claude said.

"What's the cat's name?" Rita asked as they sat down around a well-worn kitchen table. An old cat snored loudly on a windowsill just above the sink.

"That's Buster," Hazel said, pouring coffee. "He's about as old as Ben, and deaf as a stone."

She affectionately chucked the sleeping cat under the chin. "He just sleeps in the sunshine all the day long."

"Sounds good to me," Claude said. "Speaking of Ben, he looks like he's gone downhill since I was last out here."

Harry stirred cream into his coffee and nodded. "Well, like all of us he's got good days and bad. On the whole, though, the Alzheimer's has pretty well done him in." He looked at Rita. "He's got no family, no money, and no one to take care of him, so we let him stay in the office. One of these nights I expect he'll get to wandering around and fall off the dock. The tide'll take his body out and that'll be the end of it." He shook his head. "Still, I'd say that's better than spending your last year or two sitting in the holding pen out at the county home wondering what your name is."

"Hard to argue with that," Claude said. "How's business out here?"

Harry shrugged. "Nothing new. Handful of fishing boats, a few live-aboards, some houseboaters, the odd sailboat or two until the owner can get into one of the big yacht harbors. Chevron would love to get us out of here and close that road down, but the lease runs another fifteen years, so I guess we can hold out." He winked at Hazel. "Long as we can put food on the table and wood in the stove, right?"

The room was cozily warm and Rita relaxed, enjoying the friendly banter.

"We'd love to spend the afternoon," Claude finally said, "but we really do have to get Miss Rita here back to work." They stood up and started out. "Thanks for the coffee."

At the door, Hazel stopped Claude with a hand on his arm. "Rainer's back at the VA," she said in a soft voice.

Claude nodded. "Harry told me. I'll visit him in the next day or two, make sure everything's okay."

Hazel suddenly had tears in her eyes. "I don't know that he'll come out this time," she whispered.

Claude hugged her. "Rainer's a strong man."

"But I don't know that he wants to come out. I'm afraid this time he'll stay."

Out on the dock Claude shook hands with Harry. "I'll call the VA later this afternoon and talk to Rainer. I should be able to get over to see him sometime in the next couple of days. If he needs anything, I'll let you know."

Harry nodded. "Thanks. It'll mean a lot to Hazel. And me. And thanks for coming out." He turned to Rita. "It was nice meeting you. I hope Claude brings you back soon."

They left Harry on the dock and started walking back toward the harbor office. Claude suddenly turned around and called back to Harry, "Do you mind if Rita and I do a little shooting before we leave?"

Harry waved at them. "Help yourself. Won't bother anybody but the gulls."

Rita looked at Claude. "Shooting?"

"Sure," Claude said, smiling. "Harry and Rainer and I shoot out here all the time. We set up a range at the far end of the harbor, firing into a sandstone bluff. To tell you the truth, ever since we met I've been dying to find out how well the FBI trains its agents in the fine art of combat shooting."

"I don't know," Rita said doubtfully. She had never fired her weapon outside the confines of FBI-supervised firing ranges. "I've got to account for any government-issue ammunition I use and, frankly speaking, I don't know how I'd explain this to my boss, or even if I'd want to."

Claude laughed. "Not to worry. We can both use my pistol. I've got plenty of ammunition." He could see she was taken with the idea. "I'll bet you're a pretty fair shot."

"First in my class at Quantico," she replied with no little pride. "What sort of targets do you use?"

Claude shrugged. "Nothing fancy. Harry usually keeps a box of empty beer bottles on hand for whenever he or Rainer feels like target practice."

"You mean you just set up beer bottles?" Rita said, a touch scornfully, thinking of the Bureau's computer-controlled, automated pop-up targets on the combat course at Quantico.

"Lord no." Claude laughed. "Any fool could hit a bottle sitting on the ground. We throw them into the air and see if we can't hit them on the way down."

Rita smiled, thinking Claude must be joking. "Are you kidding? That's like shooting clay pigeons with a pistol."

They reached the end of the harbor and found a crate full of empty bottles. Claude took off his jacket, revealing the well-worn leather shoulder holster containing his Smith & Wesson .38 revolver.

"I'll go first," Claude said. "You stand behind me and throw a bottle as high as you can toward the bluff. Give it a good heave."

Rita bent down and picked up a long-neck Coors bottle. She had played fast-pitch softball all through high school and college and was proud of her ability to throw at least as well as most men she knew. She drew back and whistled the bottle past Claude's left ear. He stood with the pistol held lightly in his right hand, watching the bottle sail through the air until it reached its apogee. As it began falling, Claude raised the pistol and fired, his motion gentle, almost regretful. The bottle exploded. Rita's shoulders sagged ever so slightly for she knew instinctively that Claude's shot was not a lucky one and she knew further that she could not match it. He turned to her and offered her the pistol.

"Now you try it. Keep in mind that this particular pistol fires a touch high and right."

Rita took the weapon and waited until

Claude launched a bottle above and in front of her. She fired immediately and missed. He threw another bottle with the same result. She wordlessly handed the pistol back to him.

"Two things," he said kindly. "First, you've never fired this pistol before, and that makes a big difference. Second, you're *aiming*, as I'm sure you were taught, and you'll never hit a rapidly moving target by aiming at it. You've got to fire instinctively, point and shoot, point and shoot. Learn to trust yourself." He offered the pistol back to her. "I know it sounds like California-speak, but try to become one with the target."

She took the pistol and he threw another bottle high into the air. She fired and missed.

"That's good," he said, "much better. You almost hit it that time."

Rita laughed. "How could you tell?"

"I saw where you pointed the pistol in relation to the bottle," Claude said seriously. He picked up another bottle. "Relax this time and just point and shoot. Trust yourself."

He threw the bottle and this time Rita hit it, the bottle exploding into amber fragments. Claude beamed as Rita handed the pistol back to him.

"I'm going to quit while I'm ahead," she said. "But thanks for the lesson. I learned something."

Claude shook his head. "You were already a competent marksman. Or markswoman. All you need to do is make the transition to being what I call a shooter."

"How long should that take?"

"Not more than half a lifetime," Claude responded with a smile. "It's a matter of learning to do something extraordinarily difficult without thinking about it. Practitioners of the art will tell you that the *process* is far more important than the end result. Much like life itself." He rested a hand on her shoulder. "The good news is that you just took the first step."

His hand lingered a brief instant longer than necessary, a lingering they both noted.

"Come on," he said. "Time to get you back to work."

As the Volkswagen labored up the hill leading back the way they had come in, Rita watched Claude out of the corner of her eye.

"What's the story on Harry's son, Rainer?"

"No story," Claude said, concentrating on avoiding the larger of the ruts and potholes. Jesus's Volkswagen seemed to have no suspension system as that term was generally understood in El Norte. "Most of the time he's as normal as you and I"—Claude paused and smiled at Rita—"at least to the degree that one can say you and I are normal. Sometimes, though, he gets confused and can't find his way back from the past."

"What past?"

"Vietnam. Rainer never got over the war. He was a helicopter pilot with the First Cav. He came back an alcoholic and then discovered drugs. When he was discharged, the army refused to recognize his problems as service-related. He couldn't hold a job, so he ended up living back here with his dad at the harbor. I met them a few years ago when Rainer got arrested for talking to himself at a shopping mall over in El Cerrito. Bernie Beck saw that he was a veteran and called me, thinking I might be able to help get him into a treatment program at the VA."

"I take it you were able to do so," Rita said, fascinated with the story.

Claude nodded. "First we had to get the VA to agree that his condition was service related and then the rest was easy."

"Why is he back in the hospital?"

"Unfortunately the VA treats only the symptoms. Rainer can't seem to come to terms with his war experiences and so he periodically relapses."

"So what am I going to learn about Jesse Hamilton from Rainer?"

"Truthfully . . . he knows many of the same vets that know Jesse. I was hoping maybe he'd have some kind of line on where Jesse might have got to."

"Doesn't sound like Rainer has much of a line on anything. How long has he been married?"

"Rainer and Hazel got married about three years ago." Claude shook his head. "Two lost souls adrift in the night."

"What do you mean?"

"I don't know which of the two, Hazel or Rainer, has a less firm grip on reality. She drifted down to the harbor one day from God knows where, Texas she said, and just stayed. She and Rainer hit it off right away and got married five days later."

"I think that's romantic," Rita said, smiling.

"I suppose it is. Except that now Harry's got two kids to worry about."

"He doesn't seem to mind. Besides, he probably needs them as much as they need him."

Claude looked at Rita and smiled. "Would you say that everybody needs somebody?"

"Just about. Although there may be exceptions."

They both laughed.

"Amigo." Jesus walked out of his garage wiping his hands on a filthy rag, a broad grin on his face. In the garage two of his nephews were dismantling a stake-and-platform truck that looked as if it had recently run over a land mine. The boys were using an oxygen-acetylene cutting torch and shielding their eyes with the flats of their hands.

"Did you finish the brake job?"

"Sí, amigo, and what a job we did for you." Jesus held up his right hand, thumb and forefinger touching. "New master cylinder and lines, all new wheel cylinders, plus we turned all four drums. She's ready to go."

"Have you got the piece?"

Jesus nodded. Claude followed him into the Quonset-hut garage that also housed Jesus's office—a battered wooden desk and two chairs, which, if the small metal tags affixed to them could be believed, had been stolen from the Contra Costa County Family Planning Clinic. The Colt .45 was sitting on the desk on an oily rag.

"Looks fine," Claude said, working the slide mechanism to make sure there wasn't a round in the chamber and ejecting the empty clip. He expertly broke the automatic down, looking carefully at each part for excessive wear and evidence of abuse. "I'll take it," he said, quickly reassembling the weapon.

Jesus smiled.

Claude reached inside his leather jacket and pulled out a plain white envelope. "Four hundred."

Jesus took the envelope and stuffed it carelessly into the back pocket of his jeans without bothering to examine its contents.

Claude wordlessly pointed to the telephone on the desk.

"Sí." Jesus ordered his two nephews out of the Quonset hut to give Claude some quiet and privacy and then left himself.

Claude dialed the number of the VA hospital in San Francisco. "Yes," he said when the hospital operator came on the line, "I'm trying to reach a patient there, a man by the name of

Rainer Morgan." *Talk about déjà vu all over again,* he thought.

"Please hold while I check our patient directory," the operator said.

While waiting, Claude idly glanced about the garage, his eyes coming to rest on the partially dismantled stake-and-platform truck. *By God,* he thought admiringly, *it takes a third-world hunger to extract the last ounce of value from a pile of scrap metal.*

"I'm sorry, sir," the operator came back on the line, "but Mr. Morgan checked out of the hospital this morning."

"Checked out? As in discharged?"

"No, sir, not discharged. The record indicates that he left the hospital this morning with his physician's approval for a period not to exceed seventy-two hours."

"Thank you." Claude wanted to ask another question but realized that the operator was unlikely to provide any additional information over the telephone. "Would it be possible for me to leave a message?"

"Certainly, sir. I'll switch you to our automated patient voice-mail system."

After working his way laboriously through the system's exceedingly annoying automated menu, Claude finally got the ubiquitous telltale beep. "Yeah, Rainer, this is Claude McCutcheon. I hope everything's going okay. I'll call again in a couple of days. If you need anything in the meantime, give me a call." He hung up, wondering if he should call Harry and let him know that Rainer had been released on some sort of short furlough. He was about to pick up the telephone again when Jesus walked in.

"Is everything okay, amigo?"

Claude nodded and stood up. *I'll call over the weekend,* he thought. *Things couldn't have been too bad if they're giving him a weekend pass.*

Shaking hands with Jesus, he picked up the .45 and walked out to his truck. Jesus followed, waving good-bye to Claude.

The last thing Claude saw as he pulled away was the sun, glinting off the gold in Jesus's teeth.

More than anything, Jesse Hamilton missed his little boy. Earl was the last thing on God's green earth he wanted to leave behind, but after spending the past five nights in four different sleazy motels, it was amply clear that he had made the right decision in leaving Earl with Claude. The house, the clothes, the furniture, the car, all the trappings of a comfortable middle-class life, meant nothing to him, but losing Earl, even temporarily, was like having a vital organ taken from his body.

Fool, his wife had said, laughing, seeing his astonishment when she first told him she was pregnant. *What did you think was going to happen with what we been doing day and night the past three months?*

Lord, he hadn't thought about being a daddy, that was for sure. Hell, after all the years he'd stayed single, he had never thought he was going to end up married either, but then Alice had come along.

Sweet Alice, he thought, lighting a cigarette, *we sure enough had something, didn't we?*

Tired as he was, he couldn't get Alice out of his mind. If it hadn't been for having to take care of Earl, he didn't know what he'd have done when the cancer had finally taken her. He'd sure as hell never have been in this fix if she hadn't died, he knew that.

A sound out in the parking lot caught his attention and he was off the bed in a flash, gun in one hand as he peeked carefully around the curtain. Nothing. With a sigh he sank back down on the hard mattress and ran a hand over his face. He kept the room darkened, making sure that, if push came to shove, his night vision wouldn't be compromised. Besides, the light coming through the thin, raggedy curtain was more than enough to maneuver about the tiny room. He looked at his watch, saw that it was just past six o'clock, and yawned again. He hoped the hookers didn't come by again tonight—a couple of them had been turning tricks last evening in the adjoining room, and the constant coming and going, not to mention the banging of the bed against the wall, had kept him awake and on edge all night long.

Not that being alert was a bad thing—even

though he'd managed to talk to Mellon the last time he'd gotten to Sentinel, he knew Jones had a hard-on for him, bad.

He liked it that way, though.

Mr. Jones, Mr. Jones, he thought, taking another drink of beer, *you don't actually think I'm just going to take some money and leave town with my boy, do you?*

No, sir. He smiled. *It's coming up on payback time.*

10

"How's the boy doing?" Claude asked. "Earl," he added unnecessarily. He smiled, realizing that he had almost said *How's my boy doing?*

"Doing fine," Felix answered. "He's starting to talk just a little bit more, with Ruth. Don't say much to me. Told her about your cat the other day." Felix shook his head as if such domesticity were a condition he had never given much thought to. "Looks like we might be having to get a cat soon."

Claude laughed delightedly. "He's a smart boy, no doubt about it."

"When you coming over to see him?"

"Soon. In the meantime—"

The telephone rang. Felix answered it and immediately handed the receiver over to Claude.

"Claude"—it was Emma—"I'm sorry to chase you down, but Bernie Beck called and said it was an emergency."

Claude thanked her for the message and immediately dialed Bernie's number. "Bernie, it's me, Claude. Emma called and . . ." He listened for several minutes, his face hardening as the color left it. "I'll be right over." He hung up the phone, took a deep breath to steady himself.

"Trouble?" Felix asked.

"A man was just killed in my house. A neighbor called in a report of what sounded like a gunshot, and they found a body."

"Earl's father?"

Claude shook his head. "No, someone else. A friend." An image of Rainer came suddenly to mind, him with Hazel, the two of them laughing at some silly thing old Ben had said.

"You all right?"

"I have to go." Claude walked to the door, yanked it open. He was halfway through when he turned back and pointed at Felix. "You take care of that boy."

The coroner's technician folded the sheet back from the upper half of the body and looked at Claude.

"That's him," Claude said, his voice harsh in the white-tiled morgue. "Rainer Morgan."

Once back in his office, Bernie Beck pushed a pack of Camels across his desk toward Claude. "Egg drop soup."

"What do you mean?" Claude asked, puzzled.

"There was egg drop soup all over the kitchen floor. It looks like he walked into the house carrying a cardboard take-out container of egg drop soup and surprised the killer in the kitchen."

Claude lit a cigarette. "He have anything else with him?"

"What do you mean, 'anything else'? Like what?"

"Hell, I don't know, Bernie, a piece of paper, a letter, a note, something to explain why he came over to my house today."

"There was nothing. Forensics couldn't find shit. If he had anything with him, whoever killed him sure as hell took it."

Before either man could say anything further, Rita Johnson knocked on the doorjamb. Both Claude and Bernie stood up.

"Come in," Bernie said. He turned to Claude. "I believe you two know each other, don't you?"

Claude nodded. "We've met." He extended his hand to Rita.

She took it, offering a half-smile. "Claude—Mr. McCutcheon."

"Agent Johnson," he said formally.

"Claude," Bernie said, "I notified Agent Johnson's boss of Rainer's murder because I think it's connected to their investigation of your friend Jesse Hamilton and Sentinel Micro." Bernie turned to Rita. "The dead man was a friend of Claude's. We believe that he dropped by Claude's home, let himself in the front door unannounced, and confronted an intruder in the kitchen where he was murdered. Evidence at the scene leads us to believe that on the way to Claude's home he stopped briefly at a Chinese restaurant on Solano Avenue and bought a take-out serving of egg drop soup, presumably to share with Claude. The coroner believes he was shot sometime between noon and one o'clock." Bernie consulted his notes for a minute before continuing. "The neighbor across the street, a Mr. Hahn, heard the shot and phoned us. Said he saw the victim enter the house but not the perpetrator. Didn't see anyone leave." Bernie turned back to Claude. "I know you didn't do it, Claude, but as a formality I need to know your whereabouts from this morning up until sometime after, say, two o'clock."

Claude ground out his cigarette. "No problem, Bernie. At ten-thirty I left the office and went over to Felix Mackie's place for a workout. At about eleven-thirty I came back to the office. I took Emma and her sister and brother-in-law to lunch at noon. After lunch, maybe one o'clock, I drove over to the bank to see if I couldn't speed things up with the funding of Felix Mackie's business loan. I was there until two and then went back to Felix's to let him know the loan was being funded tomorrow. I was talking to Felix when Emma phoned to say you were looking for me."

"I understand from Rainer's father that he had recently been back out at the VA."

Claude nodded. "I talked to Harry out at Point Molate on Friday, and he told me that Rainer had checked himself in about a week ago, I'm not exactly sure when. I tried to call Rainer at the VA later that afternoon and was told he had checked out on a weekend pass. I figured if he got a pass, he couldn't have been in too bad a shape, so he just sort of slipped out of my mind over the weekend. I was going to try to get over to see him one day this week."

"And you have absolutely no idea why he would have just showed up at your house today?"

"Other than just stopping by on his way back out to the VA to say hello, no, I don't."

"Okay, Claude, I guess that's enough for now unless Agent Johnson wants to ask you anything."

Rita shook her head. "Was there any physical evidence at the scene?" she asked Bernie.

"Not a damned thing," Bernie said, frustration evident in his voice. "No shell casing, no prints, no fibers, no nothing. It was a clean job from start to finish. Clearly whoever was in there was not expecting to be disturbed. It was just damned bad luck that Rainer stumbled onto him."

"Or *her,*" Rita said automatically.

"Or her," Bernie said, smiling. "I stand corrected." He turned to Claude. "If you think of anything, give me a call."

"I don't know what you two think I might come up with to help you," Claude said. "I'm the only one around here that nobody seems to want to talk to." He looked at his watch. It was four-thirty. "To hell with it, I'm late for an appointment."

"Just a moment." Rita turned to Bernie. "Do you mind if I speak with Mr. McCutcheon in private?"

Bernie shook his head. "Be my guest. There's an office just across the hall that should be empty."

In the hallway outside Bernie's office Claude put a hand on Rita's arm. "I really do have to meet someone," he said, looking again at his watch. "Listen. We don't want to talk here anyway, not in a police station. There's a place just three blocks down San Pablo Avenue from here called the Last Resort. It's a low-rent little country-western bar on the left-hand side as you're driving toward Richmond. I'll meet you there in twenty minutes. If you get there before I do, tell the bartender you're waiting for me, okay?"

Rita nervously bit her lip and nodded affirmatively.

Eight people were in the Last Resort when Rita pushed through the heavy swinging door:

the bartender, one waitress, and six patrons. Of
the six patrons, four were old men sitting at the
bar, three of whom were palpably intoxicated,
and two were young men in their twenties playing pool on a poorly lit table at the rear of the
bar. Everyone turned to stare silently at Rita
when she entered.

"Claude McCutcheon asked me to meet him
here," she said to the bartender, furious at herself for feeling so nervous.

The waitress smiled and, between clicks of her
chewing gum, invited Rita to have a seat. "Would
you like anything while you're waiting?"

Before Rita could answer, Claude walked in.

"Give us a couple of Anchor Steams, Red,"
he said to the waitress. He waved in the direction of the bartender. "Sam, I need to use your
phone for a minute," he called out.

Sam nodded. "You know where it is."

Claude turned back to Rita. "This'll just take
a minute." He walked to the side of the bar and
reached over for the telephone. He dialed a
number and winked at the waitress while waiting for an answer. "Bette? This is Claude. You
asked me to give you a call." He listened
silently for several minutes, occasionally nodding his head. "Thanks a lot," he finally said. "I
appreciate it." He hung up and put the phone
back behind the bar. "Thanks, Sam."

Sam took the soggy toothpick he had been
chewing out of his mouth and pointed it at
Claude in silent acknowledgment.

"So," Claude said, back at the table, "what do you want to talk about?"

Rita waved her hand at the waitress. "Excuse me, could I get a glass, please?"

The waitress brought one over. "Sorry, honey, most folks around here just drink it right out of the bottle."

Rita held the spotted glass up to what little ambient light there was and muttered, "I can see why." She put the glass down and took a drink from the bottle. She looked at Claude. "I'm sorry about Rainer."

Claude nodded. "So am I."

"Listen. We can't continue to see each other."

Claude looked at her. "I didn't realize we were actually 'seeing' each other."

"You know what I mean, and yes, you did realize that our lunch on Friday, together with the visit out to Point Molate to meet Harry and Hazel, was not merely part of my investigation. I can't be meeting you for lunch or dinner or anything else for that matter while this investigation is ongoing. If my boss found out about it, I don't know what he'd do. At the very least my objectivity would be seriously suspect, not to mention my judgment."

Claude studied the label on his beer bottle. "One of the reasons I've always worked for myself is that I never had much interest in having someone else do my thinking for me. Do you think I'm involved in any sort of wrongdoing in this whole Jesse Hamilton thing?"

"No, I don't."

"Good, because I'm not." He reached over and took Rita's hand. "Let's be honest. We find ourselves very much attracted to each other in the midst of a difficult situation, don't we?"

Rita nodded, but did not trust herself to speak. The bar had become absolutely silent except for the click of the billiard balls as everyone strained to hear Claude's quiet words.

"We both know that I'm not responsible for whatever Jesse Hamilton, or Sentinel Micro, or whoever, might or might not have done, so I see no moral dilemma arising out of our continuing to 'see' each other." He slowly, regretfully, let go of her hand. "Give it some thought and then do what *you* think is the right thing."

Claude rose and turned toward the bartender. "Put it on the tab," he said, pointing down at the table.

He smiled once more, leaving Rita sitting alone with her thoughts.

"We've found Hamilton."

Mellon looked up from the papers on his desk, his face impassive. "Where?"

"East Palo Alto, not four miles from here." Barton Jones sat down without being asked. "A dump called—you'll love this—the Taj Mahal Motel."

"Has he been there all along?"

"Checked in yesterday afternoon. My guess is that he's moving every couple of days, so I wouldn't count on him being there much past tomorrow."

"How'd you find him?"

Jones smiled. He had known that sooner or later he'd nail Hamilton. For a not inconsiderable sum of money he'd enlisted the aid of one of the South Bay's principal cocaine distributors, a man with a "family" that extended from South San Francisco to San Jose. Once the cheese had been strategically placed, Jones had never doubted that the rats would come sniffing around. "Some lowlife that saw the picture and heard about the money spotted him buying food at a convenience store. Followed him back to the motel and made a call."

Mellon looked pointedly at Jones. "I want you to supervise this one personally."

"Everything's already in place. I've brought an experienced man up from Tijuana to provide the muscle. He'll go in first, subdue Hamilton, and then we'll get him out of there."

"Are the local police going to be a problem?"

"I don't think so. The motel is used primarily by the local working girls for turning tricks. I'm told that the East Palo Alto Police Department tends to leave it pretty much alone as long as the pimps and the motel owner keep making the nut every week." Jones smiled. "Just to be on the safe side, however, I've arranged a little diversion to occupy the police while we're dealing with Hamilton."

"What sort of diversion?"

"A noisy altercation at an after-hours club several blocks from the motel, complete with gunshots and a certain amount of, um, property damage. Several calls to 911 should keep the police dispatcher busy until well after the foolish Mr. Hamilton is safely in our hands."

11

Jesse had to laugh, if only at the ridiculousness of his situation. He'd never been one to blame others for mistakes he had made, or to talk about bad luck this or bad luck that, but lying there with a band of neon light flickering restlessly across the foot of the bed, he couldn't help thinking once again that losing his career in the army was the worst thing that could have happened to him. He had grown up in the rural South, just like Claude, and the army had been a beacon of opportunity. From the first day of basic training he knew he had found a home, a place where it didn't matter what color his skin was or what kind of high school he had or hadn't gone to or what kind of God he prayed to when the lights went out. Vietnam, of course, had opened the door for men like Jesse and Claude, men who in a peacetime army would have served two or three years as privates and then gotten out, to begin life sentences in a cotton mill or an auto plant or on a construction site, carrying bologna sandwiches in a paper bag and marking time until they just plain wore out. He and Claude often talked boldly about how they were lifers, twenty-year men with no intention of returning to civilian life. And Artie Gibson used to laugh at them as if he knew better. Artie always knew better.

"Man, this war would have to last forever for guys like us to get anywhere," Artie had repeatedly told them. "And you know as well as I do that this war ain't gonna last forever, not with all these body bags we're starting to ship home."

Artie was smart, Jesse always knew that, but maybe, if such a thing were possible, too smart for his own good. Artie liked the street life, liked getting by on being clever, living one step ahead of the Man. He had learned from a young age that to get ahead, to succeed within the system, whether in military or civilian life, a man had to have a little fear in him. Artie's only problem, Jesse had come to realize over time, his only weakness, was that he truly feared nothing.

"See," Artie had told Jesse and Claude after

he declined Claude's offer to get him promoted
to sergeant, "I'm happy right where I am. You go
making me a sergeant and I'll have to give up
my stingy brim."

Stingy brim. Jesse chuckled and lay back
against the headboard, thinking for the first
time in more years than he could remember
about Artie's stingy brim.

After two or three months in-country the battalion had been issued jungle fatigue hats,
shapeless olive-drab hats with a wide, floppy
brim. Artie had immediately had a Vietnamese
seamstress trim half the brim off, giving the hat
what he considered a more stylish look. A
"stingy brim" he called it, and he wore it tilted
to one side of his head, like a brother back on
the block. The battalion executive officer had
chewed Claude out for allowing one of his men
to wear a nonregulation hat, so Artie thereafter
wore it only in the field, a source of much
amusement to the men in his squad.

Jesse smoked his cigarette and nodded to
himself. Artie had been right about Claude too.

"They going to throw him and all these other
OCS lieutenants on the trash pile as soon as we
get out of Vietnam," Artie had told Jesse more
than once. "Listen to what I'm telling you.
Other than being white, Claude ain't no different than you and me as far as the army is concerned. And he ain't going to like it."

Thirty years later, in their last meeting at San
Quentin, after Jesse had told Artie that he was

leaving Earl with Claude, Artie had warned him about the man he hadn't seen in all those years.

"Claude and me ended up a whole lot more alike than Claude and you," Artie had said. "You both came to see the wisdom in me not wanting to be a sergeant, but you came to it in different ways. Claude was like a nine-to-five workingman in love with a beautiful woman who's stepping out on him in the afternoons. He figures that because he's in love with her, she should be in love with him, and it kills something good inside him when she finally leaves him for another man." Artie laughed. "Claude learned that you can't be loving no beautiful woman. He learned it and cut loose from all the stuff he'd been wanting in life, you understand what I'm saying? Where you differ from Claude is that you didn't pay as much as he did to learn that you can't be loving no beautiful woman. You didn't get your career in the army, but it wasn't the army's fault like it was with Claude. You got shot up and got a disability pension. You learned not to expect too much in life because you probably wouldn't get it anyway, but learning it didn't kill something inside you like it did Claude."

Once again, Jesse had to admit that Artie was most likely right, because he, Jesse, sure as hell had known better than to fall in love with Louise Griffin. At least not right away, the way he might have done when he was a kid. Alice hadn't been dead a year and he was working at

Sentinel, trying to make a new start for him and the boy. And then Louise started working there.

Jesse reached down and took a bottle of beer out of the waxed-cardboard ice bucket sitting on the floor next to the bed. No, he didn't think he would actually have fallen in love with her, but, then again, you never know. Louise was a strong woman, tall like Jesse and with a skin as black as the middle of the night. An African woman, hardheaded and proud, not a woman any man in his right mind would think to trifle with. He took a drink of beer and laughed out loud, his bass chuckle suddenly brightening the drab, darkened room like the sun unexpectedly coming out from behind a cloud. When he and Louise made love, sometimes all he could do was hold on, things got so out of hand. He still marveled at the power of her sexuality, the fire that burned in her heart.

And smart. That was the part that made him wonder if he could have actually fallen in love with her. Or her with him. She was the smartest person he had ever known, man or woman, black or white, hands down. Computers talked to her, confided in her, trusted her the way an engine will talk to a good mechanic, or a horn will come alive for a jazz musician. He saw the books in her apartment, the mathematics and physics texts, a way of thinking that was so foreign to him that it couldn't help but make him sad.

No way Louise committed suicide. Not that woman. Not in a million years. She knew some-

thing was going down when she gave me that disc to hold.

So, all right, he was going to use that disc to make life a little easier for him and Earl—nothing wrong with that—but he was going to use it to get revenge for Louise too.

He felt he was close to the end of this thing, close to making a deal with Sentinel. He had talked twice to Mellon in the past week, found the man willing to talk about a cash transaction. Mellon was a businessman, unlike Jones. *No need to make this personal,* Jesse kept repeating to Mellon.

He knew he better get things taken care of soon, though. No way he could keep hidden away like this much longer. Jones would have put the word out on the street, and somebody, a hooker, a pimp, a clerk at a convenience store, would recognize him and drop a dime in a New York minute. He knew that Mellon was getting more and more nervous, though, and felt that a deal was about to go down.

Another day, maybe two, he thought, *and this nonsense will all be over.*

Jesse yawned and sat up on the edge of the hard mattress. He looked at his watch one more time, saw that it was a little past 2 A.M., and yawned again. God alone knew how long it had been since he'd slept more than an hour or two at a time. As he got up to go into the tiny bathroom, a faint scuffling sound outside the room caught his attention.

Jesse snatched up the automatic from the table beside the bed and crouched down in the doorway between the bedroom and the bathroom. When the door burst open, he started firing, his first three bullets slamming into the large shadow that rushed into the room. Even as the first man was falling, Jesse stood up to gain a clear field of fire at the second. He saw the second shadow and got off another round, thinking he might just have a chance, then felt something smash into his solar plexus, knocking him back against the wall and driving the breath from his body. The second shadow resolved itself into a distinct form, and he realized with a shock that it was Barton Jones. He tried desperately to straighten up, to bring his pistol to bear on Jones, but knew long before the second bullet exploded into his chest, shattering his heart and one lung, that he wasn't going to make it.

Earl, he wanted to shout, but blood filled his mouth and throat and he died without making a sound.

"Mornin', Emma." Claude held the telephone to his ear with the top of his shoulder as he transferred coffee from his grinder to the coffeemaker.

"Oh, Claude, I'm so sorry about Rainer Morgan." Emma's voice sounded as if she had been crying.

"Thanks, Emma, I'll pass your condolences along to Harry and Hazel."

"Are you coming in this morning?"

Claude shook his head as if Emma could see him over the telephone. "No. Rainer's being cremated this morning and then there's going to be a private memorial out at Point Molate. After that Harry's going to sail Rainer's ashes out the Gate and scatter them somewhere beyond the Farallons. Hold on just a minute, will you?" Claude put the phone down to add water to the coffeemaker and turn it on. "Emma? Yeah, as I was saying, Harry's going to be scattering the ashes and he's asked me to come along."

"How long will you be gone?"

"Well, given how far it is out to the Farallons, probably two days. I just hope to Christ I don't get seasick. You know me and sailing."

Emma chuckled. "The thought of you on a small sailboat outside the Golden Gate . . ."

"There're few things on this earth I'd rather do less, but Harry asked and I couldn't rightly say no. Listen, do me a favor and call Felix Mackie. Tell him I'm going to be out of town for a couple of days but I'll see him as soon as I get back. And one other thing. I wouldn't be a bit surprised if the FBI didn't do a little snooping around while I'm gone. If they come by the office, you can let them see whatever they want, but don't tell anybody where I've gone—it's none of their damn business. Thanks, Emma."

Claude was pouring himself a cup of coffee when Sally Pinter knocked on the kitchen door.

"Come on in," he said. "I was just going to give you a call. Where's Bud?"

"He had to go to a sales and marketing seminar in Sacramento for the day, and little Pete's with my mother."

"He spends too much time on the road for a man with a good-looking wife," Claude teased. "Does that mean you're free to spend the afternoon with me?"

Sally blushed and tried to hide it by pouring herself a cup of coffee.

"Fortunately for Bud," Claude continued, "I've got business to take care of today. As a matter of fact I was wondering if you could do me a bit of a favor."

"What's that?"

"I'm going to be out of town for a couple of days and I was wondering if you'd look after Oscar for me. All you have to do is put out her food and give her fresh water every day."

As soon as Sally left, Claude finished packing a few things to take on the boat with Harry. Twice he walked to the front door and looked out onto the street, his anger growing because the pale blue Dodge sedan was still parked at the curb down the block. Its sole occupant, a man, sat relaxed behind the steering wheel. He appeared to be reading a newspaper. When Claude was ready to leave, he knelt down and said good-bye to Oscar.

"My daddy always said that a dog belongs to a man but a cat belongs to a place." Oscar purred loudly but did not stir from her supine position on the futon. Claude shook his head and stood up. "No telling what the old fool meant by that."

The telephone in the kitchen rang. "Now what?" Claude muttered as he walked back to the kitchen to answer it.

"This is Claude McCutcheon."

"Morning, Claude, how's everything going?" Bernie Beck asked.

"Fine, Bernie, fine. What's up?"

Bernie paused for a second. "I'm sorry to call you at home, but I've got some bad news, Claude. I just got word from the FBI. Your friend was killed early this morning."

"What?" Claude shook his head. For a moment he thought Bernie was still talking about Rainer Morgan. But that made no sense, because . . .

"Jesse Hamilton, Claude. He's dead."

"How'd it happen?" Claude heard himself ask, as if from a distance.

"I don't know too much yet. Looks like a hell of a shoot-out at a motel in East Palo Alto. Two perps, one of which Hamilton killed, the other one got away. My guess is Hamilton was expecting trouble and got it, in spades."

Claude didn't say anything. An image of Earl, note pinned to his sweater, came to mind. *Lord, Jesse, what am I going to tell that boy of yours?*

"You okay?" Bernie asked finally.

"Yeah, sure, I'm fine." Claude rubbed his eyes. "Listen, Bernie, do me a favor, will you? Call someone down at the East Palo Alto PD and tell them that I'll be responsible for the body, okay? I mean, if no relatives show up to claim him, I don't want him buried by the county or shipped over to the Stanford Medical School. Whatever else was going on, Jesse was a veteran and I'd like to see him buried properly." Claude paused for a second. "Whatever it costs, I'll take care of it."

"No problem, Claude. Consider it done."

"Thanks, Bernie. I appreciate you letting me know about Jesse." Claude hung up the telephone and stood quietly at the kitchen counter for several minutes, wondering why he didn't feel worse than he did. *Pack a bag,* he told himself. *Move.* As he did so, he remembered a conversation he had had a number of years ago with a young woman who had written a thesis on how men and women respond to death in combat situations.

"The response is quite different from that of civilian health-care professionals, doctors and nurses, who deal with mortality daily," she had said. "They accept death as the natural concomitant of life. When a patient dies, it is seldom unexpectedly, and even when the occasional unexpected death occurs, they know and are reassured by the fact that a given disease process, or response to trauma, however outwardly benign, results in death a certain percentage of the time regardless of the level of care given. Soldiers, on the other hand, almost always deny even the possibility of death, much less the reality, often to the extent of refusing to consciously acknowledge its presence.

"One man described receiving the news that a comrade had been killed as analogous to hearing the sound of distant thunder," she had added. "It's like being on the far edge of a storm front. You might see lightning and even feel the wind blow, but the reality of it remains at a distance. You know it's there but it never quite gets to where you are."

If he felt anything, Claude realized, it was anger. Anger not only at a needless death but also at being forced to be the one to deal with the ongoing tragedy.

Claude made sure the front door was locked and left the house through the kitchen and out the back. He locked the back door and walked through the yard connecting to the rear of his backyard and emerged on the street one block over. He turned to his right and walked around the block, entering onto his street to the rear of the blue Dodge. He strode quickly up to the driver's side window and reached inside the Harris Tweed jacket he was wearing for the army Colt he had purchased from Jesus Ortega. In one motion he knelt by the window and placed the muzzle of the heavy weapon just behind the ear of the man sitting at the steering wheel.

"Don't turn around," Claude said, his voice

low and menacing. "You know who I am, don't you?"

The man nodded carefully.

"Good. What you feel behind your ear is a Colt .45 automatic. Now, I'm going to be honest with you. I just bought this gun the other day, from a Mexican, and I've never fired it. That means I have no idea how light or heavy a trigger pull it has." Claude thumbed the hammer back to the cocked position, and the unmistakable sound, although by no means loud, caused the man to flinch involuntarily. "Do you get my point?"

Again, the man nodded.

"Hand me the car keys." The man complied, handing the keys out the window without turning his head. "Now answer me the truth: Are these the only keys you've got?"

"Yes."

"They better be." Claude looked over the man's shoulder and saw a cellular telephone sitting on the Dodge's console between the two bucket seats. In one swift motion Claude brought the Colt forward, in front of the man's face, aimed at the telephone unit, and fired one shot. The crashing report shook the small Dodge as the telephone exploded, the heavy .45-caliber slug obliterating the light plastic unit and continuing into and through the console, coming to rest in the automatic transmission housing. The driver jerked spasmodically and instinctively raised both arms to protect his face as the interior of the Dodge filled with the acrid smell of the smokeless powder. Claude brought the weapon's muzzle back to the rear of the man's head.

"Put your arms down," Claude hissed, jabbing the man with the pistol for emphasis. "If I catch you skulking around my house again, I'll kill you. Do you understand?"

The man, overwhelmed by the suddenness and violence of Claude's actions, nodded.

"Lie facedown across the console." When the man complied, Claude holstered the pistol under his jacket and walked quickly to the pickup truck parked in front of his house. He threw the overnight bag he had packed into the cab and, without so much as a backward glance at the Dodge, drove away.

"By the time he could get to a phone, McCutcheon was gone," Jones said, keeping his voice, face—his entire manner—perfectly calm.

"So. Once again you have failed in your assigned duties." Mellon's extraordinary basso profundo voice betrayed no emotion.

An involuntary tic above Barton Jones's left eye was the only physical manifestation of the increasing stress he felt. He was not used to failure, and having to report it via scrambled telephone line to his superiors, and then again to J. Watson Mellon, did nothing to ease his mind.

Barton Jones was the eldest of eight children born to a drunken Columbia, South Carolina, cotton mill worker and his half-witted wife. The only thing there had been enough of in his entire childhood was physical abuse. Not surprisingly, as a teenager Barton committed increasingly serious violations of the law until, in 1957, a patriotic justice of the peace in Calhoun County proposed enlistment of the seventeen-year-old in the U.S. Army in lieu of three to five years' incarceration for grand theft, auto. Almost from the first day of basic training, the army became the family Barton had never known. Assigned to the Quartermaster Corps at Ft. Lee, Virginia, the good soldier Barton Jones made a steady, if somewhat slow, climb through the enlisted ranks until, in 1965, he was promoted to staff sergeant.

In 1966 Jones went to Vietnam, assigned to the First Logistics Command in Saigon. By virtue of his years at Ft. Lee, he knew most of the quartermaster NCOs in the command and, after three months of surreptitious observation by his peers, was invited into what was known simply as the Network. The Saigon branch of the Network—run, at least as far as Jones was concerned, by a command sergeant major at USARV headquarters in Long Binh—operated as a clearinghouse for contraband war matériel stolen from the Saigon docks and from units of the South Vietnamese army for resale on the black market to the Vietcong and North Vietnamese army. Entire shipments of goods from the U.S. simply disappeared en route from the docks to the sprawling logistics facility at Long Binh. Jones was at first detailed to act as an armed guard at the weekly payoffs in Cholon, the Chinese neighborhood of Saigon. The sergeant major for whom Jones worked would compare bills of lading and manifest lists detailing the stolen matériel with the Chinese brokers who acted on behalf of the Vietcong and North Vietnamese supply officers, and the two sides would agree upon the amount to be paid. Payment was always in U.S. greenbacks, usually in excess of $100,000 at a time. Each side to these mutually beneficial transactions at once trusted and distrusted the other, and Barton Jones never allowed his attention to stray while the money was being counted and exchanged. He typically stared, unblinking, at the equally impassive Vietnamese guards who attended on behalf of the Chinese businessmen, with everyone—Jones included—armed to the teeth.

In his efforts on behalf of the Network Jones discovered an aptitude for strong-arm work, an inclination and indeed a ready willingness to use the threat of violence, and ultimately, violence itself, in the furtherance of the Network's goals. Although the vast sums of money the Network "earned" provided it with the means to subvert, via bribery, almost everyone, American or Vietnamese, needed to ensure access to the necessary matériel, an occasional stiff-necked individual was encountered. Such individuals seldom stuck to their guns after a visit from Sergeant Jones, and those who could not be bought or effectively threatened were swiftly transferred to other duties. Jones never knew exactly how far up the chain of command the Network extended, but clearly as far as general officers of both the American and South Vietnamese armies, for on several occasions his immediate superiors complained openly in his presence about how expensive it had become to maintain their patronage.

On two occasions in Vietnam, Jones was required to murder for the Network. Jones planned and carried out his duties in such an exemplary manner that he received a large bonus and, more significantly, came to the attention of several men well up the chain of command.

Throughout the remainder of his army career, until his retirement as a sergeant first class after twenty-five years of active-duty service in 1982, Jones worked first and last for the Network, becoming an integral player in its extensive criminal enterprises. Even after his retirement, he received occasional assignments, such as the one he was now engaged in for Sentinel.

"We've got one of your men, an independent contractor, killed by McCutcheon," Mellon was now recapping calmly. "Then we've got one of McCutcheon's friends killed by you personally, during the course of which murder, I might add, you failed utterly to complete your primary task. Next, you finally locate the elusive Mr. Hamilton only to kill him in the process of trying to capture him. And last but not least, we allow our only remaining link with the now-deceased Mr. Hamilton to apparently disappear off the face of the earth."

Jones shrugged involuntarily, a gesture more of frustration than resignation. "We both underestimated Jesse Hamilton, there's no question about that. As far as McCutcheon is concerned, I had absolutely no basis on which to assume that he would turn out to be as"—Jones paused for a moment, searching for the right word—"as *competent* as he has."

"When do you expect to locate Mr. McCutcheon?"

Jones shook his head. "I won't need to. Presumably he went under when he heard of Hamilton's death. My guess is that he will pick up the, ah, material stolen by Hamilton and will contact us."

"You're sure of that?"

"I think so. He hasn't been cooperating with either the police or the FBI up to this point. Now that his buddy Hamilton is dead, my guess is that he'll go freelance and try to make a deal with us."

From bad to worse, Rita thought, handing her boss the fax she'd received from Bureau headquarters. She'd already sent a copy to Bernie

Beck, trying hard not to think about what Claude must be feeling.

"Goddamnit!" Joe Bradley exploded, tossing the fax aside. "Now Hamilton's dead too?"

"Apparently he'd been holed up in a cheap motel in East Palo Alto," Rita said. "Late last night two men tried to force their way into his room and all hell broke loose. The manager said it sounded like a war." Rita shook her head. "I just got off the phone with the police down there. Mr. Hamilton was ready for action."

"What do you mean?"

"In addition to two pistols he was armed with a fully automatic MAC-10."

"Everybody on the street's better armed than we are, for Christ's sake," Joe muttered.

"Anyway, sometime after two o'clock in the morning the you-know-what hit the fan. The police figure Hamilton woke up to the sounds of the two men trying to jimmy his door and got up firing. He managed to kill one of the intruders before taking a couple of rounds himself. The second intruder fled the scene as soon as Hamilton went down. As you might expect, there was so much blood and gore at the scene the police have no way of knowing whether or not the second perp was wounded during the shoot-out. The East Palo Alto PD found a couple of vials of crack cocaine and are assuming it was a drug deal gone bad."

"What do you think?" Joe sat hunched behind his desk, his brow furrowed.

Rita met Joe's eyes. "I don't think it was drug related at all, but . . ." She shrugged. "We're missing something here, big time. Sentinel Micro calls us in to investigate an alleged interstate theft of a computer operating code by an employee, one Jesse Hamilton. Almost immediately we turn up a connection between Hamilton and Claude McCutcheon, a fellow Vietnam vet, and a lawyer. The connection isn't much, just an attempt to contact McCutcheon on the telephone. Normally we wouldn't think much of it, except, two army guys, buddies from the Nam? Who knows. Then, whammo, two bodies turn up in rapid succession at Mr. McCutcheon's house, one an intruder killed by McCutcheon himself and the other a friend of his. Then, last night, the elusive Mr. Hamilton gets killed in a reenactment of the shoot-out at the OK Corral."

"So what have we got?" Joe asked impatiently.

"A lot of questions and no answers. One scenario has Hamilton stealing the software and, fearing he's in over his head, calling his old army buddy lawyer McCutcheon for help. Did Hamilton leave the goods with McCutcheon for safekeeping while he tried to do a deal? Someone must have thought so or they wouldn't have tried breaking into McCutcheon's house not once but twice. And what about Sentinel Micro and Mellon? Are they freelancing, trying to get the software back on their own? And even if they are, since when do people start getting murdered over nothing more than a supposedly proprietary computer operating code?"

"What do you want to do?"

"First, let's get a warrant for McCutcheon's financial records. We can tie his credit card numbers and bank accounts into the mainframe back in Washington and know what he's been doing almost from minute to minute. Also, let's get some more background information on the man. What did he do between the time he got out of the army and his enrollment in law school here in the Bay Area? Let's see if we get any sort of correlation between *his* whereabouts and Hamilton's over that period of time. Maybe he and Hamilton have done a few other 'deals' together." Rita paused for a second. "Rainer Morgan's father and widow are having a memorial service today, at noon."

"So?"

"So I think we should get a covert photographer with a long lens to cover it. You never know who might show up. And, lastly, I'd like to initiate a background check on Mellon and Sentinel Micro."

Joe nodded, turning his attention to another stack of papers on his desk. "Do it."

"One more thing."

"Yeah?"

"Have you ever heard of Sir Richard Francis Burton?"

"Richard Burton? The actor?"

"No, this Richard Burton was a nineteenth-century Brit. Some sort of explorer, or government agent or something."

Joe glared at her. "Say, if you've got enough time on your hands to be reading history books, maybe we're not working you hard enough."

Rita backed out of his office, smiling. "Have no fear on that account."

12

Claude was tired. His stomach was sour from too much coffee and too little food, and his back felt as if it had been worked over with a baseball bat. There seemed to be no place on Harry's thirty-four-foot sailboat where a big man could actually stand up straight, whether in the ridiculously small cabin or on deck amidst the paraphernalia of sails, rigging, mast, and booms. Now, at midnight, after almost thirty-six hours, they were back in the Bay, tacking their way slowly in the darkness toward Point Molate and Harry's small harbor. The spreading of Rainer's ashes, the whole purpose of the voyage, had been rather less than dramatic from Claude's point of view, his main concern being to stand to windward when Harry chose to upend the small urn over the side of the boat. They had sailed out well beyond the Farallons, and in a myopic world bound closely on all sides by dense fog, Harry found himself unable to do more than mumble platitudes as Rainer's mortal remains disappeared into the greasy swells.

The so-called memorial service at the harbor before they set sail had been little better, just thinly sliced words of praise for a man whose life had been mostly destroyed by the things he had seen and done thirty years earlier in Vietnam. Only five people attended the service, including old Ben, who clearly had no idea what was going on. Three of the attendees spoke, and one of the speakers, a man who kept a fishing boat docked at the harbor and had no more than a nodding acquaintance with Rainer, took the opportunity to speak about the recent death of his own dog. The other two speakers were Harry and Rainer's wife, Hazel, neither of whom had been entirely successful in getting the words they desperately wanted to say past their overwhelming grief. Somewhere between Harry and Hazel and the clueless dog owner, Claude's mind wandered, and he thought of Jesse and Earl, and then another funeral—Verna McCutcheon's.

He had been in Vietnam almost six months when out of the blue he received the news of Verna McCutcheon's passing from an army chaplain, a straight-leg lieutenant colonel on TDY with Claude's brigade.

"I won't beat around the bush, son," the chaplain, a fat, red-faced man from Cincinnati, had said. "Your mother's dead."

"My mother?" Claude asked, confused. His mother had died when he was twelve.

"That's right, son," the chaplain said, taking Claude's confusion for shock. He waved a telegram in Claude's face. "It's right here in this Red Cross telegram. Verna McCutcheon, mother of Lieutenant Claude McCutcheon, died at 4:20 P.M., etcetera, etcetera." The chaplain looked at the date indicator on his wristwatch. He was perspiring heavily. "Two days ago. Your battalion commander has authorized a two-week emergency leave."

"Yes, sir," Claude said, wondering what he should do. The only Verna he knew was an old, cranky black woman who had occasionally cooked for his father and him after his mother died. Claude had quite frankly been afraid of her most of his life. He had known her only as "Aunt" Verna and was at a loss to explain how she could have come to have been identified as his mother.

Upon consideration he concluded that his father must have somehow arranged it and so decided to keep his own counsel and return home.

Claude's two-week emergency leave had fanned considerable envy throughout not only his platoon but indeed the entire company. To be sure, few of the men wished openly for the death of a close relative, but nonetheless, two weeks back home, in the real world, was nothing to be sneered at or dismissed out of hand. A great deal of uninformed but spirited speculation occurred as to just how close a relative the deceased would have to be to warrant an emergency leave. Most agreed that a cousin or nephew probably wouldn't do the trick, that almost certainly it would take a spouse or parent. All agreed that Lieutenant McCutcheon, the loss of his mother notwithstanding, was getting over.

The XO took over Claude's platoon and a captain at battalion lent him a set of khakis to wear home. He hopped a slick to Da Nang and from there a C-123 to Tan Son Nhut. The operations officer at Tan Son Nhut put him on the priority list and immediately got him aboard a flight to Guam. From Guam he flew to Honolulu and then on to California. With dizzying rapidity he was in and out of flight operations centers, up and down flight lines, and landing or taking off.

At home in North Carolina, his father refused to take credit for the chain of misunderstanding that had resulted in Claude's emergency leave.

"I thought you'd want to know that Verna had died," his father told Claude, "so I called the army over at Fort Bragg to ask how to get in touch with you. They told me to call the Red Cross in Raleigh. The Red Cross lady wanted to know who Verna was and I told her she was like a mother to you."

So either the telephone connection had been poor or the Red Cross official Claude's father had spoken to was inattentive, for Verna was thereafter identified as Claude's mother.

The county bureaucracy, having independently and correctly determined that Verna had died intestate and without family, had made arrangements to inter the deceased at taxpayer expense, the cost thereof to be charged back against the assets of the estate, if any. Claude's sudden and unexpected arrival and offer to pay for a Christian funeral surprised everyone at the county coroner's office.

"I'll tell you what's the truth," the coroner's clerk opined in a high-pitched, scratchy voice as Claude signed a release form relieving the county of any liability for the handling of Verna's remains. "I never knowed the army would let dern near anyone come back all the way from Veet-nam just to bury some old colored woman with no kinfolk of her own."

Claude contracted with the Marlowe Brothers Funeral Home to remove the body from the county morgue and organize the funeral. In fact, it was Bob "Your Friend in Need" Marlowe himself who lined up an employee of the funeral home, a part-time, self-ordained Pentacostal Holiness minister, when he learned that Claude had no one else in mind to conduct the services.

"He'll preach a lively service for ten dollars," Marlowe assured Claude.

The funeral turned out to be a rather simple affair, sparsely attended and quickly over. Verna had been a harsh and unyielding woman all her life, imbued with a peculiarly Southern meanness of spirit, an implacable "fuck you" approach to interpersonal relationships that seemed to spring out of the red dirt of the Carolinas along with the bright-leaf tobacco. Not many people got along with Verna while she lived, and fewer still were inclined to wish her spirit well at her burial.

It was almost 1 A.M. when Claude and Harry finished tying the sailboat up at the dock.

"Claude, I . . ."

Claude put a hand on his friend's shoulder. "You don't need to say anything, Harry. I'll give you and Hazel a week or so and then I'll stop by for a cup of coffee."

Harry nodded silently, and the two men parted without another word. As he passed by the small office at the end of the dock, Claude was surprised to see Ben wide-awake and rocking back and forth on the floor on his haunches. Claude opened the door and stepped in.

"You doing okay, Ben?"

The old man looked up at Claude, the dim light from the single low-watt bulb Harry kept burning all night revealing that the whites of his eyes had long since yellowed with age and a failing liver.

"Rainer's dead, isn't he?"

"Yes, Ben, he is," Claude replied, squatting down himself to be at the old man's level.

Ben fell silent and began rocking back and forth again. Knowing there was little else he could do, Claude reached out and put a hand on the old man's back, a gesture of shared grief and comfort stronger by far than mere words. Gradually, Ben's aching sadness settled over Claude's shoulders like a tattered shawl, and without realizing it he began to cry himself, silent tears that fell unnoticed onto the dirty wooden floor of the ramshackle office.

An errant breeze off the bay rattled a loose windowpane and startled Claude back to the present. He looked at his watch and was surprised to see that almost an hour had slipped away. Thinking about it later, he could not recall getting into his truck and leaving the harbor and, in fact, was across the Bay Bridge and in San Francisco before he consciously realized where he was going.

"Who is it?" Rita felt silly standing at her door in a cotton nightgown holding her FBI-issue .38 revolver, but it was, she told herself, almost three in the morning.

"It's me, Claude." His voice, even though muffled through the door, sounded tired.

Rita opened the door. "Claude, what in the world . . . ? Your secretary said you were out of town and she didn't know when you'd be back. I was worried about you. Where have you been?"

"I had a little business to take care of. Listen, I know it's the middle of the night, but I've been on the go for the last thirty-six hours, I'm dead beat, and I haven't been able to get you out of my mind."

Rita's shoulders sagged almost imperceptibly as Claude's words registered. Then she was in his arms, desire and sadness washing over her.

"You frighten me so," she murmured, more to herself than to Claude.

He bent down and picked her up effortlessly. In the bedroom he laid her gently on the bed. She had no recollection of taking her nightgown off, but suddenly they were both naked and Claude was in the bed beside her.

"Please," she cried out, not knowing what else to say or do as the room began to swim about her. "Please."

It became a refrain that continued throughout their lovemaking.

After making love, Claude fell asleep immediately. Rita lay awake watching him carefully, studying him, as the rising sun slowly lit the room. Her face and thighs were reddened where his two-day growth of beard had abraded them, and her breasts ached pleasantly from his not-too-tender hands. She got up at the usual time and showered, regretting having to wash his smell from her body, wishing she could spend the day in bed with him. She left him a short note explaining the eccentricities of her coffee-maker. *Call me when you wake up,* she wrote. She also left him a key to her flat, the first time she had ever indulged in such a gesture of hope.

"Emma? . . . Yeah, it's me, Claude. What's going on?"

Afternoon shadows were moving across Rita's living room floor as Claude stood nude, a towel wrapped around his waist, at the kitchen counter, telephone in his right hand. He opened a cabinet door to see what was behind it.

"Yeah, I got back safe and sound. I'm over in the City . . . They did, huh? Did you make them show you the search warrant? Did you read it?" He chuckled as Emma assured him sarcastically that she had more than just glanced at it. "No, I don't think you're an idiot. Was it Rita Johnson or did they send someone else? . . . Uh-huh. What records did they take? . . . What? . . . No, that's fine, it's what I expected. Did anybody call while I was out?" He reached over and opened the refrigerator door, idly cataloging its contents and enjoying the feel of the cool air on his bare skin while Emma went through her phone log. "Dick Kilpatrick called?" Kilpatrick was Claude's personal banker. He picked up the pencil Rita kept by the telephone. "Give me his number, would you? . . . Okay, got it. I'll call him as soon as we're done. Everyone else can wait," he assured her. "Although if Bernie Beck calls back, tell him I'll get back to him . . ."

Claude paused and thought for a moment. "Tell him I'll get back to him first thing in the morning. Oh, and do me a favor, would you? Call Felix Mackie and tell him I'll drop by and visit with him tomorrow. . . . Yeah. . . . What's that? I'll be in in the morning. . . . No, after I see Felix. Thanks, Emma." Still enjoying the cool air flowing from the open refrigerator door, he quickly dialed his banker's number. "Dick, Claude McCutcheon returning your call. What's happening?" He listened for a second, tapping on the counter with Rita's pencil. "A subpoena? Who served it?" He smiled. "Yeah, I've met her." He listened for a second and then chuckled. "I doubt they'll get much out of the records you gave them. Listen, Dick, I really appreciate you letting me know about this." He nodded as if the person on the other end of the line could see him. "No, it's nothing really. They're running an investigation on some stolen software for a company down in Menlo Park and my name accidentally got stirred into things. . . . Yeah, they're worse than the damned IRS when it comes to acting on bad information. Thanks, Dick. Lunch is on me the next time."

Claude hung the phone up and was examining the contents of Rita's refrigerator in earnest when he heard a key turn in the front-door dead bolt. The door opened and Rita walked in, balancing a grocery bag in one arm and her briefcase in the other.

"I thought you must have left," she said, stopping just inside the door.

"Why would you have thought that?" He took the bag of groceries from her arm. He put it on the counter and turned back to her.

"You didn't call." Her tone was not so much accusatory as hurt.

"I just got up. In fact"—he glanced down at the towel he was wearing—"I was just about to get into the shower. Why don't you join me?"

Claude had been in the steaming shower for several minutes when Rita shyly pulled back the curtain and gingerly got in. "Did you sleep the entire day?" she asked, as much to deflect attention from her sudden attack of modesty as to elicit an answer. She unconsciously covered her breasts with one arm.

"Pretty much." Claude sensed her discomfort. "Turn around and I'll soap your back."

The combination of the hot water and Claude's strong hands on her back caused Rita to shiver involuntarily. She gasped as his hands lingered on her buttocks and felt her knees go weak as he slowly and gently entered her.

Later, in bed, Rita lay with her head on Claude's stomach, her eyes focused on his slowly softening member. From time to time she moistened her forefinger and touched the tip of his still-weeping penis, bringing an occasional droplet of semen to her tongue.

"I had an eccentric uncle who used to say

that you could always tell a sailor by the seaman on his pants," Claude said.

Rita turned her head to look up at Claude. "What did you say?"

He smiled. "I asked what sort of information the FBI has compiled on that infamous desperado Claude McCutcheon."

"Not as much as you might think," Rita answered lazily. "We have copies of your service record, of course, your DD-214, but little else. We don't, for instance, have any record of this wonderful tattoo." She reached up and touched the back of his shoulder. On his right rear deltoid muscle, just above the shoulder blade, was a faded blue Oriental dragon's head. "Does it represent anything in particular?"

Claude closed his eyes, the memory flooding into his consciousness like sunlight through an open window. "Beyond stupidity," he murmured, as much to himself as to Rita, "it doesn't represent a thing." *What was her name?* he wondered. *Judy? Was Judy her name?* "I got it in, of all places, our nation's capital, Washington, D.C. I'm not exactly sure, but I must have been passing through on leave." He could remember that he'd picked up the woman, Judy, in a bar. They'd spent an hour or two drinking boilermakers, a shot of whiskey and a glass of beer, and she went with him to the tattoo parlor. After getting the tattoo, they'd gone to her apartment, one shabby room and a kitchenette, below the sidewalk, two miles from the White House.

Claude opened his eyes and looked at Rita. "A tattoo's a sign of ignorance, pure and simple."

"Well, I like it," Rita said. "It looks like some sort of army insignia."

"Did my credit card records from the bank provide you with much useful information?" he asked, changing the subject casually, without warning.

"Almost none," Rita answered, following Claude's lead adroitly, giving no indication of surprise or discomfort. "It's unusual these days to find someone, especially a professional like yourself, with only one credit card, and a little-used one at that. I assume you must pay most of your bills with cash."

"I do, and precisely because I don't particularly care to have my financial history and spending habits accessible to any fourteen-year-old hacker, much less government agencies and credit bureaus."

"I take it the bank manager told you I had been by with a subpoena."

"He did. To be honest, I can't imagine anyone in the East Bay you could talk to about me who wouldn't make it a point to let me know about the conversation."

"I'll keep that in mind."

"What have you found out about Jesse Hamilton's killers?"

"Not much so far. The man that Hamilton took down before he himself was killed has been identified as a Mexican national, an illegal alien, but the East Palo Alto PD has found nothing yet to indicate why he would have been involved in a strong-arm attempt on Hamilton."

"How about the other guy?"

Rita shook her head. "He got away clean. The East Palo Alto police have no leads whatever." Rita paused for a second. "I understand from Lieutenant Beck at the Albany PD that you're assuming financial responsibility for Hamilton's burial."

"That's right. To the best of my knowledge Jesse had no next of kin, so I assumed that if I didn't do something, he would end up on a dissecting table at Stanford. My secretary is working with the Veterans Administration to see if we can get him into one of the national cemeteries down on the Peninsula. What do you know about Sentinel Micro?"

"So far just annual report—type things. The chairman, Mellon, is portrayed as a captain of the high-tech industry with all the usual professional and social affiliations. Seventy-five percent of their annual sales are to the U.S. and allied governments, most of that in the classified microwave battlefield communications and laser-based weapons targeting categories. No indication of any unhappiness from either their armed services customers or the GAO."

"Four bodies lying in various morgues would

lead a reasonable person to conclude that some-body's pretty unhappy about something," Claude dryly pointed out.

Rita slid up so that her face was even with Claude's. "I have to say that I'm becoming uncomfortable talking about this case with you."

"You're worried about what your boss would say if he could see us here together," Claude said lightly, a smile on his face.

"Something like that."

"Honi soit qui mal y pense."

"And exactly what does that mean?"

"I suggest you look it up. That way you'll remember it longer than if I tell you. Are you hungry?"

Rita laughed. "Yes, a little. Are you?"

"Famished," Claude said, reaching for the telephone beside the bed, "and I know a great little Thai place over on Twenty-third and Geary that'll deliver."

13

East Oakland would make even a fool nervous. Boarded-up residences, rows of decrepit welfare housing, abandoned automobiles sitting up on cinder blocks, and trash-filled lots bore silent witness to an unconditional surrender in the so-called war against drugs. Violence ruled the streets, and automatic weapons fire under cover of darkness settled more than one turf dispute. The Oakland police seldom got out of their squad cars, and when they did so, it was generally with pieces drawn and all the slack off the trigger. The occasional predawn crack-house raid was undertaken only with the active cooperation of several agencies and was character-

ized by shows of force intended to cow even the
most wanton of street shooters. Nobody casually
motored through East Oakland, and those few
travelers who found themselves inadvertently
within its well-defined borders, especially at
night, often paid a heavy price for their careless-
ness.

Jamal Shaw, although from out of town,
found East Oakland as agreeable a spot as one
might expect to find anywhere in America.
Ratlike, he preferred to stir around after dark,
although he had no compunction about killing
in the daytime if such was necessary. Jamal had
grown up in Compton, in Los Angeles County,
and had committed his first murder at the ten-
der age of nine. Functionally illiterate and a
borderline moron by all accepted psychological
standards, Jamal was nonetheless a genius at
surviving on mean streets. He had been
approached on his home turf by a man he knew
from prison, a man known for operating an
employment agency of sorts. The job offer had
been a good one: go up to the Bay Area, to
Oakland, and snatch a black kid for some white
guy. Easy money.

Why me? Jamal had asked.

Felix Mackie, came the answer. *Bad motherfucker.*

Jamal smiled. He'd prospered around bad
motherfuckers all his life. A seasoned veteran of
the California Youth Authority and a cum laude
graduate of the big "Q," the San Quentin

Correctional Facility, Jamal knew better than to hit the streets of East Oakland with his dick in his hand and his mouth open. What he needed to know about Felix Mackie he would find out soon enough in his own way and in his own time. Questions, any sort of questions, would get you killed in East Oakland about as quickly as anything Jamal Shaw could think of.

"Kidnapping the child troubles me," Mellon said. He and Jones were seated in his office. "It is one thing to deal harshly with adults, quite another entirely to involve a small child."

Jones shrugged. "I don't see that we have any options."

"You remain convinced that McCutcheon has the disc." It was more a statement than a question.

"I do. The facts as we know them support no other conclusion. McCutcheon and Hamilton have—"

"Had."

Jones smiled. "McCutcheon and Hamilton *had* a long-term relationship going all the way back to the army and Vietnam. Just before he tried to drop out of sight, Hamilton left the boy with McCutcheon for safekeeping, and since the disc did not turn up in the wake of Hamilton's untimely demise—"

"Untimely indeed," Mellon interrupted petulantly. "Had we captured Hamilton, as you were ordered to do, instead of simply killing him, we wouldn't now be faced with the distasteful prospect of kidnapping a child."

"Since the disc did not turn up in the wake of Hamilton's death," Jones continued, his voice tight with anger, "it is reasonable to assume that McCutcheon either has it or knows its whereabouts. Since he has neither divulged its location nor physically turned it over to the FBI, I believe that he intends to offer it to us on much the same terms that Hamilton did, probably for cash and guarantees of safety for himself and the child."

"I'm not convinced," Mellon mused, more to himself than to Jones. "Mr. McCutcheon troubles me a great deal more than Hamilton ever did. As you have said, we both greatly underestimated the unlamented Mr. Hamilton. I do not intend to repeat that mistake as regards McCutcheon." Mellon swiveled his chair around and gazed out the window at the Los Altos hills. "What specific arrangements have you made?"

"Everything is set." Barton Jones was coming more and more to resent having to report the details of his activities to Mellon. "I've brought an ex-con up from L.A. to steal the child from Felix Mackie. After he's got the boy, he'll deliver him to me for payment at a rendezvous I've arranged in Berkeley."

"Is it safe to just pay this man off and let him go his own way?"

"I have no intention of doing so." Jones's tone of voice was that of an adult talking to a particularly slow child. "Even though there's no way he can make a connection back to the company, I would never leave such a loose end dangling. And, in any event, we'll be doing the rest of the human race a favor, believe me."

"Where are you putting the child while we deal with McCutcheon?" If Jones's patronizing tone of voice annoyed Mellon, he did not show it.

"I've got a safe house arranged in East Palo Alto."

A brief second of silence passed before Mellon spoke again. "Have you had any success in locating the elusive Mr. McCutcheon?"

"I was just coming to that." Jones paused for a brief instant, long enough to convey an exquisitely timed sense of insolence. "He's staying with the FBI agent, the woman." In spite of himself Jones smiled, pleased with his own perspicaciousness. "I had a hunch about her almost from the start, so when McCutcheon went under, I had one of my men plant a bug in her apartment in the City."

"What's her name?"

Whatever you do, you son of a bitch, don't acknowledge a job well done, Jones thought. "Johnson. Rita Johnson."

"Can we profit from this?"

Jones shrugged. "You never know. It sure as hell can't hurt to have this kind of information. I should have photos by Monday afternoon at the latest."

"Good, good. Between knowledge of her and

possession of the child, perhaps we can find a way to do business with McCutcheon. If, as you so strongly believe, he actually has the disc." Mellon paused for a moment, his fingers steepled under his chin. "Tell me again about the man McCutcheon left the child with—the one with whom you're going to have to deal."

"Felix Mackie. As they say in Oakland, a bad motherfucker. A San Quentin grad, nine years on a life sentence for murder. Scares a lot of people, even though it looks like he's stayed straight since he was paroled. I haven't found out yet what his connection with McCutcheon is, but it doesn't really matter."

"I do not want the child harmed, do you understand?"

Jones nodded. *What you want or don't want,* he thought as he left Mellon's office, *is going to make no difference whatever in the near future.*

Claude took a sip of coffee and made a face. He and Rita were about to leave her flat—Rita for work and Claude to meet Felix Mackie at his gym.

"I'll be honest with you. You're good at a number of things, but making coffee isn't one of them."

"Well, what would you say I *am* good at?" Rita asked, batting her eyelids.

Claude leaned in and whispered in her ear.

"Really?" In spite of herself Rita felt a blush on her throat and cheeks.

Claude nodded wordlessly, not a hint of a smile on his face.

"Will I see you tonight?" Rita asked as she and Claude walked downstairs to her car.

"Most likely. I'll call you at your office. Maybe we can have dinner over in the East Bay."

"Where are you parked?"

Claude nodded toward his truck. It was parked across the street.

"I didn't know you had a truck."

Claude smiled. *There's lots of things about me you don't know,* he thought.

"What happened to the Volkswagen?"

"That was just a loaner while I was having some work done on the truck." He laughed. "I expect that it's been repainted, had the VIN ground off, and is on its way back to Mexico City for resale even as we speak."

Rita held up her hand. "Please. I'm in the law enforcement business, remember? Don't say another word. And don't forget—call me this afternoon."

Claude stood on the sidewalk for a moment after Rita drove off. His intuition told him that someone had been watching as he and Rita had emerged from her building, and he looked carefully up and down the street. He walked slowly to the truck and got in, troubled that he had been unable to spot anything.

The truck started immediately and Claude was soon on the Bay Bridge, driving against the

East Bay commuters who were still straggling into the City. To his left as he headed toward the Treasure Island tunnel, San Francisco glowed with a pearlescent light as the rising sun burned through the fog and reflected off the high-rise office buildings in the financial district.

The gym had the usual retinue of early-morning devotees sweating and grunting when Claude walked in. He acknowledged several with a nod of the head. Felix sat impassively behind his counter, arms crossed, a giant black Buddha. He wasted no time getting to the point.

"A man's been asking around about me."

"Who?" Claude asked.

"That's what I was fixin' to ask you."

Claude nodded. "I think I can guess who it might be. They must have had a tail on me when I brought the boy over here."

Felix unfolded his arms and leaned across the counter. "You tell them they better not fuck with me," he said, his voice barely above a whisper.

"I suspect they already got that message, don't you?" Claude said with a smile. "How's the boy doing?"

"Like I said, he's doing fine." Felix resumed his position of repose. "Ruth"—his wife—"wants to know what about his peoples. She's taken with the boy."

The smile left Claude's face. "He's got no kin alive that I know of. His daddy's dead, most likely killed by the same folks that have been asking around about you. The note I got when the boy was left with me implied that there weren't any other relatives."

"You going to want him back?" Felix eyed Claude without expression.

"I'll be honest with you, Felix. That boy is my responsibility. His daddy left him with me knowing he might never see him again. My first reaction is to keep him, raise him up as my own. When I think about it, though, I've got to say that the best place for a young black boy to grow up is in a black family." Claude paused for a moment. "I can't think of two better parents than you and Ruth. What do you think?"

Felix barely nodded his head. "Ruth wants him bad."

"What about you?"

"Ain't no way the county social welfare people gonna let a man with my record adopt no child." A hint of a smile passed across Felix's lips. "You neither."

Claude laughed. "To hell with the county. And the state, for that matter. I'll decide what's best for the boy, not some civil servant with a degree in sociology. If I say you and Ruth should raise the boy as if he were your own, then that's the way it'll be. We'll dummy up a birth certificate and whatever else we need to get the job done. What do you say?"

"You better come by the house this afternoon and tell Ruth," Felix rumbled. "She won't believe me." The big man held Claude's eyes for a second longer. "This means a lot to Ruth. And me."

Claude nodded. "It does to me too. I knew the boy's daddy."

"You wanted to see me?" Rita asked.

"Yeah," Joe Bradley said, "come on in. Something interesting came in from Washington on Sentinel Micro. Two things, actually." He leaned back in his chair. "Your request for information on the company tweaked someone's memory. Several months ago the Bureau got an Information Only report from the Department of Commerce about an anonymous tip they received to the effect that Sentinel was illegally exporting their military microwave communications and laser targeting equipment to one or more countries on the State Department's restricted list. Commerce checked into it but apparently came up with nothing to warrant a full-scale investigation. The report came over to the Bureau and was promptly filed and forgotten. Until now."

"Any indication as to who Sentinel was doing business with?"

Joe shook his head. "No. Our guy in Washington called a friend of his over at Commerce and got a copy of their file, which he faxed to us." He handed the file to Rita. "Nothing more than an unsubstantiated tip. The guy at Commerce said that they get crap like that from the Silicon Valley all the time, almost always from disgruntled employees. Guy doesn't get a raise, or worse, gets fired, and whammo, off goes an anonymous letter."

"Commerce didn't ask for help from the Bureau when they originally investigated the tip?"

Joe laughed. "Are you kidding? Cooperation between agencies of the U.S. government? We're lucky they sent over the memo after they closed their file."

"What else have you got?"

"Something else interesting. It seems that although the investigator at Commerce couldn't come up with enough to substantiate the tip, he was sufficiently put off by Sentinel Micro's head of security, a guy by the name of"—Joe paused while he consulted his notes—"here it is, Barton Jones, that he did some discreet asking around on his own. Turns out that Mr. Jones's name is not an unfamiliar one over at the Criminal Investigation Division of the army's Military Police. Apparently he's been suspected of involvement with some sort of army-wide NCO Mafia going back to 1966, when he was in Vietnam."

"Vietnam?" Rita asked, thinking immediately of Claude and the now-deceased Jesse Hamilton. "Could he have been in the same unit as McCutcheon and Hamilton?"

"I don't think so, but you should probably confirm it. The file from Commerce indicates that he was a supply sergeant. The army's CID thinks he was involved in the theft and black-market sale of army matériel but could never pin anything on him. Not that they didn't try, though. They think he was behind the murder of one of their people in Saigon."

"This thing has smelled queer from the get-go." Rita chewed her lower lip. "I'm wondering if we shouldn't be more concerned with Sentinel Micro than with either McCutcheon or Hamilton," she added, thinking of something Claude had said during their first meeting: *The finger pointing at the moon is not the moon.* "What do you think?"

"What do I think?" Joe's face took on a determined set. "I think you've got a lot of work to do. I want you to find out everything you can about Sentinel's chairman and CEO. Particularly his finances. How much does he make and how much does he spend? How is he thought of in the high-tech community? What vices does he have? Is somebody blackmailing him for the technology? Get back to Commerce and find out to which companies and countries Sentinel legally exports their products. Then check out those companies, particularly the overseas ones, and see who, if anyone, they're fronting for."

"So you think that Hamilton may have stumbled onto something that implicated his boss Mellon in the illegal sale and export of high-tech military communications equipment and technology."

"I think it's a distinct possibility," Joe responded. "Or Hamilton may have been involved with Mellon all along and the two had a falling out. Maybe Hamilton wanted more money."

"One thing troubles me."

"Just one?"

"Well," Rita continued, ignoring her boss's sarcastic rejoinder, "if Sentinel's chairman, Mellon, is dirty, why in the world would he have brought the Bureau in to help him locate Jesse Hamilton?"

Joe shook his head. "Who knows? Maybe his own people weren't getting anywhere and he felt that with the FBI providing additional heat it would flush Hamilton out into the open where he could get to him before we could. If that was his plan, it may well have worked. *Somebody* sure as hell got to Hamilton before we did. In any event, a little digging into Mellon himself won't do any harm."

Rita nodded and got up to return to her office.

"Don't forget." Joe's voice stopped her.

"Don't forget what?"

"The wild card in all this—McCutcheon. Which reminds me: Did he resist giving you his office records?"

Rita shook her head. "He was out of town when I served the warrant, but his secretary was ready for us. Apparently he told her there was a good chance I'd be by and to give me everything I asked for."

"Which means he knew there was nothing in there that would do us any good. Goddamn it." Bradley shook his head, exasperated. "This McCutcheon's been around the block a few times. He's too smart to be just a penny-ante, small-time lawyer." He pointed at Rita for emphasis. "He knows his way around firearms too. I want you to be damned careful around this man."

It's a little late for that, Rita thought ruefully.

"You're certainly a sight for sore eyes," Emma Fujikawa said when Claude walked into the office.

He smiled ruefully. "What's new?"

"Well, you were right about the FBI showing up with a subpoena. That Agent Johnson who was here before showed up on Tuesday and I gave her copies of everything, like you said."

Claude nodded. "That's fine. Have you heard anything from them since?"

Emma shook her head. "Nothing."

Claude walked into his office, Emma trailing behind.

"Anything else?"

"The usual. All the mail and your messages are on your desk."

"Sit down," Claude said, indicating one of the chairs in his office. "Take a load off. Tell me what you found out from the Veterans Administration."

"Let me get my pad." When Emma returned,

she sat down with a sigh. "Oh, before I forget, you got a message from Artie Gibson at San Quentin. He would like to see you as soon as possible."

"He say about what?"

Emma shook her head. "An administrator at the prison called with the message—I didn't talk to Mr. Gibson personally."

Claude looked at his watch and nodded absently. "I'll run up and see him when I'm done here. What's the story from the Veterans Administration?"

"It's going to cost you," she said, looking at her notepad. "As you thought, both JoJo Watson and Jesse Hamilton are entitled to be buried in the National Cemetery in Colma, over on the Peninsula."

Claude nodded. "I know where Colma is."

"The VA will pay two hundred and fifty dollars toward the cost of each funeral. No more. The family, or in this case you, will have to pick up the rest. While you were gone, I arranged for the Samuels Funeral Home in East Palo Alto to pick up Mr. Hamilton's body from the county coroner's office as soon as the autopsy was completed. They're also going to pick up Mr. Watson's body at the coroner's office in San Francisco." Emma paused and consulted her notes. "That should have been done yesterday. I'll call them for you in a moment to confirm that they've done so. You'll have to talk with them about caskets and to arrange the specifics of the funeral itself. I assumed you would want both men buried at the same time."

"A double service is just what I had in mind. As to the specifics, I presume the funeral home wants to know how much money do I intend to spend."

Emma nodded. "Exactly."

"Boy, are they going to be disappointed. When can they arrange the interment?"

"I went ahead and tentatively set for this coming Tuesday, although it could be delayed with no trouble if you needed extra time or to allow any family members additional travel time."

Claude shook his head. "I don't believe either of them had any surviving family."

"I don't think so either. I spoke with Lieutenant Beck yesterday and he told me that as yet no one has come forward to claim Mr. Hamilton's body."

"Thanks, Emma. I really appreciate your help on this. When you call the funeral home to make sure they picked up both bodies, confirm that I want to go ahead with the Tuesday burial. Tell them I want both men cremated and ask them to arrange for a preacher to say a double service." Claude paused and thought for a moment. "Baptist. That ought to do it. Nothing fancy, just a straightforward Baptist funeral."

Artie Gibson was waiting when the guard showed Claude into the large visitors' room.

"I'm surprised they let you in on such short notice," Artie said, rising to shake Claude's hand.

"I told the warden's office that you had startling new information regarding the Lindbergh kidnapping."

Artie laughed. "I thought Bruno did it."

"So did the jury." The smile faded from Claude's face. "More bad news, Artie: Jesse's dead."

Artie nodded somberly. "I know. Guy called me from the City yesterday. He didn't know much, only that Jesse was found at a motel in East Palo Alto."

"There's not much to know, at least not yet. Looks like two guys tried to take him—Jesse killed one before the other got him. No leads yet, and sure as hell no ties to Sentinel or Barton Jones." Claude looked carefully at Artie. "Police are saying it looks like maybe a drug deal gone bad."

"Yeah, right. Every time a brother gets killed the first thing the police say is 'drug deal gone bad.' "

The two men sat quietly for several seconds before Claude spoke, breaking the melancholy silence.

"What have you got for me, Artie?"

"You know the guy over in the City who was telling my friend about Barton Jones and the Network?"

Claude nodded.

"Turns out the more he got to thinking about how he was hung out to dry with his dishonorable discharge, the madder he got. After talking to my friend he made a phone call or two and came up with something interesting."

"He need some . . ." Claude rubbed his thumb and forefinger together.

Artie shook his head. "Show you how mad he is, the man's giving it away."

"No honor among thieves," Claude said dryly.

"Tell me about it. Anyway, the word is that the sister, Jesse's friend, *was* killed, most likely by Jones himself."

"Who was she?"

Artie shrugged. "He didn't know exactly, but the impression he got was that she was working undercover at Sentinel."

Claude shook his head. "That doesn't make any sense, Artie. If she was heat, somebody would have jumped up when she was killed. I mean, whoever she worked for would have called the East Palo Alto PD and said, 'No way that's a suicide, she was one of us.' "

"Maybe."

"What do you mean, 'maybe'?"

Artie shrugged again. "Maybe the left hand didn't want the right hand to know what it was doing, you know what I'm saying? Maybe whoever she worked for's got something else in mind. You know as well as I do that nobody talks to anybody in the police business.

Anybody in here"—Artie waved his right arm to include all of San Quentin—"can tell you that the SFPD never knows what the FBI or the state or anybody else is doing in their own backyard. Not only that, none of these departments and agencies like one another very much, so when they do have to cooperate, they do as little as they possibly can." Artie chuckled sardonically. "Nothing the local police like better than seeing the feds fuck up, and vice versa."

"You think your source will come up with any more information?"

Artie shook his head. "My man in the City thinks he's gone as far as he's got the balls to go." Artie paused and looked at the wall behind Claude. "Jesse was a good man."

"Jesse fucked up," Claude said quietly. "He was a good man and he sure as hell didn't deserve to die in a cheap motel in East Palo Alto, but the fact of the matter is he fucked up. And left me with a big problem."

"The boy."

Claude nodded but did not speak.

"What are you going to do?"

"Probably just what Jesse did: make a stupid decision." Claude shook his head in disgust. "I can't throw that boy's life away by just turning him over to the social welfare people. The real problem is that with Felix's record as a convicted felon there's no way the county is going to let him and his wife adopt Earl, so I'll have to figure out a way to dummy up an out-of-state birth certificate and adoption papers."

"I know someone who can help you with the certificate."

"Why am I not surprised?" As soon as he said it, Claude regretted the words. "I'm sorry, Artie, I didn't mean it like it sounded. It's just that—"

"Don't worry about it. Believe it or not, I agree with what you're saying about Jesse. Listen." Artie leaned toward Claude and lowered his voice. "I've said this before: I'm a crook. That's why I'm here, in jail. The thing is, I knew what I was doing when I broke the law. I did it intentionally. Jesse was exactly like most of the idiots I have to put up with in here—he never wanted to admit that what he was doing was crooked, you know what I'm saying? That way, he never had to think about consequences, he never had to worry about the spot he was putting you in if he got killed. When I said Jesse was a good man, I didn't mean that what he did wasn't stupid." Artie leaned back in his chair. "Are you going to tell the police what you know about Jones and Sentinel?"

"What do I know?" Claude asked rhetorically. "Some cock-and-bull story cooked up by a lowlife with a dishonorable discharge and a hard-on against the military?" He held up a hand to forestall Artie's objection. "I'm not saying I don't believe it, but that's exactly how Sentinel's lawyers will characterize anything I say to the police. Without the disc the murdered woman gave to Jesse, I've got nothing to talk about. Plus, the more talking I do with the police, the greater the chance they're going to find out about Jesse's son."

"Are you thinking about going after Jones yourself?"

A muscle twitched along Claude's jawline. "I won't have to."

"How's that?"

"He's going to come after me."

Claude sat at his kitchen table and ate a light dinner of bread and cheese complemented with a fruity Napa Valley sauvignon blanc. The bread was a crisply fresh baguette he had picked up on his way back from San Quentin and the cheese a small wedge of a double cream Brie from the refrigerator. He peeled an orange and a banana for dessert and smiled at the thought of the boy, Earl, eating such a prosaic meal. The kid would've probably liked it. Claude remembered how enthusiastically the boy had attacked his oatmeal the other night. Sure, Sally had made fun of Claude, but he'd bet he and Earl would've coped quite nicely if the boy had stayed with him. *Hell,* he and his old man, who'd had no teeth to speak of and hated to wear his dentures, typically had oatmeal—or its functional vegetable equivalent, boiled okra and string beans prepared by Aunt Verna—two or three nights a week.

Lord, he thought, swirling the last of the wine in his glass, *if the old man could see me now, what in the world would he think?*

Claude finished his fruit and, still peckish, tore off another piece of the baguette and refilled his wineglass. He kept coming back in his mind to Artie's information about Jesse's friend, the murdered woman. *Who the hell could she have been working for?* he asked himself. Certainly not the FBI, or the missing disc would already be in government hands. Having thought about it at some length, he felt confident that Jesse had handed the disc off to someone, probably JoJo at the VA hospital. Then, based on the fact that the disc was nowhere to be found among JoJo's few personal belongings, and on Rainer Morgan's telephone number being on a piece of paper in JoJo's pocket, it was hardly a stretch to conclude that JoJo had given the disc to Rainer when he, JoJo, checked himself out of the hospital. Christ alone knew where it was now, but clearly Barton Jones and Mellon at Sentinel believed he, Claude, either had it or knew its whereabouts.

Claude was certain he hadn't seen the last of them.

14

She didn't give you any trouble, did she?" Claude asked, nodding toward Oscar.

"Not at all," Sally Pinter said. "I saw you come in last night, so I didn't bother to come over this morning."

The two of them were in Claude's kitchen, having a cup of coffee.

Sally finished her coffee. "Bud's due home any minute and I haven't started dinner yet. I have to get going."

"I'd like to take you and Bud out to dinner one night soon for looking after the boy that night and for feeding mouse-breath here while I was gone." He pointed at Oscar.

"You don't have to do that. Did you ever find his father?"

Claude shook his head. "I'm afraid both his parents are now deceased. I've got the boy placed with a family that wants to keep him and raise him as their own."

"Will they be allowed to adopt him?"

"Are you kidding? If the county social services people had their way, they'd shuffle that child through a series of dead-end foster homes while wringing their hands and trying desperately to avoid making a decision. Then a family law judge, probably two or three years from now, would get himself or herself involved and the process would grind to a complete halt. What they don't realize is that while they're waltzing around trying to find an absolutely perfect solution, the boy is growing up in a series of foster homes and learning all the wrong lessons out on the street. A year or two of that and he'd be lost forever."

"How can you avoid all that?"

"Easy. I'm going to dummy up some documents and give Earl a new identity, complete with some sort of out-of-state court order granting custody to the family I've placed him with." He winked at Sally. "Hey, I didn't go to law school for nothing."

Sally looked doubtful. "I know what you're saying, but it sounds awfully dangerous to me. What would happen to you if you got caught?"

Claude shrugged. "The important thing here

is not me, but the child. His father left him with me to take care of. I can assure you that I would have preferred that he hadn't, but once he did, and I accepted the responsibility, then I'm obligated, now that he's dead, to do what I think is right. For Earl, not me." He smiled at Sally. "Besides, if I couldn't ride roughshod over the county welfare department and the family law courts and get away with it, I wouldn't be much of a lawyer, now, would I?"

Claude spent the day catching up on some work he'd brought home from the office. At five o'clock he looked through his kitchen window and saw that Sally's husband, Bud, had gotten home from work. He walked out his kitchen door and across to the Pinters' house. He knocked on their back door and opened it partially.

"Hello?" he called out. "Bud?"

"Claude?" Bud answered, walking back from the front of his house. "How you doing?" he asked, pleased as always to see Claude. "How about a beer? Can you stay to dinner?"

Claude smiled and shook his head. "Not tonight. I just wondered if I could use your phone. Mine's acting a little squirrelly and the phone company hasn't gotten by to look at it yet."

"You bet. Hey, how about those A's?"

"They can't keep losing forever. Hey, it's me," Claude said when Rita answered. "I'm on someone else's phone so I can't talk too much. I'll be over at your place in"—Claude paused and looked again at his watch—"about an hour or so. How does that sound?" Claude listened for a moment and winked at Bud. "Okay, I'll see you in a bit." After hanging up the phone he turned back to Bud. "Thanks, Bud, I appreciate it."

"You bet. Listen, how about you and I go see those A's pretty soon."

Claude smiled. "You mean actually *buy* a ticket?" he said, feigning incredulity. "To watch them play?"

Bud laughed. *"Somebody's* got to pay those million-dollar salaries."

A low-pressure system off the coast coaxed a rare breath of summer into the Bay Area from the sweltering Sacramento Valley, sending large numbers of urban dwellers reflexively in search of mesquite charcoal with which to fire up little-used barbecue grills. Claude sat on Rita's small deck in blue jeans and bare feet, a bottle of Veuve Clicquot champagne on ice at his side. The deck looked out over the Presidio of San Francisco and was awash in the redolence of the thousands of blue-gum eucalyptus trees that covered the Presidio's undeveloped grounds.

"Whatever you're cooking sure smells good," he said over his shoulder.

"Coq au vin," Rita answered, stepping through the open French doors to join Claude on the deck. She had put on shorts and a T-shirt and, like Claude, was barefoot.

"You've got good-looking legs. Real good-looking."

"And the longer it cooks," Rita continued, ignoring Claude's compliment, "the better it's going to taste." She held up her glass for a refill of the dry, nutty champagne. "To Claude McCutcheon," she said with mock gravity. "An excellent judge of French champagne."

Claude accepted the toast with a nod of his head. "And legs."

"Who is Claude McCutcheon?" Rita asked rhetorically. "What does he want out of life?"

Claude laughed. "If he doesn't know by now, I'd say he's in trouble."

"Do you enjoy being a lawyer?"

Claude shrugged. "I've never really thought of myself as such. Most of what I do, or what any lawyer does for that matter, could be equally well done by any reasonably bright adult with only a modicum of training."

"What about the good that many attorneys do, like public defenders and public interest lawyers and law firms?"

Claude refilled their glasses. "You don't really want to discuss law and society, do you?" he teased.

"But isn't the law the very glue that holds us together as a society?"

"No," Claude said, shaking his head. "No, it most definitely isn't, and the relatively recent notion that it is, is one of the things that's wrong with this country."

"What do you mean?"

"I mean that we as a people seem to have lost the notion that in society individual responsibility must always be the foundation for any system of laws and governance. We've been suckered into believing that the solution for all problems lies not with the individual but with the local, state, or federal government. People think that the way to solve a problem is by passing a new law and spending more money, and why not? It's a hell of a lot safer for the politicians than facing an issue head-on and having to deal with what is often an unpleasant truth."

"How would you change things?"

Claude shook his head. "Things can't be changed. As a society we've deviated too far for too long to ever go back." He smiled. "Of course, although things can't be changed, one can adjust."

"Adjust?"

"Opt out." Claude took a sip of his champagne and smiled.

"What are you smiling at?"

"Me. Sitting here on a rare summer evening in the City, drinking chilled champagne in the company of a beautiful woman with whom I've just made love, and talking about, of all things, law and contemporary society."

"Don't change the subject," Rita admonished, wagging a finger. "Explain 'opt out.' "

" 'Opt out' means just what it sounds like: to

remove oneself as an active, participating member of the body politic."

"You can't be serious."

"Of course I am." He laughed. "Well, perhaps not entirely. But who can be serious on—"

"I know. A rare summer evening, chilled champagne, beautiful woman, etcetera, etcetera. You can't be serious about just opting out of society."

"Well, as I've always said, why should criminals be the only ones who feel free to ignore the laws of the land?" He sat forward in his chair and poured more champagne into their glasses. "Seriously, if you start with the premise that our society has become, for all intents and purposes, effectively ungovernable—"

"I don't start with that premise at all."

"Take my word for it, we have become too diverse, too contentious a nonmelting pot, and exacerbating the problem, tax revenues are shrinking at an ever increasing rate."

"The fact that the problems posed are exceedingly difficult doesn't justify 'opting out' of the system."

"Not just exceedingly difficult—insoluble. And that does justify opting out. What's more, we've always admired the man or woman who does so. In all of our literature, all of our films, all of our art, we admire the outlaw, the individual who goes it alone, who thumbs his or her nose at authority."

"I don't agree," Rita said firmly. "I think most

people are able to distinguish between the fictional antiestablishment 'ideal' and the real-life need to work together to improve society for everyone. Furthermore, any woman over the age of twenty-one could tell you that outlaws, while admittedly interesting to have around from time to time"—she smiled—"make very poor mates." She paused and took a sip of champagne. "Had Jesse Hamilton opted out? Before he was killed?"

Claude paused for a moment before answering. "Yes," he said soberly, "I think clearly he had."

"Do you think he stole the missing disc from Sentinel?"

Claude shook his head. "No, I don't."

"Do you think he had it when he was killed?"

"No."

"Do you know where it is?"

Once more Claude shook his head. "Has anyone among the law enforcement community made any progress in identifying his murderers?"

"The East Palo Alto police, who have jurisdiction, are following up the investigation into a possible drug motive for the shooting. As far as any other agencies are concerned, you know I can't discuss any of the particulars of the case, Claude."

"It doesn't matter. We both know why he was murdered and by whom, or on whose orders. Or at least I do."

"Who do you think was responsible?" Rita asked, her voice suddenly guarded.

Claude laughed, trying to break the sudden tension that had come up between them. "Why should I show you mine if you won't show me yours?" He reached out and took her hand. "Let's go see how the coq au vin is doing and you can tell me again about how outlaws are interesting to have around from time to time."

Sunshine and the sound of Rita showering woke Claude early Sunday morning. He stretched quietly, listening to the sound of the running water and enjoying the warmth of the sun as it inched across the room.

"How about some breakfast?" Rita asked from the bathroom as soon as she stepped from the shower.

"I've got a better idea," Claude called back, rising swiftly and pulling on his faded jeans. "Come with me out to the farmers' market. We can have breakfast at a little place I know in North Beach after we do some shopping." He stooped to put on his socks and shoes. "I'll shower when we get back."

The San Francisco Farmers Market was a rich mélange of sights and smells, Hispanic farmworkers mingling with well-to-do young software developers, battered pickup trucks parked next to Mercedes and BMWs. Every stall had crates of fruits and vegetables still bearing evidence of an early-morning harvest on truck farms from Salinas up to Sacramento, and the vendors sported scuffed cowboy boots, yoked denim shirts, and battered straw cowboy hats.

"Cuatro, por favor," Claude said, pointing to the large, ripe avocados. They had walked around much of the market, looking at the dizzying variety of goods for sale, before Claude started making selections. "The key to success at a large farmers' market is shoe leather," he told Rita. "If you're not willing to walk around and look at everything first, you might as well forget it and do all your shopping at the Safeway." When he had seen most of what was being offered that morning, he started to buy. *"Gracias,"* he said, taking the avocados and moving on through the large crowd with a casual confidence.

"What else are you going to buy?" Rita asked.

"The real danger here is not what to buy, but what not to buy. For anybody who likes to cook, or eat for that matter, being around such an extraordinary variety of fresh fruit and produce is precisely like being a kid in a candy store. With no trouble at all I could spend a couple of hundred dollars here this morning. Today, however, we're going to limit our purchases to the ingredients we need for supper."

"Which are?"

"Since San Francisco is in the midst of a rare heat wave, I thought I'd start us off with a chilled avocado-tomatillo soup. We'll also use the avocado for a guacamole. Then, since I'm going to buy tomatillos anyway, a chipotle-tomatillo chicken should make a nice main dish. So, we still need to get the tomatillos, a handful of dried chipotles, and, of course, the standard Mexican herbs, spices, and peppers to bring it all together."

"Did you learn to speak Spanish in school?"

"No." They stopped at another stall and Claude bought a small quantity of several varieties of peppers. "I taught myself over the past five years. Given the shift in demographics in the West, anybody who lives in California and doesn't speak at least a passable Spanish is going to be in a minority very shortly. Besides"—he stopped and smiled at Rita—"it comes off the tongue so much more warmly than English, don't you think?" He gestured suddenly to a boy pushing a cart with a large thermos of rich, darkly roasted Mexican coffee. *"Dos café, por favor."* He handed Rita a paper cup of the steaming, black coffee with a flourish. "Getting hungry?"

"Famished."

Breakfast was a high-fat, high-calorie affair at a small mom-and-pop diner off Union Street in San Francisco's North Beach district. Everyone in the place seemed to know Claude, from the old men sipping coffee at the counter, to the middle-aged but muscular grill cook who wore a Giants baseball cap, to the young waitress in cutoff blue jeans and a tube top. No menus were produced, no specials recited, and no check prepared. The waitress, Alyce, brought two mugs of coffee and, after being introduced to Rita, plopped herself down on Claude's lap and scolded him for not having been in for a while.

"You're putting on weight," Claude observed.

"No way, José," Alyce answered, punching him in the chest as she got up. She winked at Rita. "He *never* brings women in here."

In short order food began to arrive at the table: large plates filled with soft scrambled eggs, home fried potatoes, and spicy Italian sausage. Additionally, there was a fresh sourdough baguette and, for each of them, a crisply cooked waffle.

"Good Lord," Rita sighed, slowing down as they neared the end of the huge meal. "It's going to take me a month to recover from the damage I'm doing here this morning."

Claude laughed. "Yeah, but when have you had so much fun?"

Never, Rita started to say, but didn't.

"What made you join the FBI?" Claude asked after the plates had been cleared away and Alyce had refilled their coffee cups.

"I don't know. I can't remember not wanting to be an agent." Rita smiled. "Even as a little kid I wanted to be a G-girl."

"Was your father in law enforcement?"

Rita shook her head. "No, he sold insurance. My mother was, is, a housewife." She took a piece of bread and lightly buttered it. "What about your parents?" she asked, looking down at the bread. "What do they do?"

"They're both dead. My mother died when I was twelve and the old man died when I was in Vietnam."

"I'm sorry," Rita said automatically.

"No need to be. They've both been dead a long time now."

"Any brothers or sisters?"

Claude shook his head. "No, after my mother died it was just me and the old man. I guess we did okay." He paused and thought for a moment. "Anyway, we did the best we could."

"What kind of work did he do?"

"Not much of anything. He was shot up pretty badly in the Second World War and drew a disability pension. Oh, he did occasional odd jobs when he felt like it, and people from all over our part of North Carolina were always wanting to pay him to train their hunting dogs, so we never wanted for anything." Claude laughed. "Every now and again he'd tease me, say that he was going to get me a new mother, but the fact of the matter was we both liked things just the way they were."

"How do you mean?"

Claude shrugged. "Hard to say. Mostly I remember it was quiet when I was growing up. There wasn't any family around to annoy us, folks like aunts or uncles or nephews. The old man originally came from West Virginia—'by God West Virginia' he called it—near

Bluefield, and if he had any family still alive up there, he never mentioned them to me. All of my mother's people died out before she did. Most evenings me and the old man'd sit together after supper. I'd be reading or doing schoolwork, and he'd be working on his guns or fishing tackle, doing something with his hands, and we wouldn't need to talk or even play the radio. I guess we just always knew what the other was thinking so there was no need to say anything."

"Did you hate to leave him when you went into the army?"

"No, I really didn't. Not at the time. You know how it is when you're young. I was dying to get out of North Carolina and see the world. And I suppose I just assumed he would always be there whenever I wanted to come back. It never occurred to me that he might die and leave me on my own. I remember when I left, he drove me down to the recruiting station in Raleigh. We got up early, before daylight, and the lights flooding back into the backyard woke up the old man's dogs and set them to barking." Claude paused and shook his head. "Funny how you remember something like that, isn't it? Anyway, we stopped for breakfast on the way to Raleigh, and neither one of us could think of a thing to say. When we got to the recruiting station, we sat in the car for a minute and smoked a cigarette. Finally, when I had to leave, he told me that he had hitchhiked into Bluefield when he joined the army during the Depression. That was all."

Rita laughed, thinking suddenly about her father. "You know, I think it actually embarrassed my father when I joined the Bureau after law school. I guess he thought I would join a large law firm and practice corporate or tax law."

"And meet a nice young man."

"Especially that. My father was no different from most men of his generation. I suspect his continuing nightmare throughout my adolescence was the imagined sight of me in the backseat of some boy's automobile."

"Are you still close to your parents?"

"Yes and no. I talk to them every week or so on the telephone, mostly to reassure them that I'm not constantly involved in shoot-outs with bank robbers and South American drug dealers." She paused for a minute before continuing. "I'm afraid we've reached a point where we have so little in common we actually have to work at having a conversation. That must sound terrible." She looked at Claude. "Have you ever wanted children?"

"No. Oh, from time to time I've thought about it, mostly in a fantasy about having grown sons and daughters gathered about to cherish and respect me in my old age, but I've never really been able to delude myself into believing it possible." He laughed. "I know I would have been a competent parent, though, because I was always able to spot the mistakes various friends were making with their children." He looked over at Rita. "How about you? Is that old biological clock starting to tick ever more loudly?"

"I can't say that it is, although my parents seem to be able to hear every tick a continent away."

Claude laughed and stood up. "Well, listening to your clock ticking no doubt gives them something to do in their retirement."

15

"Mornin', Emma."

Claude smiled at the surprised look on his secretary's face as he came into the office.

"My God," Emma cried, "will wonders never cease? Claude McCutcheon in the office before ten o'clock and on a Monday morning no less." She feigned a worried look. "We're not being investigated by the Bar Association today, are we?"

Claude sneered. "Don't get me started on the Bar Association this early in the morning. Just thinking about the money I'm forced to pour down that rathole every year supporting that leftist bureaucracy is enough to make me wish

I'd listened to my mother and become a violinist. Or something."

Emma made a rude face and busied herself with grinding beans to make a fresh pot of coffee. "Sam Ratliff called just a few minutes ago and so did Bernie Beck. I told both of them you'd call back later today."

"Did either one of them sound important?"

Emma shook her head. "No, I got the feeling both calls were social. Did you ever call Sam back Friday afternoon?"

Claude nodded. "Yeah, he was having a small problem at his new construction site. Nothing major. Bring me in a cup of coffee when you get it made." Claude walked into his office and sat down. Before he could do anything, the phone in the outer office rang. He heard Emma answer it and place the caller on hold.

"It's Special Agent Johnson, the FBI lady," Emma called out. "Are you in?"

"Yeah, I'll take it." Claude punched the appropriate button on his telephone and said hello.

"Good morning," Rita said. "I called your home, and when you didn't answer, I thought I'd try the office. I didn't think you went to work so early."

"I don't normally, but I've got some things that need attending to. What can I do for you?"

"Well, nothing, really," Rita said, nonplussed

by the way Claude asked her, implying she needed a reason to call him. "I just called to say hello and to thank you for the weekend. Am I calling at a bad time?"

"There's never a bad time for you to call, although aren't you concerned about the security of this line?"

Rita chuckled. "Not as of this morning. I had the surveillance terminated."

"Both I and the ACLU are forever in your debt. As for the weekend, it *was* a good one, wasn't it?"

"Would you like to come over to the City for dinner tonight?"

"I'd love to, but I've been promising some friends that I'd have dinner with them and tonight's the night."

"Some other time then. By the way," Rita added casually, "when is Jesse Hamilton's funeral?"

"Tomorrow. Listen, I'd like to chat but I need to get a couple of things done here this morning. I'll call you later."

"Call me tonight, when you get home."

"Good-bye." Claude hung up and called out to Emma, "Get Bernie Beck on the line for me, will you?" He reached into his pocket and pulled out the key to Rita's flat, looking at it contemplatively for several seconds before replacing it.

"Lieutenant Beck's on the phone," Emma called out. "Line two."

Claude snatched the receiver off its cradle. "Bernie, how're things going?"

"Fine, Claude, fine. Thanks for getting back to me. We haven't talked for a couple of days, so I was just calling to see how you were doing. When's Jesse Hamilton's funeral?"

"Tomorrow. He's going to be buried in the national cemetery in Colma."

"I'm pleased to hear that worked out. Was it much trouble?"

"No, it really wasn't. The VA helped out some and Emma took care of the paperwork and the details."

"Is it going to cost you much?"

"Surprisingly little, actually." Claude laughed. "Once Emma and I were able to convince the funeral parlor that they weren't burying a wealthy East Palo Alto drug dealer, that is. Not to change the subject, but have you heard anything new on the man I shot in my house?"

"Not a thing on motive, but you'll be pleased to hear that the district attorney has tentatively concluded that the shooting was a clear case of self-defense."

"I'm glad to hear it," Claude said sarcastically.

"You should be," Bernie said, a hint of annoyance creeping into his voice. "It means he won't be pursuing a criminal indictment against you. It wasn't as big a slam dunk as you might have thought, Claude—DAs, especially in the Bay Area, mightily hate to see private citizens engaging in gunplay. Even in their own homes in the middle of the night. You might eventually have beaten the rap if he'd decided to indict, but it would have cost you a whole lot of money and heartache, believe me."

"I understand, Bernie. I know that you worked hard to help me out on this and I want you to know that I appreciate it. I mean it."

"If you'd like to demonstrate your appreciation in a more tangible fashion, you can buy me lunch at Bette's next week."

"You got it. I'll talk to you soon."

Emma walked into the office, a large mug of coffee in her hand. "Coffee's ready."

"Music to my ears." Claude looked at his watch. "One more call and then I've got to get some work done. See if you can get Sam Ratliff on the line for me." He leaned back in his chair and sipped the hot coffee contentedly.

Barton Jones watched from across the street as Jamal Shaw sauntered insolently down the sidewalk toward the corner. Barton had chosen their meeting place at the intersection of San Pablo Avenue and Gilman Street and the time, midday, with care. Numerous men began gathering at that particular intersection every day just before noon to drink wine, smoke cigarettes, and discuss the afternoon racing program at Golden Gate Fields, a thoroughbred racetrack located on the Albany mudflats just half a mile down Gilman from San Pablo Avenue. Barton knew that he and Jamal Shaw would not be looked at twice by the other "sportsmen" as the two of them finalized the details of the kidnapping of Jesse Hamilton's orphaned son. For verisimilitude Barton carried a copy of the racing form clutched in his left hand, a pencil stub behind his right ear. He noted with pleasure as he crossed the street that Jamal, upon arriving at the designated intersection, did not overtly look around for him, but rather leaned against the wall of the corner building and closed his eyes, just another player soaking up a bit of sunshine.

"Got a light?" Barton asked, a pack of Marlboros in his hand.

Jamal reached silently into his pants pocket and pulled out a crumpled book of matches. He accepted the cigarette offered by Barton and lit both with one match.

"Have you had an opportunity to check out the situation?"

Jamal indicated that he had with the barest nod of his head. Neither man looked at the other.

"Do you anticipate any problems?"

Jamal responded no with an almost indiscernible shaking of his head.

"Good." Barton ground out his cigarette on the pavement. "I'll pick him up from you at five o'clock tomorrow morning." Barton reached into his pocket and withdrew a small, white envelope. "There are two pills in here," he said, giving the envelope to Jamal. "One should suffice to keep him sleeping all night. Give him the second one tomorrow morning before we meet. Do you understand?"

Jamal silently indicated that he did.

"When I have the child, alive and unharmed, I'll pay you the full amount we agreed upon, in cash." Barton turned to leave.

"It's not enough," Jamal said, so quietly that Barton almost didn't hear him.

Barton stopped but did not turn around to look at Jamal.

"I want ten thousand dollars," Jamal said.

An observer standing more than five or six feet away would not have known that the two men were talking to each other.

Barton smiled, a thin, mirthless pulling back of the lips. Jamal's demand was not unexpected. The two men had previously agreed upon five thousand dollars for the snatch. After pausing for an appropriate moment to indicate that he was considering this new development and was displeased with it, he turned partially around so that he could see Jamal out of the corner of his right eye. The amount to be paid was immaterial to him, but he knew that he had to make at least a token show of resistance to the new demand. "Eight thousand."

Jamal felt a warmth come over his body. "Ten," he repeated, knowing that Jones was in no position to negotiate.

Barton nodded and turned briefly to look directly in Jamal's eyes. "Don't fuck it up," he said, and was quickly gone.

For just a second a tiny crab of doubt gnawed at Jamal, the thought that perhaps the man he had bargained with was somehow different from most other men he had encountered in his short, violent life. Almost as quickly as the doubt came, however, it went, and he strolled easily down the street to a bus stop, the thought of ten thousand dollars in cash overriding all concern.

"Kitty!"

Claude laughed and nodded his head. "That's right," he said to the boy, "kitty." He smiled at Felix and Ruth. "He remembers my cat."

"Earl, do you remember Mr. McCutcheon?" Ruth asked. The boy, his eyes wide with curiosity, nodded but did not speak. "You run along and wash up now," Ruth told him. "Dinner's going to be ready soon."

Claude watched him leave the room and then turned to Felix.

The big man nodded. "Ruth's got him almost to talking. A few words here and there, anyway. You want anything to drink?"

"Beer's fine, whatever you've got. Has he said anything about his father?"

Ruth shook her head. "No, he hasn't. That boy's powerfully troubled and most likely was long before he was left with you. You don't know anything about his mother?"

Claude accepted a beer from Felix. "Thanks.

No, I don't know anything about her, except that Jesse's note to me said she had been dead for several years." He paused and took a drink of his beer. "She must not have had any close relatives, or at least none that Jesse wanted his son left with, because he didn't indicate anything like that to me." Claude looked from Ruth to Felix. "He knew he was in trouble when he sent that boy to me. I suspect he even knew that there was a good chance he would never see his son again. In all the world he trusted me to do right by him, and that's what I've done. As far as I'm concerned, he's your son now."

After dinner Earl was put to bed and Claude, Felix, and Ruth sat with coffee in the living room.

"What have you told the neighbors?" Claude asked.

"I told them that Earl was my sister's boy, from Virginia," Ruth said. "I said she was sick with the cancer and that she asked me to take the boy until she got better."

"What about his father?"

Ruth shook her head. "I said he didn't have no father."

"Good," Claude said. "We'll have to come up with a Virginia birth certificate but that shouldn't be too much of a problem. I'll dummy up a court order from Virginia giving both of you temporary legal custody of the boy based on the mother's illness. That should be enough for you to get him enrolled in kinder-

garten this fall. After that, say nine months to a
year from now, we'll put together a full-scale set
of Virginia adoption papers and it'll be case
closed." Claude lifted his coffee cup in a salute
to Ruth and Felix. "I believe that Jesse, had he
had the opportunity to get to know both of you,
would be pleased to have you raising his son as
your own."

Felix wasn't sure he could trust his voice not
to crack. "I, we, owe you for this, Claude." He
didn't have to look at his wife to know that she
was crying.

A third of the way down the block from Felix
Mackie's house, on the other side of the street, a
pair of ratlike eyes glowed from the front seat of
a late-model Toyota. Jamal Shaw had stolen the
car an hour earlier in Berkeley. He watched as a
white man stepped out of the Mackies' house
and stood out on the stoop for a moment,
bathed in a square of yellow light coming from
inside the house. Jamal had no idea what sort of
white man, other than the police, would be visiting Felix Mackie at home, but the very fact
troubled him because it was, in Jamal's experience, something unusual. He started the Toyota
and drove quickly away, the need for a hit of
crack cocaine suddenly overwhelming.

"Who is it?" Rita's voice was muffled by the
closed door of her apartment.

"It's me," Claude said softly.

The door opened partway, framing Rita's face between its edge and the doorjamb.

"I thought you said you were busy tonight."

Claude shrugged. "I finished up my business early. Thought you might like to see me."

When he returned from the East Oakland crack house in which he had spent three relatively pleasant hours, Jamal insolently parked almost directly across the street from Felix's house. The dash clock in the stolen Toyota indicated that it was just a little past 1 A.M. Jamal got out of the car and stood quietly on the sidewalk for several minutes, sniffing the air for danger like a particularly large and unattractive rodent. Stuffed into the waistband of his trousers was a 9mm Bulgarian-made automatic, a weapon he had purchased that very night from a fellow sportsman and hunting enthusiast he met at the crack house. Although quite prepared to use it, Jamal hoped that he would be able to snatch the child without arousing Felix or his wife, for even in East Oakland gunfire could, on the odd occasion, attract the attention of the authorities.

Jamal knew from his informal surveillance of the one-story, wood-frame house that the child's bedroom had a single double-hung window facing the vacant lot to the left of the house. He paused again at the window, listening to a breeze blowing trash along the street. He opened the window and quickly lifted himself into the bedroom, the residue of crack cocaine in his body masking the pain of dragging his shins across the windowsill. A night-light was plugged into an outlet near the door, and Jamal could clearly see the boy sleeping soundly on a small cot. He reached into his pocket for the sleeping pills he had been given and carefully placed one in the child's mouth. The boy swallowed instinctively and did not wake up. Jamal immediately relaxed somewhat, the first and, in his mind, most difficult part of the job completed with no problem. He decided to wait several minutes before taking the child out the window, reasoning that the pill he had given him would need at least that much time to begin to have an effect.

Felix Mackie was awake. He seldom slept soundly, a legacy of his years in prison where it behooved a man never to have more than one eye closed at any time. He didn't know exactly what sound had awakened him, but something clearly had and he had not survived in a harsh, unforgiving environment by ignoring such things. After a short time he got up, thinking perhaps the boy might be stirring around the house. Ironically, Felix Mackie kept no weapons in or around his house, so secure was he that his reputation alone was sufficient deterrent. Ruth turned in the bed and asked if anything was wrong.

"Go back to sleep," he said, not unkindly, "I'm just up checking on the boy."

Ruth smiled and said nothing, her spirit moved by her husband's love for the child. *Thank you, Lord Jesus,* she prayed, pulling the woolen blanket up around her neck.

Through the thin Sheetrock walls Jamal heard every word of the short conversation between Felix and Ruth. He drew the Bulgarian pistol from his trousers and stood behind the door. When Felix opened the door and walked into the child's bedroom, Jamal stepped up behind him and brought the pistol crashing down on the big man's head. Stunned, Felix staggered for two short steps and then steadied himself against the far wall.

He snarled, "You're a dead man, mother—"

Jamal, his heart racing, brought the pistol up and shot him, the bullet entering Felix's chest and piercing the right lung. Felix, although rocked by the impact of the bullet, didn't go down. In fact, he took a step toward Jamal, his face a frightful thing to see.

Jamal fired again. The second bullet, striking a rib, ricocheted downward and pierced Felix's left kidney before exiting near the small of his back. Felix, slowed but not yet ready to go down, lurched toward Jamal, who fired yet again. The third shot hit in the lower waist, the bullet disintegrating as it shattered the heavy pelvic bone. Felix toppled to the floor just as Ruth burst into the room. Jamal turned the weapon on her and pulled the trigger. When the pistol failed to fire, he cursed madly and grabbed the still-sleeping child from his cot.

"I'll kill the motherfucker," he kept repeating, holding the jammed automatic against the boy's head. "I'll kill the motherfucker."

Ruth, shocked almost senseless by the sight of Felix, dead for all she knew, lying motionless on the floor, froze. Jamal took one step and pushed her roughly aside, trying once more to shoot her. Cursing the useless pistol, he held the boy under one arm and dashed out of the house through the front door.

16

Barton Jones yawned as he turned off Grizzly Peak Boulevard above the University of California campus into Tilden Park. It was 5 A.M. and he had risen two hours earlier at his rented condominium in Menlo Park on the peninsula south of San Francisco. He had directed Jamal Shaw to meet him in the park above Berkeley, knowing that the likelihood of someone's stumbling onto their "exchange" at that hour of the morning was small indeed. As he pulled into the parking lot adjacent to the park's restored turn-of-the-century merry-go-round, he noted a single car, a late-model Toyota, already parked there. Tendrils of fog drifted through the stand of redwood and eucalyptus trees surrounding the parking lot as Barton parked and identified Jamal Shaw as the sole visible occupant of the Toyota. He got out of his car and walked quickly to the Japanese import. Standing abreast of the open driver's side window, he could see a young child sleeping on the backseat. Jamal did not bother to get out of his car.

What a moron, Barton thought. "Did everything go all right?"

Jamal inclined his head to look up at Barton, contempt on his face. He opened his jacket so Barton could see the pistol in his waistband. Jamal had not been able to figure out why the weapon had jammed but was not concerned because, in his considerable experience, just the sight of a weapon was sufficient to cow most men. Also, the crack cocaine he had smoked within the past half hour while waiting for Jones had considerably enhanced his sense of well-being and control.

"You gots the money?" he asked insolently, ignoring Barton's question.

Barton smiled and nodded. "Did you give the boy the sleeping pills?"

"Yeah, I gave him two. One when I snatched him and another one about ten minutes ago."

Barton reached into his jacket pocket and pulled out a small-caliber revolver. Before Jamal could react, Barton placed the muzzle of the pistol against his temple and pulled the trigger. Jamal jerked spasmodically as the bullet ripped through brain tissue and his body came to rest slumped against the Toyota's steering wheel. Barton reached in with the pistol and placed the muzzle against the base of Jamal's skull. He fired twice more, Jamal's body jerking once each time a bullet smashed upward into his brainpan. Barton dropped the pistol into Jamal's lap and walked quickly around to the passenger side of the car. He easily lifted the still-sleeping boy out of the backseat and carried him to his own car. He opened the trunk and placed the child in a large cardboard box he had lined with blankets. He closed the trunk and skinned off the latex surgical gloves he was wearing.

" 'If the gloves don't fit, you must acquit,' " he said to Jamal Shaw's corpse as he dropped them on the ground next to the stolen Toyota. *Just like stepping on a cockroach,* he thought, driving out of the park and down to the Bay.

Claude woke to the smell of coffee brewing. He was alone in the bed and it took him just a second to place exactly where he was. When he remembered, he nestled back amongst the pillows, content not to rush waking up.

"Coffee," Rita said, sitting on the edge of the bed with two cups in her hands. *"Real* coffee," she added. "I made a special trip to your pretentious coffee store and bought a pound of their best."

Claude sat up against the headboard and sipped the coffee. "Perfect. And you're right, they are pretentious." Claude shook his head and winked at Rita. "But they do roast and sell good coffee." He patted the side of the bed next to where he reclined. "You're not in any great rush this morning, are you?"

The telephone woke them for the second time at a quarter past nine. It was Rita's secretary, calling to find out why she wasn't in the office. As she stammered an excuse, Claude got up and went into the bathroom. He came out and watched as she dashed about the bedroom, dressing.

"Aren't you going to shower?" he asked, teasing her.

"No time. We have an office staff meeting every Tuesday morning, and if I don't leave in the next two minutes, I'm going to have to walk in late." She stopped long enough to give Claude a quick kiss. "Besides, this way I get to smell you on my skin all day long." She looked at her watch. "I'll have to splurge on a cab, but at least I can put my makeup on, on the way to the Federal Building." At the front door she looked back at Claude. "Lock up when you leave and call me tonight."

Claude waved good-bye and walked into the kitchen for a fresh cup of coffee. He pulled the window blind back enough to see Rita running up the sidewalk to catch her cab. *Claude, my boy*, he said to himself as he walked back into the bedroom, *you made the right decision never to work for anyone but yourself. All this rushing about to punch time clocks is hard on the system*. Taking a sip of coffee, he dialed his office.

"Hello, Emma? Claude here. Just calling to make sure you got to work on time."

"Claude, Ruth Mackie's been trying to reach you since early this morning. She even called me at home to see if I knew where you might be."

"What did she want?"

Emma paused for a second. "Felix was shot last night," she said, her voice shaky. "Ruth said something about a burglar or something. They took Felix over to the Kaiser Hospital in Oakland."

"How is he?" Claude asked, his heart pounding with dread.

"It sounded pretty bad. She said he was shot three times. Oh, Claude, what's going on?"

"I don't know, Emma," he said soothingly, "but we'll try to find out. Did Ruth say anything else?"

"No, just that she had to talk to you as soon as possible. She said to tell you she would be at the hospital all morning. Felix was still in surgery when she spoke with me."

"Okay, if she calls again, tell her I'm on the way to the hospital. Then call Bernie Beck at the Albany Police Department and tell him what happened. Ask him to check with the Oakland PD for any information they might have and tell him I'll call him later this morning. Got that?"

"Yes. Claude, I'm worried. Does Felix getting shot have anything to do with the shootings at your house?"

"I don't see how they can," Claude lied. "You know how things are in East Oakland. I expect Felix was just unlucky and confronted a burglar in his home last night, don't you think?"

"I guess so," Emma said, her tone of voice telling Claude that she guessed nothing of the sort.

"I'll talk to you later. Don't forget to call Bernie."

"How is he?"

Claude found Ruth in the surgical waiting room at Kaiser Hospital. She looked drawn and haggard. As soon as she saw Claude, she started crying again.

"He took him," she sobbed, "he took little Earl."

"Who took him?" Claude asked, although he knew in his heart who was behind the kidnapping.

"The man who shot Felix. He told me he'd kill Earl if I did anything."

Claude took Ruth into his arms, comforting her as best he could. "Have the doctors told you anything yet about Felix?"

"Not yet," she said, her face buried in Claude's shoulder. "He should be coming out of surgery before long." She looked up at Claude. "What are we going to do about Earl?"

"Don't worry about Earl," Claude said, knowing how hollow his words sounded. "The men who took him want something from me, something they think I have. As soon as they get what they want, they'll release the boy, believe me." Claude thought for a second. "Did you tell the police anything about Earl?"

Ruth shook her head. "No, I told them Felix was shot by a burglar, but beyond that I thought I better not do or say anything until I talked with you. Did I do right?"

"Perfect. Let's leave it at that for the time being."

"Mrs. Mackie?" A surgeon walked into the waiting room.

"Over here," Claude said.

"Who are you?" the doctor asked, looking first at Claude and then at Ruth.

"I'm a friend of the family. This"—Claude nodded toward Ruth—"is Mrs. Mackie."

"Your husband is a tough man," the doctor said with the lilting accent of a high-caste New Delhian. He held his hand out and introduced himself to both Claude and Ruth. "I'm Doctor Patel, and I ought to know." He smiled. "Mr. Mackie should, barring unforeseen complications, recover nicely, although he will be hospitalized for some time. Unfortunately, we did have to remove one kidney, but most people do quite nicely with only one. We'll just have to

see how that goes. He has a broken pelvis and
two broken ribs as well as a punctured lung.
Troublesome, but again, your husband appears
to be a man with an iron constitution. He came
through the surgery with all his vital signs in
great shape."

"May I see him now?" Ruth asked.

The doctor shook his head. "Soon. He's in
the recovery room under heavy sedation. I'd say
in three or four hours you should be able to look
in on him, although of course he won't be doing
much talking."

"Why don't you let me take you home?"
Claude suggested. "You could use the time to
rest a little and then come back later."

Ruth shook her head firmly. "No. I'm not
leaving here until I see Felix."

"That's fine," the doctor said. "You can make
yourself comfortable here if you'd like. I'll send
a nurse out for you as soon as we're sure things
have stabilized."

After the doctor left, Claude walked Ruth over
to a well-worn sofa on the far side of the room.

"Are you sure you're going to be okay here,"
he asked, "on your own?"

"I'll be fine. You worry about little Earl."

"I'll have him back soon. Count on it."

Claude drove directly to his office from the
hospital. "Did you get hold of Bernie Beck?" he
asked Emma as soon as he got to the top of the
stairs.

"Yes. He hadn't heard about the shooting when I spoke to him but promised he would look into it immediately."

"How long ago was that?"

Emma looked at her watch. "About an hour."

"See if you can get him on the line for me, would you?"

Emma nodded and picked up the phone. "I just brewed a fresh pot of coffee. Go on into your office and I'll bring you a cup as soon as I get you through to Lieutenant Beck."

Emma had Bernie on the phone and a cup of coffee on Claude's desk in less than a minute.

"Bernie? Claude here. . . . Yeah, great. Listen, Bernie, have you found out anything on the Felix Mackie shooting yet?"

"Not much, Claude. My man in Burglary at the Oakland PD said it looks like a hot job that turned bad when Felix confronted the burglar."

"Anything in the way of physical evidence?"

"Nothing to speak of. Two nine-millimeter shell casings on the floor, so we know the pistol was an automatic. My man said Felix was shot three times so he guesses that the weapon jammed on the third shot, probably trying to eject the spent casing. He figures it was just a cheap street gun, probably Chinese or Eastern European manufacture."

Claude thought for a minute. "Anything else unusual around the East Bay last night?"

"What are you getting at, Claude? Does Felix

Mackie getting shot have anything to do with you?"

"What do you mean?"

"You know goddamn well what I mean," Bernie said, irritation obvious in his voice. "Don't be pulling my dick on this, Claude, we're friends, remember? If something's going on, if there's a connection here, I want to know about it."

"I don't know, Bernie," Claude lied, "I really don't. It might be a coincidence and it might not. That's why I asked about anything else you might have heard of."

"There was one thing," Bernie said reluctantly.

"Yeah?"

"A park ranger up in Tilden Park found a stiff this morning sitting in a stolen car near the carousel. Black male, no ID, we're running a fingerprint check now. It was a professional hit, three slugs in the brain, the murder weapon left on the scene with the body. Real clean."

"And?"

"There was another weapon in the car with the stiff. A Bulgarian-made automatic with a spent shell casing jammed in the ejector mechanism."

"Bingo."

"Yeah, looks like it. Oakland PD has the pistol now. They're going to try to match it to one of the slugs they dug out of Felix. My guess is it'll be a match."

"So what have you got?"

"Nothing but questions, and a feeling that neither you nor the FBI is telling me everything. And I've got to tell you, Claude, I don't much like it."

"Have you talked to the FBI? About this?"

"Just before you called. I spoke with Agent Johnson and she claims not to know anything either." Bernie thought for a moment. "Say, isn't today the day of your friend's funeral? Jesse Hamilton?"

"Yeah, but he's not exactly my friend. Just an old army buddy."

"Whatever. You watch yourself, Claude. I don't want to be going to *your* funeral anytime soon, you hear?"

"Glad you could make it," Joe Bradley said sarcastically, looking at his watch. Rita's fellow agents attending the weekly staff conference smiled.

Rita sat down at the large conference table and assumed an expression of pained innocence. "I was on the telephone with Lieutenant Beck of the Albany PD. Another development in the Sentinel Micro case."

Joe shook his head. "I was just coming to that matter on the agenda. I got notified late yesterday afternoon that we are to close our file on that investigation."

"What?" Rita couldn't hide her astonishment.

"You heard me. Sentinel Micro has notified

the Bureau that the death of Jesse Hamilton amounts to a de facto resolution of the case."

"What about the alleged stolen technology?"

Her boss shrugged. "Who knows? Presumably Sentinel has satisfied itself on that aspect of the matter." He smiled. "So, as they love to say in the movies, case closed."

"But, Joe, there was another murder last night, and an attempted murder as well. Both, I believe, tied in to McCutcheon and this case."

Joe was unimpressed. "Believe it or not, the local authorities are perfectly well equipped and staffed to solve local crimes. The murder of Jesse Hamilton, the shootings at McCutcheon's house, and now these latest shootings you've brought up are all within the purview of said local authorities. Besides"—Joe fixed his young agent with an amused look—"if I remember correctly, you didn't think much of this case from the get-go. Why all the interest now?"

Rita bit her lip. "I just hate to see an investigation closed with so many loose ends. Nothing more."

"Well, as it just so happens, so do I. Have we gotten anything back from Commerce on who Sentinel's doing business with internationally?"

Rita shook her head. "Not yet."

"Then light a fire under someone back there. If you don't turn up something of interest soon, and I mean real soon, I'm going to have to close it down. In the meantime I want you to give Martin"—Joe inclined his head in the direction of one of Rita's fellow agents—"a hand on his Wells Fargo robbery investigation."

Claude dressed carefully, as if he were putting on a uniform instead of a suit. He bathed and shaved, using his great-grandfather's shaving mug as he did almost every day. The suit was a dark gray wool, conservatively cut and tailored perfectly to Claude's body, with just enough extra room under the left armpit to accommodate the underarm shoulder holster he wore on occasion. The pants were held up with a pair of wine red woven-silk suspenders. Instead of the cowboy boots he normally wore, he shoehorned on a pair of burnished oxblood wing tips, a pair he had owned for almost fifteen years and which fit like the familiar grasp of an old and valued friend's handshake. His shirt was white and plain-collared, and he wore a dark burgundy silk tie. *Not bad,* he thought, admiring himself in the bathroom mirror. *In fact, too nice for a funeral.*

In the kitchen he picked up the telephone and dialed Sentinel Micro's number.

"This is Claude McCutcheon," he said when Sentinel's switchboard operator answered, "and I'd like to speak to Mr. Mellon. . . . Yes, ma'am, that's right, Claude McCutcheon. I believe he's expecting my call." Claude lit a Camel while he waited, recorded music, white noise, coming from the telephone. Oscar walked into the kitchen and meowed loudly. Claude shook his head. "I don't like it either," he said to the cat, flicking the ash from his cigarette into the sink. A familiar basso profundo voice came on the line.

"Mr. McCutcheon, how nice to hear from you. Give me the number you're calling from and I'll call you right back on a private line."

Claude gave his telephone number and hung up. He looked at the cat. "Big deal, huh, Oscar?" Before the cat could answer, the phone rang. He picked it up. "McCutcheon."

"Mr. McCutcheon, I am so pleased you decided to get in touch with me. May I presume—"

"You've got something I want and I believe I have something you want," Claude brusquely interrupted. "Since I've got to be down your way later this afternoon, I suggest we get together and trade."

"I concur, but not here. Sentinel owns a boat that we keep moored at the St. Francis Yacht Club in San Francisco. You know the St. Francis, don't you? Opposite the Marina Green in the City."

"I know where it is."

"Good. Meet me there this evening at eight o'clock."

Before Mellon could say anything else Claude hung up. "Eight o'clock it is," he said to himself. He picked up the telephone once again and called his office. "Emma? Claude. Listen, Emma, do me a favor, will you? Call Ruth

Mackie for me and tell her I want to see her at her home this evening at about nine o'clock."

"She's not going to want to leave the hospital that early, Claude. In fact, I think they're having a hard time getting her to leave at all."

"I know, but tell her that I said she has to meet me at her home tonight. Whether she wants to leave Felix's bedside or not." He paused for a second. "I'm leaving for JoJo and Jesse's funeral now."

"Agent Johnson called not too long ago. Do you want me to call her back for you?"

"Please. Tell her I've left for the funeral and will call her tomorrow. Thanks, Emma."

Claude walked back into his bedroom and strapped on his shoulder holster. He removed the .38 revolver and checked the loads, expecting everything to be in order but knowing better than to trust to memory when his life was involved. That done, he slipped the revolver back into the holster. Next, he reached under the futon and drew out the big Colt .45 automatic Jesus Ortega had sold him. He released the clip into his palm and with his thumb ejected each of the blunt rounds onto the futon. Oscar leaped up onto the comforter and began batting at the loose bullets. Drawing on a pair of white cotton gloves, Claude wiped each shell casing free of fingerprints and then reloaded the clip. He reinserted the clip into the automatic and chambered a round, taking pleasure in the authoritative manner in which the slide rammed the bullet home. Standing up from the futon, he slid the heavy weapon into the waistband of his suit trousers opposite the small of his back. Drawing on his suit coat, he took a last look in the mirror and then quickly left the house.

17

They must be putting a hell of a lot of water on this cemetery grass to keep it so green, Claude thought, his attention wandering during the reading of the service. For JoJo, freed now from the remorseless grip of addiction, he felt relief fully as much as sorrow at his passing. He could only hope JoJo had found some measure of peace. He suddenly remembered that Jesse Hamilton had fallen in love in Fayetteville, North Carolina, with a young, dark-skinned girl he met at the NCO club. *Could she have been the boy's, Earl's, mother?* Claude wondered. Jesse had wanted to meet her in Hawaii on R and R, just like all the married guys met their wives, and borrowed money from Claude to send to her for the airfare. *Did he ever pay me back?* Claude wondered, smiling in spite of himself. *I'm sure he must have.* Claude ignored the preacher's droning voice and allowed himself to slip deeper into his reverie. *What did Jesse look like twenty-five years after Vietnam?* he wondered. *Was he a handsome man, bold with the ladies?* Claude had only a vague recollection of Jesse as a young man, in the squad bay and in the field, but of course no idea whatever of the man in his later, adult years. *It's strange,* he thought, *how quickly we're gone, men like Jesse and JoJo and me. Not a trace, not a ripple to mark our passage. He might as well not have had a son, for not even the boy will remember him, not really, not like he was.*

It was a thought almost too sad to be borne and Claude involuntarily shook his head, trying to put it out of his mind. *What did you dream of, Jesse, late at night when you were all alone? What did you hope for?* Claude looked at his watch and almost signaled to the preacher to wind things up, but then thought better of it. *I guess a man really shouldn't get buried in too big a hurry. He'll be long enough in the ground that a little extra time getting him there shouldn't matter.*

A helicopter passed overhead, tacking south along the freeway that ran adjacent to the cemetery. Claude looked up, an involuntary reaction cued more by the feel of the aircraft than its sound, and the memory of the last time he saw Jesse flooded into his consciousness.

As the lead Huey settled down, Claude could see the pilot and copilot sitting impassively at the controls, their flight helmets and dark goggles making them look like giant locusts, their heads swiveling about in short, hexapod movements. In contrast to the apparently indifferent serenity of the pilots, the door gunners grinned maniacally and waved Claude and the lead squad aboard, anxious to be back in the relative safety of the sky. Sgt. Jesse Hamilton stood with the rest of the platoon, bent away from the violent wash of the first helicopter's landing and takeoff. The landing pad at the artillery firebase from which they were leaving could only accommodate one slick at a time so the remaining three Hueys orbited until the first one was back in the air. The operation made the artillerymen exceedingly nervous, for the camp was frequently mortared whenever helicopters were resupplying them. Fortunately, the second, third, and fourth slicks made their pickups without incident, and all four helicopters were soon tacking across the valley, climbing to mission altitude.

The morning had started quietly enough, with a hot breakfast choppered out from the brigade's base camp outside Tay Ninh. Claude's platoon had been detailed to spend a week at the artillery firebase camp, providing perimeter security. It was considered something of a lark, particularly compared to active patrolling, and the duty was rotated through the brigade's three battalions.

A little before noon the artillery battery commander, a young second lieutenant, woke Claude to tell him that the battalion XO was inbound on a slick. *Can't be good news,* Claude muttered as he rose, the tropical midday humidity making his body feel as if it were coated with 30-weight motor oil.

"Brigade has gotten a report that there may be an NVA unit infiltrating the area around this village." The XO's finger stabbed at the map spread out on a sandbag between them. Jesse stood behind Claude, peering over his right shoulder. The village indicated was only five klicks east of the firebase camp. "We don't think there's much likelihood of such an infiltration, but brigade wants it checked out nonetheless. Since you're so close, Colonel Weatherby"—their battalion commander—"decided to use your platoon." The XO looked at his watch. "Four slicks will pick you up at thirteen hundred and drop you south of the village. Sweep through the village and its environs and, assuming you don't step into any shit, radio for extraction at sixteen hundred." The XO looked at Claude and didn't quite smile. "You should be back in time for dinner."

From the air things always looked so peaceful. Making no attempt to mislead or confuse,

the helicopters flew directly east to the
unnamed village, orbiting once at Claude's
request to give them an aerial overview of the
terrain. The helicopters were barely off the LZ,
on their way home to hot coffee and cigarettes,
when Claude and Jesse began looking for land-
marks from which to orient their map. The
squad leaders set up a quick defensive perimeter and urged everyone to stay alert. Claude
pointed to a small hill on a diagonal to their
intended line of march to the village.

"We'll move on a line with that hill," he told
Jesse. "Get the points and flanks out."

The platoon spread out in a staggered line
and started walking, the village partially visible
ahead and slightly to their left, the route of
march paralleling a row of scrub trees on their
right flank that terminated at the northern end
of the village. The plan was to approach the village from the south, move through it, and sweep
three hundred and sixty degrees around it, looking for any sign of enemy activity. It was hot
and quiet, the sun just past vertical as the platoon moved through the open field south of the
village. Almost immediately a sense of unease
swept through the platoon, a feeling that something wasn't quite right. Jesse quickly moved
down the line, admonishing everyone to look
sharp, while Claude moved up to the head of
the first squad. The platoon slowly approached
the village, extremely conscious of the tree line
some fifty yards to the right. Claude called a

halt, agitated by the lack of any activity in the village, now just a hundred yards in front of them. He motioned for Jesse.

"Something's queer," Claude said as soon as Jesse joined him. "Tell Artie"—the second squad leader—"to take five men and scuff around that tree line."

Before Jesse could answer, the quiet afternoon erupted with the sound of massed automatic weapons fire. A third of the platoon were instant casualties, Jesse among them. The battle lasted almost three days, with two of the brigade's three battalions ultimately involved in hunting down and wiping out the NVA battalion that had in fact infiltrated the area. Jesse had been hit three times: twice in the left leg, badly shattering the femur, and once in the right shoulder, snapping his collarbone like a twig. Because of the intensity of the battle it was almost six hours before he could be medevac'd.

Claude was so busy with other things that he never got a chance to tell his friend and platoon sergeant good-bye.

The helicopter quickly passed over the cemetery. The preacher, sensing what he thought was Claude's impatience, quickly concluded the service.

"Would you care to say a few words?" he asked Claude.

Claude started to shake his head, then changed his mind, then changed it back again.

"No," he said, an aching sadness coming over him, "I guess you've about said it all."

"Amen," the preacher said, and then both he and Claude stood silently while the honor guard from a local reserve unit was called to attention by their sergeant. They quickly fired three volleys into the air and then stood at attention while the bugler, a nineteen-year-old Sixth Army Band member from Hays, Kansas, played taps.

And there's an end to it, thought Claude as the buck sergeant in charge of the honor guard handed him the folded American flags that had been sitting atop the urns containing Jesse's and JoJo's ashes. Claude nodded and tucked the two flags under his left arm as the sergeant mumbled the words about a grateful nation.

"Just a minute, Sergeant," Claude said as the man started to turn away to dismiss the bugler and the honor guard. "I'd like to stake you and the boys"—Claude indicated all the soldiers with a nod of his head—"to a round of beers and maybe some ribs." He handed the startled young sergeant a hundred-dollar bill. "I know, I know," he added as the sergeant started to protest, "but take it from me, Jesse and JoJo there"—another nod, this time in the direction of the two urns—"would be tickled plumb to death to think of you guys having a few beers after their funeral. And you can rest assured that no one will be the wiser."

The sergeant quickly pocketed the money

and saluted Claude. "Thank you, sir. I, we, appreciate it." He turned to his small command and shepherded them into the van that had brought them down from the Presidio.

"Hot damn!" Claude heard one of the soldiers gleefully exclaim, and he smiled, knowing what a couple of free beers would have meant when he was a private in the ranks. He turned to the Baptist preacher, who was standing with his hands folded over his Bible, and took another hundred-dollar bill out of his pocket. "Here you go, Reverend," he said, noting that the man's pupils dilated slightly at the sight of the money. *I'll bet damned few of your flock have ever given you a hundred dollars for a service, even a double funeral,* he thought without rancor. "Do me a favor," Claude continued. "I'd appreciate it if you'd spend a little time this evening telling the Lord that both of these men were good, kindhearted souls. They may have come to hard ends, but I believe that when everything is said and done, they'll both be good men to have in heaven."

"I'll tell Him," the preacher said, quickly pocketing the money and turning to leave as if afraid Claude might ask for its return. "I surely will."

Claude presently stood alone at the gravesite, two workmen watching from a distance as he spoke to the two urns. A cold wind was whipping over the hills that stood between the cemetery and the road to Half Moon Bay, carrying the

ubiquitous tendrils of fog that turned everything
they touched to an emotionless, monochromatic
gray. A quarter of a mile away, under a large
eucalyptus tree, Barton Jones watched through a
pair of binoculars.

Nothing bored J. Watson Mellon like being at
sea, although, in point of fact, leisure activities
of all kinds bored him. He maintained the corporate yacht strictly because it seemed to
appeal to many of his customers and suppliers.
It was peculiar, he often thought, how men and
women making a great deal of money every
year, executives with substantial personal
assets, actually seemed to enjoy being treated,
generally with their spouses, to inane little
cruises around the San Francisco Bay and out
through the Golden Gate.

"Will you require anything further, sir?" the
steward asked as he placed on the desk in the
main cabin a lacquered tray on which sat a delicate Wedgwood china cup and saucer together
with a sterling silver pot of coffee.

Mellon did not immediately look up from
the report he was reading. "No," he said, shaking his head, "that will be all." He glanced at
his watch and then looked up at the steward. It
was six o'clock. "Please inform the captain that
you both may leave now." He didn't want anyone else—other than the involved parties, of
course—on board for the meeting this evening.

Mellon worked steadily, the cabin admirably

suited for use as a mobile office, complete with cellular telephones, three computers with high-speed modems, and two fax machines. His face remained impassive as he reviewed various documents and reports, his only response to the written words being an occasional marginal note scribbled furiously with his fat, black Mont Blanc. At 7:20 P.M. he heard footsteps on the deck above the main cabin. Seconds later the door opened and Barton Jones walked in carrying a sleeping Earl Hamilton wrapped loosely in a blanket. Mellon looked up and motioned over his shoulder with his fountain pen.

"Put him in there." He pointed to the master bedroom, which lay off the main cabin.

Jones walked around the desk and through the indicated door, whistling when he saw the ornately finished master suite, polished mahogany gleaming in the muted overhead lighting. A king-size bed sat on a slightly raised platform. He laid the sedated child on the bed and returned to the main cabin, sitting down on one of the overstuffed leather sofas fronting the desk.

Mellon looked up at him and frowned. "Get out to the parking lot and wait for McCutcheon."

A slight flush came over Barton's face as he rose to obey the order. Mellon thought of saying something to him about his attitude, but decided against it. The exchange was what was important now, not personality clashes. Later, though, he would have to do something about Jones.

Claude had been sitting in the yacht club's parking lot since slightly before six o'clock. He parked the truck at the far end of the lot, near the employees' parking area, in a spot where he could see most of the yacht harbor. Claude saw Mellon arrive in a large Mercedes that he drove himself. He watched as the executive walked out along the slips until he came to an ostentatiously large motor yacht, the very one Claude had guessed would belong to Sentinel Micro. Shortly after Mellon arrived, Claude watched the crew leave the boat. He lit a cigarette and sat back to wait for Jones's arrival.

It was not quite dark when Barton Jones pulled into the parking lot. Claude watched him take the bundle he assumed was Earl from the trunk of his car and walk quickly out the slip to the large boat. As soon as Jones disappeared from the slip, Claude got out of his truck cab. He unconsciously checked the big Colt to make sure a round was chambered and resettled it once again in the waistband of his suit trousers. He walked quickly to the entrance to the slip area, his eyes busily seeking out every corner of the parking lot for human activity. Satisfied that he was alone, Claude crouched down behind a large BMW sedan and waited.

Barton Jones was steaming as he walked along the slip from the yacht to the parking lot, so mad, in fact, that he paid scant attention to anything other than his own anger. When he reached the parking lot, he paused to light a cigarette. The sudden flare of the match in the growing darkness of late evening robbed him of any effective night vision for several seconds, more than enough time for Claude to step up behind him and place the muzzle of the Colt firmly against his lower back.

"Make a sound," Claude growled, "and I'll shoot you down like a fucking dog."

Jones stiffened but remained silent.

"Drop the cigarette," Claude said, maintaining firm contact with the pistol, "and let's go get this over with." When they reached the moored yacht, Claude stopped Jones before he could step on board. "Reach into your jacket and take out your pistol. Slowly." Claude emphasized his instructions with a slight additional pressure of the Colt's muzzle against Jones's back. "Now drop it over the side." When his last order was complied with, Claude indicated that Jones could board the vessel. "Nice boat," Claude murmured as the two men descended the broad teak staircase that led from the deck down to the main cabin.

Mellon looked up as first Jones, then Claude entered the cabin. His sphincter muscle contracted ever so slightly when he realized that Claude, not Jones, was in control.

Jones began to speak. "I—"

"Shut up," Mellon said brusquely. "Neither Mr. McCutcheon nor I are the least bit interested in what you have to say." Jones flushed red, barely able to control himself. Mellon turned his attention to Claude. "Welcome, Mr. McCutcheon. I apologize—"

"Get the boy," Claude interrupted, his voice flinty hard.

Mellon smiled. "I do like a man who gets right down to business. The boy is here and well. Do you plan to honor your half of the bargain?"

"I don't bargain with kidnappers." A sardonic smile passed quickly across Claude's face. "And even if I did, I don't have whatever it is you're looking for. Your fantasies notwithstanding, Jesse Hamilton gave me nothing before he was killed." He pointed the Colt at Mellon. "Now get the boy out here."

Mellon inclined his head toward Jones. "Bring the child out." Mellon continued, speaking again to Claude, "You know, I could use a man of your resourcefulness in my business. I think you're being a bit hasty in dismissing my overtures to you. In fact, your friend Mr. Hamilton was quite content working for me for a number of years." Mellon shook his head, and disappointment edged into his voice. "I still don't understand why he suddenly felt the need to foul his own nest."

"My advice is to shut up about Jesse

Hamilton," Claude said. "In fact, my advice is to just shut up entirely."

Before either man could say anything further, Barton Jones reentered the cabin, Earl Hamilton, still sedated and asleep, in his arms. He laid the boy none too gently on the leather sofa adjacent to the desk. When he straightened up, drawing his right arm from underneath the child, he had a pistol in his right hand. Claude, his attention momentarily diverted by a flash of anger at the roughness with which Jones treated the sleeping child, realized that Jones would be able to shoot him well before he could bring the big Colt around from Mellon's general direction.

"Put it down on the desk, asshole," Jones snarled.

Claude hesitated for just a second and then laid the Colt down as ordered.

"Now sit over there," Jones said, a twisted smile on his face, "next to the kid."

"Well done, Mr. Jones," Mellon said. "I was afraid for a moment there that you might once again have underestimated our Mr. McCutcheon. Where did you have the extra pistol hidden?"

"In the kid's blankets." Jones was flushed and, Claude could see, nearly out of control.

"How appropriate." Mellon looked at Claude. "I'm afraid we have something of a problem here, Mr. McCutcheon. You see, if it were up to me, I would be more than happy to rely on your word as a gentleman that you don't have"—he waved vaguely in the direction of the personal computer sitting on the side of his desk—"the stolen disc, but unfortunately it isn't up to just me." Mellon smiled. "You see, in today's complicated business world one must have partners, and my partners are, quite frankly, concerned that you might not be a man of your word, that perhaps you might, upon reflection, decide to do what the unfortunate Mr. Hamilton attempted."

"Who are your partners?" Claude asked, hoping to keep Mellon talking for as long as possible while he tried to figure out how he was going to get to the .38 in his underarm holster without getting shot.

Mellon smiled. "Let's just say that they're concerned military men."

"Concerned?" Claude asked contemptuously. "Concerned with what? Building up their net asset positions?"

"That and more," Mellon answered dryly. "Certainly they view Sentinel as a for-profit venture, but beyond that—"

"I think you've done enough talking now," Jones said to Mellon, his voice anything but subordinate in tone.

Mellon raised his eyebrows, his irritation at Jones's tone of voice evident. "To whom do you think you're speaking?"

Jones stepped quickly to where Mellon was

seated and abruptly slashed him across the face with the barrel of the pistol he was holding. Mellon fell backward out of his chair onto the carpeting. Jones reached over and picked up the Colt that Claude had laid on the desk. Jones looked down at Mellon, who was holding the side of his face in pain and astonishment, and laughed.

Uh-oh, Claude thought. *The worm has turned. Big time.*

"Get up," Jones barked at his erstwhile employer. "Get up, you miserable cocksucker, or I'll shoot you right there." Keeping his eyes on Claude, Jones reached down and roughly pulled Mellon to his feet by his collar. He shoved the still shaken man over to the sofa where Claude sat. "Sit down. Partners my ass." Jones laughed. "Your so-called partners have decided to put you out of business. Permanently."

Claude looked at Mellon. He was bleeding heavily from the deep gash Jones's pistol had made across his forehead and appeared to be in shock, his eyes wide but not registering a great deal of what was going on.

"I don't imagine this technique of partnership dissolution was covered in the usual case studies at the Harvard Business School, was it?" Claude asked.

Mellon didn't respond.

Claude looked back at Jones. "Why'd you kill Rainer Morgan?"

"Who the hell is Rainer Morgan?" Jones asked, puzzled.

"The man who was murdered in my house. It *was* you that killed him, wasn't it?"

"Oh, him. Yeah, I killed him. Bad fucking luck was what it was. He burst into the place before I had a chance to duck out the back. I guess he must have heard me inside and, thinking it was you, walked right in without bothering to knock or anything. I felt a little bad about it, but what could I do?"

"And the guy up in Tilden Park this morning? I take it he was the one you got to snatch the kid from Felix Mackie?"

Jones smiled, pleased at the memory of putting three bullets into Jamal Shaw's worthless head. "Bingo. No regrets there."

"How about Jesse Hamilton?"

Jones nodded. "Unfortunately, the operation itself was a spectacular failure, given that the intention was not to kill him, certainly not there at the motel, before I could have a little chat with him. As it was, he damned near killed me. At least I had the good sense to send my hired muscle in first. Hamilton put three slugs into him before he got a foot in the door." Jones shook his head and laughed. "Believe me, if the guy hadn't been so damned big, Hamilton would have gotten me too. Luckily, I was able to use him like a shield and managed to get a couple shots off as he was going down. Barely. I'll be honest with you, I hadn't expected Hamilton to be so, um, determined."

"And the woman? Louise Griffin? Her death wasn't suicide, was it?"

"No, indeed, it wasn't, and that was my handiwork too. Ms. Griffin, as it turned out, was Army CID and came this close"—Jones held up his left hand, forefinger and thumb barely apart—"to blowing Mellon and his partners completely out of the water. Fortunately, somebody in CID back at the Pentagon ratted the undercover operation out to Mellon's partners, and I was brought in to see what could be salvaged. I'll tell you this much, she was one tough lady. Smart too." He shook his head in perverse admiration. "And that was what did her in. She suspected who I was right from the start, but thought she could string it along for a few more days, get just a little more data on the Pentagon end of things. I knew she had taken a disc with incriminating evidence on it, but she died without telling me who she gave it to. It didn't take long to put two and two together and come up with Hamilton, though."

"Is that when you decided to get the FBI involved?"

Jones nodded. "Griffin's death sent Hamilton under cover. I figured maybe the FBI could flush him out and I could get to him first. From that point, however, things admittedly got a little out of control." Jones smiled, but there was no mirth in his eyes. "You, Mr. McCutcheon, have caused me no end of grief."

"You should have listened to me when I first told you that I didn't have the disc."

"Perhaps, but the fact that Hamilton left his son with you confused everybody." Jones smiled again. "Except those incompetents at the FBI. Hell, they never even knew about the kid, did they? Anyway, whether you had the disc or not, from the perspective of my employers you were irrevocably involved by virtue of the fact that you had the boy."

"What about the real disc? Aren't the folks in Washington worried about the fact that it hasn't been recovered?"

"Can't be helped. This leak has to be stopped somewhere, and you two get to be the fingers in the dike, so to speak. Sentinel is going to be shut down, the technology moved offshore to the Far East." Jones took a computer disc from his coat pocket and tossed it onto Mellon's desk. "Not the disc he"—Jones nodded toward Mellon—"stupidly allowed to be stolen, but an interesting one in its own right. It contains data that indicate that Mellon was stealing from the company. The police will conclude that Hamilton stole it for blackmail purposes and gave it to you"—a nod to McCutcheon—"for safekeeping. When Hamilton was killed, you foolishly decided to play out the hand. Mellon had the boy kidnapped and you came here tonight to make a trade. Something went wrong, a shoot-out took place, and no one's left to tell the sad tale."

"What about Mellon's soon-to-be ex-partners?" Claude continued. "Aren't you just a little worried that they might view you as the sole remaining loose end in this whole sorry affair?"

Jones shook his head. "My people have been working with Mellon's so-called partners"—he sneered as he spat out the word *partners*—"ever since the good old days in Vietnam. You can believe me when I tell you that this is just another assignment." He laughed, a tension-filled, joyless sound. "So you see, you two—or I should say you *three*, counting the kid—are the only loose ends we're concerned with." He thumbed back the hammer of his pistol and aimed at Mellon. "At least you'll have the distinct pleasure of seeing Mellon die first."

Claude realized that he would have only a split second to get to the revolver in his shoulder holster while Jones was occupied with shooting Mellon. While drawing the pistol, he intended to throw himself in front of Earl, hoping that even if Jones managed to shoot him, he might nonetheless get a round off himself while protecting the drugged child. He began by subtly shifting his weight to his left, turning his left shoulder imperceptibly away from Jones to reduce the arc through which he would have to swing his hand to bring the weapon to bear. He knew there wasn't much chance he could pull it off, but—

"Freeze! FBI!"

Startled, his right arm and hand already starting for his revolver, Claude swung his gaze to the cabin's door. Rita Johnson stood there, her service revolver aimed at Barton Jones. Jones stood rigidly, his back to Rita, his pistol still aimed at the semiconscious Mellon. Claude looked back at Jones and saw the right side of his face twitching uncontrollably. "It's over, Jones," Claude said quietly, sliding to his right on the sofa to get in front of Earl. "Put the gun down and we'll all get out of this alive."

"Fuck you!" Jones screamed, and whirled around toward Rita, his finger already tightening spasmodically on the trigger.

"Shoot him!" Claude yelled at Rita, knowing he would never be able to draw his own pistol, aim, and shoot it before Jones killed Rita.

The crashing report of Jones's first shot filled the cabin, and the rich oak paneling scant inches from Rita's head exploded into splinters as the bullet disintegrated on impact.

With almost insane lucidity Claude saw the cylinder of Jones's revolver turning, bringing a fresh bullet into the firing position.

Claude struggled to free his own weapon from the shoulder holster.

A second gunshot almost deafened him. Jones's upper torso snapped backward as if he had been struck by a sledgehammer. The back of Jones's head exploded in a red mist as the bullet, which had taken him in the throat, directly beneath his chin, turned upward and exited several inches above his brain stem. He was dead long before he hit the floor. Stunned, Claude turned and saw Rita, still in a combat stance, a wisp of white smoke drifting up from the barrel of her service revolver.

18

"Lieutenant Beck on the line," Emma called out.

"Lieutenant Beck on the line," Emma called out.

Claude leaned forward in his chair and picked up the phone. "Yeah, Bernie, what can I do for you?"

"I thought I'd call and let you know that Mellon just cut a deal with the U.S. attorney's office over in the City. He's going to cop a conspiracy plea in exchange for full cooperation and testimony against the army officers involved at the Pentagon. Among others, apparently two admirals and five generals were involved to one degree or another."

"Yeah, right," Claude said, "if he lives long enough. How about felony murder?"

"Nope. Conspiracy only, with incarceration limited to not more than five years at Club Fed. Right now they've got him in the Federal Witness Protection Program. The U.S. attorney and the Justice Department back in Washington both feel that cleaning house at the Pentagon is far more important than dropping a big load on a white-collar perp like Mellon."

"I guess I can see how they'd feel that way. Besides, they're probably counting on the fact that one of his old 'partners' will pop Mellon sooner or later."

Bernie laughed. "You never know. Say, Claude, one last thing."

"Yeah?"

"I also heard a rumor about a little boy being mixed up in all this. The rumor has it that Jesse Hamilton had a son. You wouldn't happen to know anything about that, would you?"

Claude shook his head as if his friend could see him. "No, I guess I wouldn't."

"I didn't think so. I also heard that Felix Mackie was being discharged from the hospital this morning. I'd say that three weeks is a damned quick recovery given the wounds he had."

"Even so, I don't expect he'll be doing any heavy lifting down at the gym for a while yet."

Bernie chuckled. "Give him my regards when you see him. Oh, and tell him I can help him get the boy that you don't know anything about into the Oakland PAL Little League program whenever he wants."

"I appreciate it, Bernie, and I know Felix will too."

"You bet. Say, what do you hear from that FBI agent, Rita Johnson? I understand she got back from Washington a few days ago."

"Not much," Claude replied carefully. "I guess she's been pretty busy back there since breaking the case and the shooting and all."

"She seemed like a pretty solid woman. A man could do a lot worse than hooking up with someone like that."

"I'll tell her you said so. Maybe she's looking for a husband."

"Good-bye, Claude," Bernie said dryly. "Call me sometime when nothing's going on for a change. Maybe we'll try to catch an A's game before the season's over."

Claude hung up the phone and walked out to Emma's desk, the keys to his truck in his right hand. "I won't be back this afternoon, so you can go ahead and close up for the day. I'll see you in the morning."

"No, you won't," Emma replied, shaking her head. "I'm taking a week off starting tomorrow, remember?"

"I remember you asking but I don't remember giving my consent," Claude teased. "And anyway, who ever heard of someone starting a vacation on a Thursday?"

"Consent," Emma muttered sarcastically as

she turned off her computer. "I'll see you next week." She pointed a threatening finger at him. "Stay out of trouble at least until I get back."

The Bay Area was still in the midst of an unusual summer warm spell, and Claude rolled both of the truck's windows down as he eased into traffic.

"Artie."

"Claude." Artie rose from the metal folding chair and greeted Claude with a firm handshake. "Good to see you again," he said, meaning it. "Tell me about Jesse and JoJo's funeral."

Claude smiled and described the startled look on the preacher's face when he gave the hundred-dollar bill.

"Man, I'd have liked to have seen that." Artie chuckled and shook his head. "Jesse and JoJo would have too." He coughed quietly and the smile left his face. "Man told me about what happened with Jones and Sentinel."

"What man?"

"Nobody said nothing about no boy, though," Artie pointed out, ignoring Claude's question. "Earl okay?"

"He's doing just fine. In fact, I want to tell you something about him, but first I want to say that I think you were right."

"Right about what?"

"About Jesse's motives. It wasn't about money at all." Claude shook his head for emphasis. "It was about Barton Jones killing

Louise Griffin. It had to have been, or Jesse would have turned the disc over to the police as soon as she was killed."

"I didn't exactly say that I thought his motive in trying to deal the disc he got from her was to get Jones."

"No, but it's what you were thinking."

"Maybe. But the money he thought Sentinel would be willing to pay, or at least the idea of it, tripped him up. See, if all Jesse wanted was to see Jones pay for killing the woman, he could have simply turned the disc over to the police, like you just said. That would have put the hurt on both Jones *and* Sentinel. I told him so myself, a couple of times. 'Think about your boy,' I told him. 'You go killing Jones, they'll lock you up for the rest of your life. Who's going to look after Earl?' So then he started thinking that if he could deal the disc to Sentinel for enough money, he and Earl could split after he killed Jones, be safe someplace." Artie smiled sardonically. "Most of these fools in here"—he waved his right arm vaguely to indicate the entire prison population—"could tell you right quick that a man can have either revenge or money, but not generally both as a part of the same deal." Claude started to say something, but Artie reached out and put a hand on his arm, a surprisingly intimate gesture. "Let him go, Claude. It's done and over." Then, a second later: "Tell me about the boy."

"It may be done and over for Jesse, but not for Earl. And here's where you come in."

"Me?"

Claude nodded. "It won't be a problem dummying up the documents we'll need to give legal custody of Earl to Felix Mackie and his wife. The problem is that they didn't know Jesse and can't tell the boy anything about his father when he gets old enough to want to know. So I told them that part of the deal is that you get made the boy's godfather."

"I don't know if that was such a good idea," Artie said quietly, looking down at the floor. "How's he going to feel about a godfather locked up in prison?" Artie looked up at Claude. "Why can't you be his godfather?"

"Because I didn't know Jesse, not like you did. Not as a grown man. I'll be honest with you, Artie—in a ridiculously short time I've come to love that boy. I wouldn't have thought it possible, but it's true. He's fragile and he's damaged and all he wants is to love somebody and be loved in return. You and I and Felix and Ruth are going to see that he gets everything he needs, and one of the things he's going to need is a role model—particularly one who knew his daddy."

"Role model?" Artie didn't quite laugh.

"Technically, you're eligible for parole in another year. I spoke yesterday with the judge who sentenced you and the DA's office over in the City, and I think that both can be con-

vinced to support you at the parole hearing."
Claude looked at his watch and stood up. "I've
got to go."

"I'll think about what you said. About the
boy and all."

Claude shook his head. "I wasn't asking you
to think about it, Artie."

"Hello? Anybody home?"

"Come on in," Claude called out. "I'm back
in the kitchen."

Rita walked slowly through the great room,
her mind recording every detail: the slightly
raised sleeping alcove with its futon and
armoire, the three plain shoji screens defining
the bath and toilet, the unexpected transition
from the gleaming hardwood to the sensuous
texture of the Mexican paver tiles on the
kitchen floor. Later, she knew, she would want
to be able to remember it all. In the kitchen
Claude stood at the counter in blue jeans and a
linen shirt chopping carrots, celery, and onions.
A bottle of Perrier-Jouët sat in a clear glass ice
bucket next to two long-stemmed champagne
flutes.

"Claude McCutcheon wearing an apron?"
Rita teased.

Claude threw up his hands in mock surrender. "You have penetrated my darkest secret:
domestication."

"I doubt it. Here." She handed him a bouquet
of bright red and orange gladiolas.

"I thought you might call from Washington," Claude said casually as he put the gladiolas in a pitcher with warm water.

"Did you miss me?"

" 'Sweet meter maid.' " Claude smiled. "I thought of little else." He busied himself for a second opening the bottle of champagne and pouring two glasses.

Rita took a pack of cigarettes out of her purse and held one up for a light. Seeing Claude's inquiring look, she shrugged. "You got me started on bad habits again, I guess." She leaned forward toward the Zippo in Claude's hand. "I hadn't smoked since college." She exhaled and smiled ruefully. "Still, after Washington, I figured, why not?"

Claude frowned and handed her a glass of wine. "I'm sorry to hear that. What happened?"

"I resigned from the Bureau."

"What?" Claude was shocked.

"There wasn't much else I could do." She shook her head ruefully. "Talk about a babe in the woods. The old boy network at the Pentagon and the West Point and Annapolis Protective Associations didn't take too kindly to two admirals and five generals, not to mention an odd sprinkling of field-grade officers, getting bagged in our follow-up investigation of Sentinel Micro, so an anonymous source sent a couple of audiotapes to the director of the Bureau." She paused to take a sip of champagne.

"Audiotapes?"

Rita nodded. "Someone, presumably either the good folks at Sentinel or their Pentagon partners, planted an extremely sensitive listening device in my apartment." She took a drag on her cigarette. "Actually, the sound quality during your visits was quite good." She smiled at Claude and, in spite of herself, blushed. "I had no idea lovemaking was so noisy and so, um, distinctive. The director felt that fraternization by an agent, me, with a subject under investigation, you, was, to say the least, unacceptable behavior."

"Hard to argue with that," Claude said, attempting humor.

Rita didn't smile.

"Listen," he continued, "you didn't do anything wrong. Large organizations have to have rules that are applied generally across the board. Individuals, particularly those who are expected to exercise independent judgment such as you are, are always faced with having to modify their adherence to those rules based upon changing circumstances. Your becoming my lover did not in any way compromise your investigation."

"Claude," Rita said, shaking her head, "in some ways you're like a child. Our becoming lovers *did* compromise my investigation. It had to have, by virtue of the very fact that it happened. To say nothing of the obvious appearance of impropriety. Suppose you *had* been somehow involved with Mellon or your friend

Jesse Hamilton. You could have used our relationship to shield yourself, to divert my attention away from you."

"But I wasn't involved. And I didn't use it in such a way. Why punish yourself with what might have been."

"Who said I was punishing myself? A perfect example was the child. Jesse Hamilton's son. You never told me about him and you *knew* that it was a vital piece of information. You *knew* that the man you killed in your house was there to kidnap the child and that he was sent by Sentinel Micro. That fact alone would have entirely changed the focus of my investigation, and yet you didn't tell me."

Claude shrugged. "I couldn't tell you about him and you know why. The authorities would have immediately removed him from my home and placed him in a county facility or foster home. I couldn't allow that to happen."

"You couldn't allow that to happen? Claude, you're an attorney, an officer of the court, for God's sake. You don't have the right to make decisions like that."

"Before we get sidetracked talking about who had the right to do what, let's back up a moment and look at the actual sequence of events involving the child. When he first was left with me, Jesse, his father, was still alive and competent to make such a decision regarding his own child. When I killed the would-be kidnapper, even though Jesse was still alive at that point, you know as well as I do that the Alameda County juvenile authorities would have taken the boy from me. I had what I considered then, and continue to believe, to be an unambiguous moral obligation to do what I thought was best for the child, and the worst possible thing in my mind would have been to have just turned him over to the authorities."

"You could have done so and then petitioned the court for custody and adoption after Mr. Hamilton was killed."

Claude didn't quite laugh. "Yeah, right."

"And you never said anything about Jesse Hamilton talking to Joseph Watson out at the Veterans Administration hospital. Had I known about that meeting, perhaps I could have interviewed Mr. Watson before he died of a drug overdose. It could well be that Hamilton left the disc with him for safekeeping, and the fact that you found Rainer Morgan's telephone number among his belongings after his death at least raises the possibility that the disc was passed along to Rainer when Watson decided to leave the VA."

"Some big ifs there."

"Yes," Rita responded, exasperation evident in her voice, "there are, but that's the very nature of the law enforcement business. You follow every lead, regardless of how improbable or far-fetched it might seem at the time. We know that Jesse Hamilton had in his possession, at least temporarily, the disc taken by the Army

CID undercover agent Louise Griffin. It was not recovered by Jones when Hamilton was killed, so we may presume that he gave it to someone prior to his murder. Before leaving his son with you, he visited Watson at the VA hospital. Rainer Morgan coincidentally was an inpatient at about that same time and was killed in your home shortly thereafter. It is not wild speculation to suggest that the chain of possession of the computer disc ran from Louise Griffin to Jesse Hamilton to Joseph Watson to Rainer Morgan, and that Morgan was planning to give it to you."

"My thinking exactly. Unfortunately, if Rainer had it, the secret of its whereabouts died with him. His father, Harry, found neither the disc nor anything that would have suggested what Rainer did with it, *if* he ever had it, among his belongings." Claude took a sip of champagne. "What about Louise Griffin? Why didn't the FBI connect her to the army and its CID investigation of Sentinel? Didn't her death look suspicious to anyone besides Jesse Hamilton?"

"There was no reason it should have. Nobody, not the FBI, and certainly not the local police, knew she was working under cover. The CID, when she died, should have immediately brought us into the picture to investigate her death, but nothing was said. Part of the ongoing FBI investigation back in Washington is focused on certain CID personnel, in a concentrated effort to determine who compromised the undercover investigation in the first place, and whether that person or persons also conspired to keep the significance of her death from the FBI." Rita shook her head. "In hindsight, I admit that I should have at least been mildly curious about the seeming coincidence of her death."

"Meanwhile, when Jesse was killed, I was left with the question of what to do with Earl for the rest of his life, how to protect him while at the same time keeping his paternity a secret from the authorities. I thought I had solved that problem by allowing Felix Mackie and his wife to 'adopt' him, but as you know, Jones managed to snatch him."

"Killing another man in the process."

"Almost two," Claude corrected. "If Felix Mackie hadn't been so damned tough, he'd be dead right now as well. And, by the way, I never got a chance to thank you properly for letting me get Earl off the boat before the San Francisco police got there."

"Think nothing of it. One more stupid decision on my part wasn't going to make any difference one way or the other, not at that point."

"Don't say that," Claude said heatedly. "Your decision was anything but stupid. You gave that boy his best possible chance to have caring, responsible parents and an opportunity to make something of himself. Listen"—Claude softened his tone considerably—"I probably made a few bad decisions, I'll grant you that. But you can't fairly judge yesterday's actions in light of today's knowledge. Everything I did, literally everything, was informed by the responsibility I had for Jesse Hamilton's child."

"But—"

"Wait, please, let me finish. We can argue all night about whether or not I should have immediately turned the child over to the authorities, but I will not change my way of thinking. The fact of the matter is that *I* made the decision to be responsible for the boy, and having done so, I was left with very little room for maneuvering."

"So little that you told me nothing."

"That's not entirely true. The first evening we spent together I cautioned you against focusing all of your attention on Jesse Hamilton. Remember? 'The finger pointing at the moon—' "

" '—is not the moon.' " Rita smiled. "I remember. Not exactly a smoking gun as far as clues are concerned."

"Granted, but not exactly insignificant either. But beyond that, what could I tell you? A few minutes ago you said that there was a danger that I might have used our growing relationship to interfere with your, the FBI's, investigation. And yet that's precisely what I would have done had I told you about the boy and then asked you not to say anything."

Claude got up and got the bottle of champagne from the counter before speaking again.

"By the way, Hazel Morgan, Rainer's wife, has disappeared."

"What?" Rita looked up in surprise. "What do you mean?"

"I drove out to the harbor to visit the two of them last week, and Harry told me she had been gone five or six days already."

"Gone where?"

"God only knows. Neither he nor Rainer ever really knew much of anything about her, where exactly she was from, who her people were, that sort of thing. She was pretty spaced-out when she first showed up at the harbor, and Harry figures that the loss of Rainer drove her a little crazy again and so she just took off." Claude shook his head. "He doesn't figure he'll ever hear from her again."

"That's terrible. How is Harry doing?"

"He's put his lease on the harbor up for sale. He said that if he can sell it, he's going to sail his boat down the coast to Mexico or Central America, maybe just keep going." Claude looked at Rita. "A big part of Harry died with Rainer, and now with Hazel taking off . . ." Claude's voice trailed off and both he and Rita sat quietly for several minutes.

"Tell me something," Claude asked, breaking the silence. "How did you know I was meeting Jones on the Sentinel yacht in San Francisco?"

"I didn't. I was at the cemetery when you buried Jesse Hamilton and I saw him watching you. Of course I didn't know what he was doing at the time, but I decided to follow him when he left the cemetery. Eventually he led me to East

Palo Alto where he picked up Hamilton's son and then out to the yacht harbor. I parked a block away, on Marina Boulevard, and watched the two of you walk out to the yacht."

"And you followed us onto the boat?"

Rita nodded. "I was listening behind the door to the cabin the whole time, waiting for the right moment." Rita paused and lit another cigarette. "What would you have done if I hadn't been there?"

"I don't know. I expect something would have worked out." Claude smiled. "The foolish Mr. Jones hadn't quite seen all my cards, don't you know." He finished his wine before speaking again. "What are your plans?"

"I don't really have any as yet. I'm going to travel for a month or two, see the UK and some of Europe, come back to the East Coast and drive across the country, that sort of thing. Then, well, who knows? Maybe come back to San Francisco and get a job with a law firm. I am a lawyer, after all."

"Why get a job working for someone else? Set up your own practice. In fact"—Claude toyed with his champagne glass, not looking at Rita—"I was sort of thinking about asking whether you might be interested in throwing in with me."

Rita laughed, a sound oddly devoid of humor. "Is that an offer of employment or an offer of marriage?"

"Neither. I just thought you might want . . ."

He paused and looked across the table at Rita. "Hell, I don't know what I thought. Maybe I just hate to see you leave. 'McCutcheon and Johnson, Attorneys at Law.' How does that sound?"

"I'll be honest with you, Claude, it's not what I had in mind."

"Well, it's something to think about. When are you taking off?"

"Tomorrow afternoon. I'm on the five o'clock British Airways flight to London."

"I'll be damned. You know, all the traveling I've done, I've not yet been to London."

Rita stood up. "I'll send you a postcard," she said, her smile barely taking the sting out of the words.

Claude rose. "I take it you're not staying for dinner?"

Rita shook her head, refusing to meet Claude's eyes. "I have to go." *While I still can.* "I haven't packed yet and I still have bills to pay, that sort of thing." Her voice dropped as she spoke, her last few words barely a whisper.

Neither of them spoke as Claude walked her to the door. "It really *was* for the boy," he murmured to himself, watching her get into her car and drive away. As she turned the corner at the end of his street and passed from his line of sight, the telephone beside the futon began to ring. He walked back to the kitchen and opened a fresh can of food for Oscar. By the time he had poured himself another glass of wine and sat down once again at the table, the telephone had stopped ringing. Through the open kitchen window he heard the muted sounds of his neighbors enjoying the summer evening, and a radio playing somewhere in the middle distance. The telephone began to ring again.

"Claude, thanks for coming by."

"No problem, Harry." Claude looked around the small harbor as the two men walked out along the breakwater. "I doubt I'll get out this way much once you've taken off. The place won't be the same without you. Plus, you know what I think about sailing. When are you leaving?"

Harry smiled, remembering the one or two times he had been able to talk Claude into taking a sail with him. "Tomorrow. Everything's been pretty much taken care of, so I thought I might as well hoist the sails."

"Did you get what you wanted for the lease on the harbor?"

"Got exactly what I asked for. And the fellow that bought the lease also bought the houseboat. He's moving his family in day after tomorrow."

"Have you heard anything from Hazel?"

"Not a word. You know, as much as I miss Rainer, I feel just as bad about Hazel taking off like that. I know she's in trouble up here"—he tapped the side of his head—"and yet there's nothing I can do about it."

Claude put a hand on Harry's shoulder. "I'll

ask Bernie Beck over at the Albany PD to keep his ear to the ground. If she turns up, or we hear anything at all, I'll get word to you."

Harry wiped his hands on a rag and looked down at his feet. "One reason I asked you to stop by was to tell you that old Ben died last night. I found him this morning, just before I called you."

"I'm sorry, Harry. I know you were fond of him."

"It was way overdue. And besides, with me selling the lease and moving away, I don't know who would have looked after him. The fire department rescue squad took the call and picked up his body about an hour ago. After they left, I cleaned out the office where he stayed."

"He couldn't have had much in the way of personal possessions."

"No, just some ragged old clothes, most of which I gave him over the past few years. I did find this, though." Harry held up a small computer disc. "I remember you asking if there was anything like this among Rainer's stuff."

Claude took the disc and turned it over in his hands. *How many lives,* he wondered, *how many lives wasted for this?*

"Did that have anything to do with Rainer's death?" Harry asked in a quiet voice.

Claude shook his head, unable to add to his friend's grief by suggesting that his son had died for nothing more than a digital collection of 1s and 0s. "No, it's just a disc that JoJo Watson gave to Rainer to give to me. I don't know how in the world Ben ended up with it."

"What's on it?"

"Nothing," Claude said, turning to face the Golden Gate. He cocked his right arm back and suddenly whipped it forward, sending the disc skimming out over San Pablo Bay like a flat stone. It skipped twice and then sank, disappearing immediately from sight. "Not a damned thing."

Acknowledgments

If the story contained in these pages can in any way be said to be well told, a great deal of the credit must go to Dave Stern, my editor at Pocket Books. With a sure touch and much good humor, he insisted, page by page, that it be everything it possibly could be.